Bella Andre has always l
and then non-fiction bo
her first romance novel, s
career. Since selling her f
sixteen "sensual, empowered stories enveloped in heady romance" (*Publisher's Weekly*) about sizzling alpha heroes and the strong women they'll love forever.

She is the author of: *Wild Heat, Hot as Sin* and *Never Too Hot*, all available from *Rouge*.

www.bellaandre.com

NEVER TOO HOT

BELLA ANDRE

NEVER TOO HOT

1 3 5 7 9 10 8 6 4 2

Published in the UK in 2012 by Rouge, an imprint of Ebury Publishing
A Random House Group Company

First published in the United States in 2010 by Bantam Dell,
A Division of Random House, Inc. New York

This novel is a work of fiction. Names and characters are the product of the author's imagination and any resemblance to actual persons, living or dead, is entirely coincidental.

The Random House Group Limited Reg. No. 954009

Addresses for companies within the Random House Group can be found at www.randomhouse.co.uk

A CIP catalogue record for this book is available from the British Library

The Random House Group Limited supports The Forest Stewardship Council (FSC®), the leading international forest certification organisation. Our books carrying the FSC label are printed on FSC® certified paper. FSC is the only forest certification scheme endorsed by the leading environmental organisations, including Greenpeace. Our paper procurement policy can be found at:
www.randomhouse.co.uk/environment

Printed and bound in Great Britain by Clays Ltd, St Ives PLC

ISBN 9780091949099

To all of the songwriters and singers who take me right to the heart of it every time I sit down to write.

And, always . . .
To Paul

ACKNOWLEDGMENTS

EVERY BOOK is an adventure and it's a thrill to take it with so many wonderful people on my team. Thank you to my husband and kids, my parents, and my mother-in-law, who are always there for me when I'm imagining and writing a book. And a special thank-you to my sister-in-law, Linda. Thank you to the fabulous women in my posse: Shelley Adina, Jami Alden, Carol Culver, Theresa Grant, Jasmine Haynes, Rachael Herron, Anne Mallory, Monica McCarty, Poppy Reiffen, Penelope Williamson, Veronica Wolff, and Jackie Yau. Thank you to Ellen Higuchi and the entire Thursday night romance readers' group for the endless support, great book recommendations, and laughter. Thank you to Jeannie Ruesch for my beautiful website. Thank you to my editor, Shauna Summers, who sees all the things that need to be seen, and to Jessica Sebor as well. And, yet again, huge thanks to my agent, Jessica Faust, who constantly goes above and beyond the call of duty.

And last, but certainly not least, big, juicy thank you's to each and every one of you who told me how eagerly you were waiting for Connor's story. I absolutely loved writing this book and I hope you love reading it just as much.

Enjoy your trip to Blue Mountain Lake,
Bella Andre

CHAPTER ONE

CONNOR MACKENZIE slid his rental car into the gravel driveway behind the old log cabin and was pulling the keys out of the ignition when the cheap metal key ring scraped against his palm. He swore as it bit into the bumpy, scarred flesh, skin that still felt too tight every time he flexed his hands or made a fist.

Still, today was one of the good days. All through the flight and the two-hour drive from the airport through winding back roads he'd been able to feel everything he touched.

The worst days were the ones where the numbness won. Days when it took everything in him to fight back the angry roars, when he felt like a wounded lion crammed into a four-by-four-foot cage in some zoo, just waiting for the chance to escape and run free again. To be whole and king of the jungle again.

His hand stung as he pulled off his seat belt and slammed the driver's-side door shut. He needed to get out to where he could see the water, breathe it in. Calm the fuck down. Get a grip.

This lake, deep in the heart of the thick Adirondack woods, would set him straight.

It had to.

He'd come from another lake, from twelve years in California's Lake Tahoe fighting wildfires. But he couldn't stay there another summer, couldn't stand to watch his brother and friends head out to fight fire after fire while he went to physical therapy and worked with rookies in the classroom, teaching them from books and trying not to notice the way they stared at the thick scars running up and down his arms from his multiple grafts.

Coming to Blue Mountain Lake had been his brother's idea. *"Dianna and I want to get married at Poplar Cove end of July,"* Sam had said. They'd been planning a big wedding for late fall, at the end of fire season, but now that Dianna was pregnant, their schedule had moved up several months. *"After all these years, especially with Gram and Gramps down in Florida full-time, I'm sure the cabin needs work. Might be a good project for the next few weeks. Better than hanging around here, anyway."*

Connor had wanted to camp outside the Forest Service headquarters until they agreed to sign his umpteenth round of appeal papers, the papers that would put him back on his Tahoe Pines hotshot crew. He'd been jumping through one Forest Service hoop after another for two long years, working like hell to convince the powers that

be that he was ready—both mentally and physically—to resume his duties as a hotshot. Up until now they'd said there was too much risk. They thought it was too likely that he'd freeze, that he might not only take himself out, but a civilian too.

Bullshit. He was ready. More than ready. And he was sure this time his appeal would be approved.

But he could see what Sam was saying. Getting at the log cabin with a saw and hammer and paintbrush, running the trails around the lake and going for long, cool swims might do something to settle the agitation that had been running through his veins for two years.

Things were going to be different here. This summer was going to be better than the last, a sure bet it would be a hell of a lot better than the two that he'd spent in a hospital.

This summer the monkey that had latched itself onto his back, the persistent monster that had been slowly but steadily strangling Connor, was going to finally hop off and leave him the fuck alone.

Moving off the gravel driveway, Connor walked past the grass and through the sand until he was at the water's edge. He looked out at the calm lake, the perfectly still surface reflecting the thick white clouds and the green mountains that surrounded it, waiting for the release in his chest, for the fist to uncoil in his gut.

A cigarette boat whipped out from around the point and into the bay, creating a huge wake on the silent midday shore, and the cold water splashed high, up over Connor's shoes, soaking him to the knees.

Fuck.

Who was he trying to kid? He wasn't here for laughs this summer. He was here to push past the lingering pain in his hands and arms.

He was here to force himself into peak physical shape, to prove his worth to the Forest Service when he got back to California after Sam's wedding.

He was here to renovate his great-grandparents' one-hundred-year-old log cabin, to work such long, hard hours on it that when he slept he would outrun his nightmares, the god-awful reminders of the day he'd almost died on the mountain in Lake Tahoe.

He was here to be alone. Completely alone.

And no matter what he had to do, he was going to find the inner calm, the control that had always been so effortless, so innate before the Desolation fire.

Turning away from the water, he stared back at the log cabin. The words POPLAR COVE were etched on one of the logs, the name his great-grandparents had given the Adirondack camp in 1910. He forced himself to look for its flaws, for everything he'd need to tear down and rebuild this summer. The paint was peeling beneath the screened-in porch on the front where the storms hit hardest. Some of the roof's shingles were askew.

But even as he worked to be dispassionate, he mostly saw the precision detailing his great-grandfather had put into the cabin a hundred years ago: the perfect logs holding up the heavy corners of the building, the smaller logs and twigs that framed the porch almost artistically.

Eighteen summers he'd spent in this cabin. Ten weeks

every summer with Sam and their friends under the watchful but loving eyes of their grandparents. The only people missing were his parents. One time he'd asked his mother why they couldn't come too, but she'd gotten that funny, breathless, watery-eyed look that he hated seeing—the same look that she usually got when she was talking to his dad about his long work hours—so he'd dropped it.

He couldn't believe it had been twelve years since he'd stood here.

After signing up to be a hotshot at eighteen, Connor's summers had been full fighting wildfires. Any normal July 1st this past decade would have seen him in a west coast forest with a 150-pound pack on his back, a chain saw in his hand, surrounded by his twenty-man, wildland firefighting crew. But the last couple of years had been anything but normal.

Connor had never thought to see the word disability next to his name. Seven hundred thirty days after getting caught in a blowup on Desolation Wilderness and he still couldn't.

Still, even though he belonged in Tahoe beating back flames, as he stood on the sand, the humid air making his T-shirt stick to his chest, he felt in his bones how much he'd missed Blue Mountain Lake.

Heading back to his car, he grabbed his bag from the truck, slung it over one shoulder and headed for the steps off the side of the screened-in porch that stretched from one side of the house to the other.

Most of his indoor time as a kid had been spent on this porch, protected from the bugs and the rain, but open to the breeze. His grandparents had served all their meals on the porch's Formica table. He hadn't cared that his teeth had chattered on cool mornings in early summer while he downed a bowl of Cheerios out there. He and Sam had lived in T-shirts and swim shorts regardless of the cold fronts that frequently blew in.

One of the porch steps nearly split beneath his foot and he frowned as he bent down to inspect it. Guilt gnawed at his gut as he silently acknowledged that his grandparents could have hurt themselves on these stairs. He should have come out here in the off-season, should have checked to make sure everything was okay. But fire had always come first.

Always.

Something grated at him there, so he reminded himself that the bones of the log cabin were sound. He'd heard the stories a hundred times of how his great-grandfather had cut each one of the logs himself from the thick forest of pine trees a half mile from the lake. Still, time took its toll on every building eventually, no matter how well constructed.

Taking the rest of the stairs two at a time, ready now to see what other problems awaited him inside, Connor reached for the handle on the screen door.

But instead of turning it, he stopped cold.

What the hell?

A woman was dancing in front of an easel, swinging around what looked like a paintbrush, white cables dangling from her ears as she sang in a wildly off-tune voice.

Every few seconds she dipped into her paint and took a swipe at the oversized canvas.

He couldn't believe what he was seeing. Some strange singing, painting woman on his porch was the last thing he wanted to deal with today.

Still, he couldn't help but be struck by how pretty she was as she did a little spin before squirting more paint onto her easel and sweeping her brush through it. He was close enough to see that she wasn't wearing a bra under her red tank top and when she wiped at the damp skin on her neck and the deep vee between her breasts with a white rag, his body immediately responded in a painful reminder that it had been too long since he'd been with a woman.

He quickly filled in the rest of the sensual, unexpected picture. Curly hair piled on top of her head and held with some sort of plastic clip, cutoff jeans, tanned legs, and bright orange toenails on bare feet.

It took far longer than it should have for him to snap himself out of the haze of animal lust that was wrapping itself around his cock. Another time he might have walked in with a smile and charmed the panties right off her. But he hadn't come to the lake to get laid.

A woman had no place in his summer, no matter how well she filled out every one of the boxes on his checklist.

For whatever reason, the woman was trespassing.

And she had to go.

* * *

It was, Ginger thought with a smile as she mixed Cinnabar Red and Ocean Blue, a perfect summer day. She'd started it off with a walk along the beach, then took a bagel out to the end of the dock to munch while reading a sexy paperback, and now here she was painting like crazy on the porch.

The pop song streaming into her ears at top volume hit the crescendo of the big final chorus and she had to stop painting altogether to play air drums and sing harmony. She felt so happy, so carefree, and it hit her suddenly, powerfully that she could never—*never!*—have done this in her old life.

Oh, the way her ex-husband and their "friends" would have reacted if they could see her now. Her whole life she'd been perfectly buttoned up, overly coiffed and made up, and elegantly outfitted despite the fact that the tag on her clothes had always been in the teens rather than the single digits. Discounting the fact that her body refused to shrink even if she ate nothing but heads of lettuce, in every other way she'd been the perfect rich girl turned businessman's wife.

But not anymore. Not at Blue Mountain Lake.

She didn't have to be that woman here.

Sure, she was still doing a lot of fund-raising for the school's art program, but she loved knowing she was helping people. Besides, it had always been a rush to know that she was good at getting people to reach into their pocketbooks and do good. Great at it, actually. The joke back home—shouldn't she stop thinking of the city as home, already?—was that all she had to do was walk into a room full of millionaires and they'd start throwing money at her as fast as she could catch it.

Helping out at the Blue Mountain Lake schools had been a great way to get involved with the town, to not feel so alone as she started over. What the locals lacked in dollars they made up for in enthusiasm. And so although she'd come to this small town to focus on painting, she couldn't help but be swept up in her work with the kids and parents.

The day she'd moved into Poplar Cove she'd vowed not to waste any time looking into her past. She'd rather live in the moment. Take each day as it came. And everything would really be perfect, if only she had a . . .

The song ended and in the silence between tracks she could hear a mama bird announce her arrival to a nest full of baby birds on the underside of the eave. Ginger leaned forward to watch as a little head poked out of the nest and took food from its mother's beak in what looked like a kiss.

Another bouncy pop song started up, but Ginger pulled out her earphones. She wasn't in the mood anymore. She stared at her canvas, but instead of seeing the painting she'd been working on all day, she saw an image of the cute baby that had been playing on the beach during her morning walk.

The little girl had been positively gleeful as she jabbed a pink shovel into the sand, her sweet round cheeks and chubby little legs poking out of her pink polka-dot swimsuit. Her mother had looked tired, almost frazzled, and yet, as she watched her daughter play on the beach, perfectly content at the same time.

Her husband, Jeremy, had held her off for years. *"One day,"* was what he told her. *"When the time is right, then we'll see."*

By the time she'd realized the time was never going to be right, that his "one day" didn't work for her, she'd had to face up to the fact that the marriage didn't either.

Lately, she wondered more and more when it was going to happen. *If* it was going to happen. She knew plenty of women who had to do in vitro at thirty. Three years past that, Ginger sometimes wondered if her viable eggs were all drying up one by one.

But there was more. Because if she were in one of her foolish I-should-know-better romantic moods (which usually involved several glasses of wine), the truth was she still wanted a wonderful husband to have the family with. Yes, her first marriage hadn't been great. But that didn't mean the second couldn't be the love she'd been searching for.

This was perhaps the only problem about settling into a small town as a single woman. The available men (who weren't ordering from the senior menu) were pretty slim pickings.

She'd been set up by one of the local biddies with Sean Murphy, who co-owned the Inn with his younger brother, but there'd been no chemistry. Yes, he was a great-looking guy. Tall, dark, chiseled. But even though she'd enjoyed his company, she couldn't shake how much he reminded her of her older brother.

One day in the not too distant future was she going to have to pull up stakes again, simply for the chance to start a family?

She sighed. Maybe it was time to get a refill on her iced tea. It was pretty darn hot after all. And she had only thirty minutes left to paint before she had to leave for her shift at the diner. No point in spinning off in her head with what-ifs and worries when she should be enjoying the time to herself.

But just as she was about to put down her brush, the screen door to her left abruptly swung open.

She spun around to see a large man standing in the doorway, his face tight and grim, his eyes narrowed. Fear hit her square across the chest.

How long had he been standing on the steps? Had he been watching her?

She'd never met him before. He wasn't the kind of man she would have forgotten. So why was he looking at her like that, like he'd come to get revenge?

Oh God, her parents had told her this would happen, hadn't they? They'd told her it was crazy to live out so far in the woods. Her nearest neighbors were nearly an acre away, far enough that they wouldn't be able to hear her screams. Maybe, she thought wildly, the biggest problem about being a single woman in a small town wasn't having trouble finding dates, it was being murdered.

Ginger gulped in air, swallowed hard, tried to remember how to breathe. She gripped the paintbrush like a weapon despite the fact that she knew it wouldn't do a lick of good in beating back the wall of muscle staring her down.

"Who are you? What do you want?"

He moved all the way onto the porch, the door banging closed behind him. "What are you doing in my house?"

His house? What was he talking about?

Huge and nuts. Not a good a combination. She was in big trouble here. Too far from the phone to place an emergency call to a friend, or even the police. Was her only choice to try to bluff him with some tough-chick act?

She was toast.

Widening her stance, lifting the paintbrush as if it were a knife, she growled, "Get off my porch," just as the sun moved out from behind a cloud and landed on his torso.

She sucked in a sharp breath. She hadn't been able to see his arms and hands clearly at first, but now she couldn't take her eyes off them. His skin was a mess, beneath the short sleeves of his T-shirt, raised and bumpy, covered with red lashes and lines. In the glimmering sunlight streaming in through the porch screen, it looked fresh and raw and terribly painful.

"Oh my God, what happened to you?" She dropped her paintbrush and moved toward him.

If anything, his expression became even more fierce. "I'm fine."

She continued across the porch. He was obviously in shock. In denial about the pain he had to be in.

"You don't need to pretend you're okay. I can see your arms, they . . ."

By then she was only a handful of feet away from him, close enough to see the true damage. She swallowed the rest of her words as her eyes and brain finally made the connection.

She'd just made a terrible mistake. Yes, he'd been hurt. Badly. But it wasn't recent. They were old wounds.

His words were low and hard. "I was burned two years ago. I'm fine now."

She bit her lip. Nodded. "Oh. Yes. I can see that now. It's just when the sun hit you, I thought—" She should stop talking now; the hole she'd dug was already big enough. "I'm sorry. I didn't mean to make such a big deal about your . . . your scars."

The silence that followed her horrible words was long. Borderline painful. He must hate it when people freaked out over his scars and here she'd practically been wrapping gauze around them.

And of course, now she couldn't stop wondering how he'd gotten so badly burned. Even though it was none of her business.

Finally, he said, "I'm Connor MacKenzie. And this is my house. I thought it was empty. I just flew all the way from California. It should be empty."

His name registered quickly. At last, something that made sense. "Are you related to Helen and George MacKenzie?"

"They're my grandparents."

She breathed her first sigh of relief. He wasn't a serial killer. He was related to the cabin's owner.

"I'm Ginger. Why don't you come in." She tentatively

smiled. "Maybe we can start over and I could offer you a glass of iced tea?"

He didn't smile back. "How do you know my grandparents?"

Did he realize that every word out of his mouth sounded like an accusation? Like she'd screwed up all of his big plans when she didn't know him from Adam.

"I'm renting this cabin from them. Didn't they tell you?"

He stared at her for a long moment, and she got the uncomfortable feeling that he was trying to assess whether she was telling him the truth.

"No."

There would have been a time when a big, strong man of few words like this would have had her trembling and weak-kneed. She would have assumed she was the one in the wrong even when she clearly had it all right. Fortunately, a lot had changed in this past year. And she, frankly, wasn't in the mood to be pushed around.

"Wait here." Sixty seconds later she was back with the signed lease. "Here it is."

He took the document from her and as he read through it, she was able to take a good long look at him for the first time. Golden-brown hair, deeply tanned skin, thickly lashed eyes, a full yet masculine mouth and strong chin, presently covered with a half-day's stubble.

Now that she was no longer worried that he was going to attack her, on an elemental level, her body suddenly recognized his beauty.

His innate power.

Up close, not only was he strikingly handsome, but he was even bigger than she'd first thought. Between the wide breadth of his chest and the muscles flexing beneath his T-shirt, from the size of his biceps and the way his chest tapered down to slim, tight hips, she could feel her breath slowly leaving her body, quickly being replaced with something that felt—uncomfortably—like desire.

It wasn't until several long moments later that she realized he was staring back at her. His eyes were making a lazy path from her face to her partially covered breasts, then farther down to her hips and legs before slowly moving back up to her face.

Suddenly, she remembered what she was wearing. Or, more to the point, wasn't wearing.

She'd never go out in public without a bra, but here, in the privacy of her own house, she did as she wished. It was one of the things she enjoyed most about having her own place. The freedom to not only do whatever she wanted, but to wear whatever she wanted.

A tank top and cutoff jeans had never been part of her city vernacular. But here at the lake, especially when she was getting down and dirty with her paints, when the thermometer read eighty and the humidity was ratcheting up all day in preparation for a rainstorm, she liked the bohemian feel of cutoffs.

Not thrilled about flashing some stranger—even less thrilled about him taking any surreptitious pleasure from looking at her—she crossed her arms over her breasts to stop the peep show. But then she realized he hadn't given her the lease back yet, so she had to unfold one arm and reach for it.

The corners of the papers crumpled in his fist. Damn it, he'd already cut into most of her dwindling painting time for the afternoon. She wasn't in any mood for games.

Switching into a stern demeanor that had been known to make billionaires quiver in their Ferragamos when they "forgot" to give one of her charities the money they'd publicly promised, she said, "Now that you have your proof, I'd very much appreciate it if you'd give me back my lease."

But this man didn't quiver. He didn't shake. Instead his eyes continued to hold hers and she was almost certain she saw a challenge in the blue depths.

And wouldn't you know it, her heart started leaping around in her chest. She supposed it was some sort of instinctual response to the combination of his devastating looks and the threat that he clearly posed to her perfect summer on the lake.

"Lucky you," he drawled. "Getting this place all to yourself this summer."

She was caught off guard by the way his low, rough voice slipped and slid through her veins so seductively. How the hell had he managed to almost make her toes curl on the porch floors with nothing but a few words?

Up until now he'd been hard. Unyielding. Definitely not in a bargaining mood. But now that she'd not only staked but proved her claim, it looked like he'd decided to change tactics by stunning her with the full force of his sensual power.

Well, just because she liked what she saw (she'd have to be drained of all hormones not to), didn't mean she had any intention of touching. Which meant she was immune.

Mostly, anyway.

"You're right," she agreed, and even though she wouldn't normally feel the need to rub in her win over a virtual stranger, she couldn't resist adding, "It's breathtaking."

He looked out at the lake. "Not many views this good, even on this lake. My grandfather used to call it the million-dollar beach."

When he turned back to her his lips were curled up on one side in what might have been a half smile under other circumstances. But right at that moment it was colored more with a sneer than anything even remotely connected to happiness.

"I'm just wondering one thing. How did you know my grandparents were thinking of renting it when they didn't even remember to tell their own family?"

It was a sucker punch. Oh no, he wasn't going to get away with that. Because Ginger Sinclair was no longer afraid to call people on their shit. And this guy was fairly brimming over with it.

"Are you accusing me of something?"

The half-not-a-smile dropped. "Only if you've got something to be guilty about."

Jesus. What was with good-looking guys? Were they so used to getting their own way all the time that they thought they could say and do whatever they wanted, whenever the mood struck? Someone should have taken this one down a peg a long time ago. Looked like the job was all hers.

Twisting her mouth into that same half smile, half sneer he'd just graced her with, she said, "Well, since I've already been living here for eight months without your knowledge, it's clearly been a long while since you've had a chat with your grandparents. Seems to me I'm not the one who should have the guilty conscience."

She braced herself for his next parry, but instead there was that flash in his eyes again, not angry now, more intrigued. The way her pulse jumped confused her, made her head feel like it was spinning. What was it about this guy that had her body turning traitor on her?

It had to be the muggy weather. All the dancing on the porch must have depleted her electrolytes. She was dehydrated. That's all it was.

"You're right," he finally said. "I need to call them."

Ginger couldn't believe it. Was he actually agreeing with her? Well, that was that. Now that they'd cleared everything up, he'd go and leave her alone. Good.

She couldn't wait.

But then, she noticed the large bag at his feet, presumably full of his clothes. Clearly, he'd been planning on staying in the cabin tonight. Because he'd thought it was vacant. Which meant he didn't have any other place to stay.

Oh no.

She looked at his face again, immediately getting snared in his dark blue eyes.

Definitely no.

This log cabin was hers and hers alone. The cuckoo clock chimed four times over the fireplace in the living room and she was hit by a sudden rush of anger at her perfect day falling to shreds.

"Look, I'm sorry that you didn't know someone was living in the house, but I've got a twelve-month agreement, so you're going to have to find another place to stay." Tonight and thereafter, thank you very much. "And I'm afraid I'm going to be late for work if I don't leave soon, so . . ."

She looked at the door, making it perfectly clear that it was time for him to leave.

He nodded, picked up his bag and said, "Okay."

She was midway through releasing the breath she'd been holding when he added, "I'll come back tomorrow. So that we can figure out something that will work for both of us."

What? He was coming back?

She should have known a guy like this wouldn't back down so easily.

"I'll say it one last time. *I've got a lease through the summer.* Good-bye."

There. She couldn't have been clearer.

But he still wasn't leaving. Instead his eyes were scanning the cabin and then he was walking over to a log that held up the wall between the porch and the living room. Without warning, he slammed his fist into it.

She half screamed in surprise. "What the hell are you doing?"

Calm as anything, he used his fingertips to brush away the crumbled wood chips.

"See that?"

She swallowed hard. "You just made a hole in the log."

A perfect fist-sized hole. How strong did he have to be to hit it like that without even flinching?

"This rotten log is just one of the half-dozen ways this old house could come down around your head." He turned back to her, raised an eyebrow. "I'm sure my grandparents would be happy to give you a refund on your rent."

Her heart was still pounding from the shock of seeing him knock a huge chunk out of the log. But she was bound and determined not to let his scare tactics work.

"I'm not going anywhere."

"Then we'll talk tomorrow."

The screen door slammed shut behind him as he left. Ginger couldn't stop herself from moving over to the log to get a better look at it. And as she put her hand into the hole he'd left, she hated how Connor had made her look at the cabin that had been her refuge with different eyes.

With doubt.

CHAPTER TWO

MOST DAYS Ginger's five-mile drive to the small downtown strip on the opposite side of Blue Mountain Lake was a leisurely, relaxing one. As winter had turned to spring and spring had shifted into summer, the trees were bursting with bright green new growth that she'd never failed to appreciate.

Until today.

What on earth was she going to do about Connor? About the fact that he clearly wanted an all-access pass to her home? She wasn't ready for her lakefront idyll to come to an end.

She was finally getting the hang of, well, hanging out. Her paintings were starting to look the way she pictured them in her head.

And Blue Mountain Lake—but especially Poplar

Cove—felt more like home than any home she'd ever had before.

It was a whole different world out here in the woods as compared to her previous life in New York City. She loved everything about it. The past eight months at Poplar Cove had been the happiest of her life. The setting, of course, was spectacular, but her joy was inspired by far more than the beautiful natural surroundings.

Freedom was a revelation. For the first time in her life, she answered to no one but herself. Not a husband, not her parents, not the committee members of umpteen charity boards.

Sure, she'd had to get a job waiting tables in town to pay for her canvases and paints and groceries, and it had taken a little while to get used to taking orders and delivering food and drinks, but waitressing was a small price to pay for not having to take her parent's money while her ex-husband kept their money tied up with lawyers.

As she parked her car behind the diner and got out into the fresh air, she took a few seconds to breathe it in as she reminded herself that there was no reason to freak out.

So the owner's grandson had showed up out of the blue. So what? The most important thing was that she'd held her ground. And would continue to do so. Unfortunately, she had to admit that he'd done a good job of making his point about the old cabin. Something would have to be done there.

Isabel, her closest friend in town who also happened to own the Blue Mountain Lake Diner, always gave good advice. If anyone would know what to do in a situation like this, it was Isabel.

Ginger was halfway across the parking lot when Josh, Isabel's fifteen-year-old son, nearly knocked her over as he shot past her to join a pretty blonde on the sidewalk. Ginger called out a hello, but he didn't hear her as he rounded the corner.

She pushed through the back door into the kitchen to find Isabel chopping a couple of bell peppers into thin slivers. "Who was that cute girl Josh was leaving with? He couldn't take his eyes off her."

Isabel sighed, not looking up from her task. "Who knows? I'm the last person he'd introduce her to."

From the first, Ginger had been struck by how attractive Isabel was. Slim and blond, nearly fifty, she looked easily a decade younger. Today, however, she looked tired. Worn out. Probably because things had been rough lately between Isabel and her teenage son.

"What happened this time?"

Isabel's words came out in a rush. "He slammed in through the door, even though I've told him at least a hundred times that he's going to pull the door clean off its hinges, and when I asked him to grab the silverware from the dishwasher, he told me he wasn't going to work today."

For the past few months Josh had been helping out for a couple of hours in the afternoon to earn some spending money. Apart from a tray of dropped wine glasses, he'd done great. A little lazy sometimes, but he was only fifteen.

"Hmm." Ginger didn't want to take sides, even if it did sound like Josh might be out of line. "Did he say why?"

"Evidently his father told him he should be out having fun with his friends because there's plenty of time for him to work when he grows up."

Isabel blew out an angry breath. "I'm going to kill Brian. He feels guilty because he only sees his son a handful of weeks every year and doesn't have a clue how much harder all of his endless *generosity* makes my day-to-day. You should have heard Josh last night going on and on about all the 'totally awesome' things he did with his father in the city the past couple of weeks."

"Must be hard to compete with that."

"Impossible. So I told Josh he'd better stay or else and you'll never guess what the little shit said?"

Ginger had a pretty good idea what a fifteen-year-old boy might come up with. Especially after working with them for the past months at school.

"He said the only way he was going to stay was if I chained him to the stove. And then he blasted out of here with that girl to go see a movie."

Ginger leaned on the counter. "I still have nightmares about fifteen. Braces. Bad skin. All I needed was the ponytail and glasses to perfect the look. The extra fifteen pounds didn't help any, either."

Isabel grunted and Ginger knew she was being no help at all. "What I'm trying to say is that fifteen is a hard age for everyone. And you've got to know that Josh is a great kid. All year up at the school when I was doing art with his class, he was always really polite. Amazingly focused.

There was this one kid I almost smacked a couple of times when he repeatedly flicked paint on the—" She realized she was heading off on a tangent and switched back to Josh. "Anyway, compared to some of the other kids, Josh is practically an angel."

All the fight seemed to go out of her friend. "Thanks for that. It helps to hear that he's not turning into a complete screwup. A lot, actually."

"You're welcome. I wish I could help more, but without a kid of my own to practice on I'm pretty much just standing here blowing smoke."

Knowing this was a touchy subject for her, Isabel said, "Oh honey, I shouldn't complain. It's just that days like this make me wish I had a partner in this whole parenting thing. Someone to share the decisions with. To make it all easier. I thought it was hard when Josh was a baby and I was up all night with him, then had to pretend to be a fully functioning human being the next morning. But I'll tell you what—this moody teenager crap is even harder."

"And totally normal," Ginger had to remind her.

Isabel nodded. "You're right. If I keep letting the little things get to me I'll be completely out of my mind by the time he goes to college. Remind me to get you five cents out of the tip jar later. Counseling session officially over."

Ginger hesitated for a moment, even though that was her cue to go to the storage room to hang up her bag and change into her black pants and button-down shirt.

She'd hoped to chat with Isabel about Connor. But it was clear that her friend already had enough on her mind with her son.

No big deal. A lot had changed in the eight months Ginger had been at the lake. She'd learned to speak up. Not to let people steamroll her. She'd been clear with Connor. Poplar Cove might have been his house as a kid, but it was her house now. If any work was going to be done on it while she held the lease, she'd say when, she'd say how much.

She didn't need Isabel to tell her that.

The traffic was crazy on Main Street and Connor had to park on the far end of the street from the Blue Mountain Lake Inn. Main Street was only one block long, but even though he hadn't been to the lake in over a decade, it felt like stepping back in time. Some of the storefronts were newer, shinier than he remembered, and there hadn't been brick-paved sidewalks when he was a kid, but the huge flower baskets were still hanging from the old-fashioned lampposts and the hardware and grocery stores were right where they'd always been.

He caught sight of himself in the window of a yarn store. Jesus, he looked like he was hunkering down for a storm, hunched and tense. The five a.m. cross-country flight was taking its toll. Connor was used to constant movement, not being cramped in a tiny seat for so many hours. A long hard run would help burn off some of the aggravations of the day. But first he'd get a room at the Inn.

Just for tonight. By tomorrow he'd make damn sure

he'd worked out a way to get back into his own damn lakefront cabin.

Walking around the front of the Inn, he remembered going to piano and popcorn nights in the oversized great room with a fireplace big enough that a half dozen of them could stand up inside it. Looking at it now, he could hardly believe it was the same place. It now sported weatherproof windows, a new wing off the back, and extensive landscaping.

He pulled open the door and was surprised to see his old friend Stu Murphy standing behind the front desk. They'd both been big fans of superhero comic books and had spent endless hours up in the Poplar Cove lofts reading by flashlight.

But Connor wasn't in any mood for a walk down memory lane. He should have known better than to come downtown, to the Inn, where he would run in to all these people who knew him as a kid. In a small town where everyone knew everything about everyone else, they'd all want to know about his scars. About what he was doing out here.

"Connor MacKenzie. How long has it been?" Stu said. "Glad to see you back in the Adirondacks."

Connor worked to cover his black mood as he shook his friend's hand. "You work here now?"

"Actually, I own it. Sean and I bought the Inn a couple years ago." Stu did a double take at Connor's scars and paled. "I heard you were a firefighter out west."

"Yup. Sam and I are hotshots in Lake Tahoe."

"Sounds great," Stu said easily, his relief at not having to go there palpable. Just as Connor had known it would be.

Putting street clothes on the day he'd left the hospital, Connor had made the decision that he wasn't going to hide his scars from anyone, even if most people probably wished he would. He'd always been more comfortable in T-shirts. He ran hot, even in cold weather, always had.

His burns weren't some sort of battle scars that he would forever wear with pride, but he wasn't ashamed of what had happened either. Firefighters often got burned. It was the risk of the job. But also part of the adrenaline rush, the reason they were all out there. Because there was nothing better than bringing a fiery bitch to her knees, nothing more satisfying than knowing he'd saved another forest, another house, another life.

Still, he hadn't realized just how uncomfortable most people would be with his scars. Even people he'd thought were friends.

Ginger was one of the only people he'd ever come across who hadn't pretended not to notice. Instead, she'd blurted the first things that came into her head.

Her reaction almost felt like a welcome change.

"So what are you doing out here?" Stu asked.

"Sam's getting married here end of this month. I was planning to take the next few weeks to fix up Poplar Cove."

Once he got Ginger to grant him access to his own house, that was.

"I'm getting married too." Stu backed away from the

counter and poked his head into the office behind the front desk. "Rebecca, do you have a minute? There's an old friend of mine I'd like you to meet."

A pretty brunette came out and shook his hand. "Hi there," she said as Stu made the introductions.

"It's always nice to meet another one of Stu's friends. I'm sure the two of you got up to a lot of trouble as kids."

Just then Stu's cell phone rang. "Shoot. It's the bride again. I swear this is the last wedding we're having here. Ever again."

Stu's fiancée lowered her voice, grinning as he walked away. "At least I now know exactly the kind of bride I don't want to be." She cocked her head to the side. "Were you just coming by to see Stu, or did you need something else?"

"I need a room. Just for tonight."

Her face fell. "Oh, I'm so sorry, Connor. I wish we had one, but this wedding has simply taken over. Every single room. Even the ones that we don't usually rent out. These people have practically moved into the supply closets. And all the local B&Bs are booked too for the next few days. But I can make a few calls to some of the nearby towns if you have a few minutes."

It didn't take long for her to confirm that the nearest opening was an hour away at a motel on Piseco Lake at the southern tip of the Adirondacks.

"Don't worry about it," he said. "I'll figure something out."

Damn it, he should be sleeping at Poplar Cove. He could just imagine Ginger's face if she found him kicking his feet up with a beer on her porch when she got off work, how her eyes would get big, the way her cheeks would flush with outrage.

What was he thinking? He'd just met her. He didn't know her at all. And beyond getting her to agree to let him work on the cabin, he didn't plan to. She was just some random woman who happened to be living in his family's lake house.

The fact that there was something intriguing about her—he hadn't expected a woman as soft and artsy-looking as her to have such backbone—was irrelevant.

But Stu's fiancée clearly couldn't stand to think of him being homeless for the night. "I'm sure Stu wouldn't want you going all the way to Piseco. If you wouldn't mind sleeping on his couch, you could stay with him until a room opens up when this wedding is finally over."

He knew a good offer when he heard one and after she brought him upstairs and showed him into Stu's suite of rooms and his couch for the night, he quickly changed into his running gear. Five minutes later he was sprinting away from Main Street.

He should have known this trip would turn into a total clusterfuck. For twenty-eight years, everything he'd wanted had come right to him. The perfect job. Gorgeous women. Life had been easy. Fun. Exhilarating.

Two years after his accident everything should be back on track. Not unraveling more every day. So many times in Lake Tahoe he'd wanted to get in his car and just drive. Anywhere. Just to get away. To get out of his head. To leave what had happened on the mountain behind. Especially on those nights when sleep didn't come, when all he could do was replay those sixty seconds in Desolation Wilderness when everything had changed.

But that was the wimp's way out. So he'd held tight. Waited for the Forest Service to get it right and put him back with his crew. Waited until this morning, when he'd gotten on the plane to New York.

Was it too much to ask for a little peace and quiet? For some space to get his shit together and push his body until it finally gave up the fight and did what he goddamned wanted it to do? Was it too much to want to help his brother with his wedding and bring his great-grandparents' cabin back to its former glory?

His lungs were burning, but it was the good kind of burn, the kind of pain that reminded him how lucky he was to be alive. Sprinting like this was what had gotten him off that trail in Lake Tahoe with nothing more than a couple of fucked-up hands and arms, some nasty scars on his shoulders and neck.

And that was why he was going to run past the pain, run until he was too exhausted to notice it anymore.

Two hours later, he limped upstairs in the near state of exhaustion he'd been shooting for and found a message on Stu's fridge telling him to grab whatever he wanted. He downed one beer before his shower and was already halfway through the second as he made his way out to the end of the Inn's long dock. Searching for a spot with cell service.

Ginger had been right about one thing. It was long past time to check in with his grandparents.

Standing out on the edge of the dock in the fading light, he watched a small sailboat drift by. He'd just spent a couple of hours running through cedar and poplar trees, but he hadn't really taken in his surroundings yet.

His whole life he'd been a doer, a mover. But sometimes as a kid, late at night after the campfires were out and the moon was high in the sky, he'd learned to be still. To sit quietly and listen for the call of the loon. To watch the water lap softly at the shore.

Right here, in this moment of perfect silence on the lake, he should be feeling it in his solar plexus.

But he didn't. Couldn't.

Pulling his phone out of his pocket, he dialed his grandparents in Florida. "MacKenzie residence."

"It's Connor."

"Who? I used to have a grandson with that name. But I haven't heard from him in so long I've forgotten all about him."

He wasn't in any mood to give his grandmother the apology she was fishing for. Not after she'd gone and rented Poplar Cove out from under him.

"I'm at the lake. At the Inn. Where I'm going to be sleeping on Stu Murphy's couch."

"Get over it, Connor. You and your brother haven't used the cabin since you were kids. And is that any way to talk to your grandmother?"

He should have known she wouldn't let him get away with being an ass. Hell, she'd single-handedly controlled two crazy-active kids every summer for eighteen years. A tiny woman, she was deceptively tough. She didn't care if he was three or thirty. She wasn't going to put up with his shit.

"The young woman we rented it to came highly recommended by the Miller girl. You know, the one who manages all of the summer places? In any case, it's been a blessing knowing someone is there to make sure the place doesn't fall down."

Her admonishment was loud and clear. Given that his grandparents now lived full-time in Florida and had stopped making the drive back and forth to the Adirondacks every six months, it made sense to rent the place out. Not because his grandparents needed the money, but because the log cabin hadn't been built to remain empty for years on end.

Poplar Cove was the kind of place kids should be running through, dripping on the porch in wet bathing suits, leaving a trail of sand from their feet all the way up the stairs to the bedrooms. And, on a more practical note, it certainly didn't hurt to have someone in residence who could alert the owners if something broke and needed fixing.

"Have you met our tenant?" she asked. "Is she pretty?"

"Yes, I've met her," he said, not bothering to answer the second question. His grandmother would get far too much satisfaction from knowing just how pretty Ginger was.

"What does she think of you?"

"Not much. Told me to get off her porch."

"Good for her. Sounds like a girl with a good head on her shoulders."

"The place needs work, Grandma. Lots of work. Far as I can tell, it'll take me most of the next month to get it all taken care of."

His grandmother made a sound of irritation. "Here's the deal, kid. Ms. Sinclair has a lease with us through Labor Day and I intend to honor it."

He rolled the woman's last name around on his tongue. Sinclair. It sounded fancy. Posh. Even a little stuck-up. Funny how none of those tags seemed to fit the barely dressed, out-of-tune singer with the paintbrushes and wild curls.

"If you really think you need to get in there to fix anything," she continued, "work it out with her. And FYI, if this phone call is any indication as to your approach, I'd think about putting on some of the charm you used to be famous for." In the background he could hear his grandfather speaking. "It's cocktail hour, honey, got to go. Love you!"

Connor hung up the phone, staring out at the sun slowly setting over the lake as he pondered the unexpected complication to his summer plans.

His grandmother was right. His best bet for getting Ginger to give him what he wanted would be to yank the old charming Connor out of the rubble. But it had been a long time since he'd been with a woman, since the days when all he had to do was grin and they'd fall into his arms.

That first time he'd gone back to one of the usual firefighter groupie haunts after his grafts had healed, he'd barely been in the bar ten minutes when he realized he didn't belong there anymore. Not because the women looked repulsed, even though he knew that would come if they got too close and made the mistake of running their fingers over his scars.

He didn't belong there, because he wasn't fighting fire anymore. And he wouldn't belong in that world again until he convinced the Forest Service to put him back on his crew.

The sun kept falling, the clouds turning a brilliant red-orange that he remembered so well from childhood. But then, suddenly they weren't clouds anymore.

They were red-orange flames.

He was back in California, out on the mountain, in the deadly heat, running, running, running but not getting anywhere. Not getting away.

God, he'd never felt heat like this. Never run so hard. His lungs were running on fumes and then he was choking, gasping, his lungs shutting down as he tried to breathe in oxygen that wasn't there anymore.

This was it.

He'd finally met the fire he couldn't outrun.

He could practically hear the flames laughing at him as they blew him down, pulling him in, dragging him backward, dragging him under, taking him straight into hell.

Oh shit, his hands were melting. The pain took him over as every goddamned cell broke apart and all he could think was Fuck. Fuck. Fuck.

Death would be a sweet release from this torture, but he didn't want it, was fighting with everything he had.

He wasn't done yet, damn it!

And then, he realized he couldn't feel his hands anymore, couldn't hold on to his Pulaski. It dropped out of his hands, fell in a loud crash . . .

Connor abruptly found himself standing back on the dock. The empty beer bottle was lying on the dock between his feet. The breeze had picked up, cooling the sweat that was covering his face.

What had just happened? One moment he was looking out at the lake and the next . . .

Fucking PTSD. The episodes hadn't started up right away, not until the pain from his skin grafts had become unbearable. His first Forest Service reinstatement denial had made them worse. With every appeal that had been denied, his episodes had grown bigger, more intense.

And he'd had to work harder and harder to deny their existence.

CHAPTER THREE

"HEY SWEETHEART, you brought me the wrong pie."

Ginger looked down at the thick slice of lemon meringue she'd just set in front of Mr. Sherman. He was one of the diner's regulars, an old-timer whose wife had passed away long before Ginger arrived at Blue Mountain Lake. Either he didn't know how to cook or didn't want to. Most nights, he arrived at six p.m. on the dot and sat down at the table in the back corner. Sometimes he was joined by a friend. Tonight, he'd dined alone on meat loaf and mashed potatoes. Cherry pie was his standing dessert order.

"I'm sorry about that, Mr. Sherman," she said as she picked up the offending plate. "I don't know where my mind is tonight."

A blatant lie.

Ginger took the lemon pie back, switched it with a slice of cherry, gave it to Mr. Sherman, and was wiping down the counter with more force than necessary when the bells on the front door chimed. She put down her rag and she was reaching into the menu box when she looked up.

And saw him.

Connor.

The immediate instinct to smooth down her hair and check her shirt for stains was so strong her hands were halfway to her head by the time she realized what she was doing.

What was she doing? Why was she worrying about impressing Connor?

That part of her life, the one where she made sure to be primped and polished just in case she ran into an acquaintance in an overpriced chichi grocery store was over and done with. She was simply going to show Connor to a seat, take his order and then deliver his food as she would any other customer.

And no matter what, she wasn't going to have any kind of hormonal reaction to his broad shoulders or chiseled jaw.

Cold as ice. That was her.

He sat down right in front of her, looking just as dangerous as he had on her porch.

"You're here. Ginger Sinclair."

She'd never heard anyone say her name like that, almost like it was a curse, but with a distinct sensual vibration beneath it.

Her heart jumped in response and she watched in

horror as his eyes honed in on the pulse point at her neck. And then, as Elvis sang about how he couldn't help falling in love, she swore she could hear Connor's breathing speed up as he watched her body react to his close proximity.

She felt herself lean in toward him, saw him shift closer to her on the bar stool even as her fingers were itching to reach out, to touch him and see if he would feel as hot as he looked.

The menu she'd been holding smacked into the underside of the counter and snapped her out of the crazy spell just in time. Connor looked a little stunned too.

What had just happened to her? To both of them? Had they both become unwilling participants in some sort of mad scientist's chemistry experiment to combine Man A with Woman B to see how quickly they'd combust?

Annoyed by her ridiculous lack of self-control, Ginger slapped the menu down on the gleaming Formica counter harder and louder than she'd planned.

"Tonight's special is meat loaf and mashed potatoes. I'll give you a few minutes to look at the menu and decide what you want."

But instead of looking at the menu he said, "I know exactly what I want."

She knew he had to be talking about food, and yet the way he said it felt like—

"I didn't know you worked here. I'm glad you do. Now I don't have to wait until morning to see you again."

Oh. Oh my. A half dozen ceiling fans kept the diner cool. She shouldn't be feeling so warm.

"I've been wanting to tell you that I was a complete jerk this afternoon."

She could feel herself softening, melting down from her core outward. But then she looked at him and realized her reaction was probably exactly what he'd been expecting.

This afternoon she could have sworn he wanted to throw her bodily off the porch. He had to have an ulterior motive. A second later it hit her.

"I take it you spoke with your grandparents?"

"I did. But my grandmother isn't the only one who thinks I misbehaved. Earlier today you asked if we could start over. Any chance that offer still stands?"

Her body screamed *Yes!* at the exact same time that her brain shouted *Don't you dare, he's playing you!*

Frankly, she had a hell of lot more faith in her brain to steer her right.

He thought he could come in here smelling like fresh soap and pine needles and blink those shockingly blue eyes at her and get her to dumbly agree to whatever he wanted.

Like hell.

He might be saying all the right things, but she very much doubted his heart was in it. He wanted Poplar Cove. Period.

She narrowed her eyes, widened her stance behind the counter. "Enough with the charm. Let's get down to it. What exactly do you want from me?"

"Poplar Cove hasn't been overhauled in two decades at least. Logs need to be replaced before they crumble. The roof is on the verge of blowing off. I need to get in there, do the work."

She was glad that he'd finally dropped any pretense of trying to patch up their rough start. An honest discussion she could do. Not this smoldering, try-to-make-her-swoon stuff. Still, there was no way she was going to let him hang out in the cabin day in, day out, for weeks on end.

"The cabin has held this long," she insisted. "I'm sure it'll make it another few months."

"Ever use the stove? The microwave? A blow dryer?"

Knowing his questions had to be a trick, that with every word he said her perfect summer was disappearing day by day, hour by hour, she reluctantly said, "Of course, all of them."

"The wiring is ancient. Anyone of those appliances could start a fire. You wouldn't know the house was burning at first. The sparks would start behind the walls. They wouldn't kick into overdrive until you were asleep. That's when smoke would start flooding into the room."

He paused. Gave her plenty of time to color in the picture he'd just sketched.

"Odds are you'd never wake up."

He was doing it again. Trying to scare her into giving up her home. To him.

She leaned in closer over the top of the counter, too angry now to remember to keep her distance from all those muscles, all that heat.

"You were sure I wouldn't be able to say no to that, weren't you?" Especially when he was practically a walking billboard for the necessity of fire safety. "Well, guess what? The answer is still no. I can hire an electrician to work on the cabin. I don't need you to do it."

"My grandparents aren't going to pay to rewire the place from the ground up. Not when I'm here and able to do the work for free."

Unfortunately, she didn't have the money either. Not anymore, damn it. Not unless she wanted to ask her parents for a loan, which she definitely didn't.

"Fine," she snapped, loud enough that a couple of customers looked up from their plates to see what the problem was. "You can redo the wiring. And then I want you out." She propped her pencil point hard enough against the paper to make a small hole. "Now what do you want to eat?"

But instead of looking at the menu, he said, "We're not done yet. I'm not just here to fix the cabin's safety issues."

"There's more?" she said, amazed by his nerve. Almost impressed by it, in fact.

"My brother's fianceé is pregnant. It was a long road for them to get there."

"Good for them. But since I don't know your brother or his fianceé," she said, knowing she was being harsh, but hating herself for giving in about letting him redo the wiring, "I'm missing the part where any of this matters to me."

"They want to get married on the beach at Poplar Cove. End of July."

How was it that he seemed to know right where to aim to hit her most vulnerable spots?

He had to mention marriage, didn't he? That elusive happily ever after they were all searching for. That she was searching for. Because even though her own marriage had crumbled to pieces, in her heart of hearts she still wanted to believe that lasting happiness was possible.

Worse, after living at Blue Mountain Lake for eight months she agreed that Poplar Cove would be the perfect place to host a wedding.

Beyond frustrated, the words, "Next thing I know you're going to be telling me you couldn't get a room at the Inn," came pouring out.

"You're right. A big wedding has taken over."

Oh no, she'd completely forgotten that her friend Sue said a Bridezilla was in residence for the next few days.

"What about one of the B&Bs?" she tried, feeling the situation slip even further out of her hands.

"Nope. Nothing on the lake. But there's a room open in Piseco."

"Piseco? That's an hour away."

"At least," he agreed, finally picking up the menu.

The movement drew her eyes down to his hands and she was stunned by how bad his scars were up close. She couldn't pull her eyes away from them, couldn't stop thinking about how much pain he must have endured from not only the burns, but the grafts as well. And then, he rubbed his left hand with his right, as if he were trying to work out the kinks in the muscles and tendons beneath the rough skin.

"When I was a little girl," she found herself saying in a much softer voice, "I reached up to the stove and knocked over a pot of boiling water onto my shoulder. I still remember how much it hurt."

It had been only a first degree burn, and the scar had almost completely disappeared by now, but it had been one of the most painful physical experiences in her life.

"For so long afterward," she continued, "it hurt. So badly. Do your hands hurt anymore?"

When he didn't reply, she looked back up into an expression so intense her skin prickled, her palms started to sweat. She couldn't look away as his eyes dilated, the black pushing nearly all the blue away. She held her breath, waiting for his answer. And then she heard it, low and raw.

"Yes."

From the tense lines of his shoulders, the tendon jumping in his forehead, she could see how much the admission had cost him. And that was when she realized, for the first time, that he wasn't just some big, gorgeous guy intent on ruining her summer.

Connor was human.

He was a man who had obviously survived something horrific, who was just trying to deal with what life threw at him.

She had to ask herself why she'd decided she needed to act like such a bitch about letting him work on the cabin. Even staying there a couple of nights until the Inn opened up.

Was she being strong? Tough? Taking a stand, claiming what was hers because she wasn't a pushover anymore?

Or—and this was the worst possible option—was it the exact opposite? Was she afraid of herself? Afraid that her new life wasn't quite as settled and solid as she thought it was? That the addition of a stranger into her cocoon might break it apart completely?

No, she told herself. The life she was building at Blue Mountain Lake was a good one. And really, the more she thought about it, Connor had come all the way from California with no idea that his grandparents had rented out their house. Under the fluorescent lights she could see how tired he looked.

"You know what, this is stupid. You're not going to drive all the way to Piseco tonight. There are plenty of empty bedrooms upstairs at Poplar Cove. Until the Inn empties out again."

He was silent for a long moment and although she'd been expecting to see victory in his eyes, there wasn't even a hint of it.

"I appreciate that, Ginger."

Knowing she was repeating herself, but wanting to make sure she was being perfectly clear—not only for his sake, but for hers too—she said again, "But just until you find a new place to stay."

"Sure." He smiled, then, for the very first time, and even though it was only the smallest upturn of his lips her breath went. "Only until then. And I'll have the special."

Going back into the kitchen, she gave Isabel the order, then said "I need to get some air," and walked out the back door into the parking lot.

The sun had set and in the darkness Ginger looked up

at the thick clouds that were blanketing the sky while wind whipped her ponytail against her face.

A storm would be hitting soon.

Tonight.

Normally, Ginger loved the changing weather. She got such a thrill every time she watched the crashing thunder duel with the lightning while she sat safe and cozy beneath a thick blanket on the screened porch.

But she didn't feel safe anymore.

All these months she'd thought she was so perfectly settled. That Blue Mountain Lake was an impenetrable retreat. She'd told herself nothing could rock her again, that she was steady now, that she was the one in control.

Had she been living a fantasy?

And yet, thinking of Connor sitting at the counter waiting for her to come back with his food sent a shiver of sudden anticipation running through her. Almost as if some secret part of her, deep inside, was hoping for trouble. For something to shake up her lakeside idyll.

Which was crazy. She was perfectly happy. Of course she wasn't looking for anything—or anyone—to shake things up.

But if that was totally true, she had to wonder, then why was she buzzing head to toe at the thought of Connor sleeping under her roof?

He wanted her.

The moment he walked into the diner and saw Ginger standing behind the counter, desire had hit Connor square in the groin. And all the while they were talking, while he'd been hammering on her about getting into Poplar Cove, sex had been running a constant current between them.

She'd changed out of the skimpy tank and shorts combo she'd had on earlier, but the fitted white shirt and black pants weren't too bad either, managing to nicely highlight her ample breasts. The half-mirrored walls gave him a good opportunity to appreciate the curve of her hips, the slight bounce of her breasts as she sparred with him.

Not only was Ginger his perfect type, lush and soft and sure to be wild in bed, but she was clearly smart too. Tough. He couldn't stop himself from appreciating—despite his irritation at having to work for it—how quick she was to cut his attempt at charm off at the pass, when any other woman would have folded at his initial apology.

And then there was the way she'd responded to his scars, the fact that she experienced some of the hell he'd lived through personally.

No one knew how much his hands still bothered him. No one had the guts to ask him outright if they hurt. He'd been surprised enough by her question to answer.

And afterward, he'd actually been disappointed when their conversation had ended and she'd gone back into the kitchen.

Since puberty he'd had plenty of experience with lust, but rarely had any of his attractions gone beyond the superficial, beyond the bedroom.

Fuck. He couldn't afford any distractions from his ultimate goals for the summer: continuing his intense training regimen so that he would be in peak physical condition for his upcoming Forest Service reinstatement, first, and fixing up Poplar Cove for the wedding, second.

There was no room for third.

He took a twenty out of his wallet and threw it down on the counter, then got the hell out of the diner.

CHAPTER FOUR

ALL NIGHT, Isabel had thought there was something not quite right with Ginger. She hadn't been able to put her finger on it exactly. Just that she looked different. Brighter, somehow. But also, unsettled.

Eight months ago, when Isabel first met Ginger, she'd had the same impression—that Ginger was a woman in dire need of calm. Living on Blue Mountain Lake had clearly done wonders for Ginger's nerves, just as it did for most people who settled in long enough to slow down to the pace of local life. So, then, what on earth could have happened to Ginger to send her back to that unsettled place?

Telling Scott, her fry cook, to man the stove for a minute, Isabel headed out after Ginger.

"What's wrong?"

Ginger shoved the curly hair that had escaped her

ponytail back from her face. "I had an unexpected visitor this afternoon."

Unexpected visitors were rather common in a place as beautiful as Blue Mountain Lake. Friends from the city who'd decided to drop by for a couple of days and relatives looking for a private beach to park their kids while they raided the liquor cabinet were par for the course. But Ginger wouldn't be looking so worried if a gaggle of girlfriends had descended on her.

"Who? Don't tell me your ex came all the way out here?"

Ginger had told her all about her marriage to Jeremy, that her relationship had fizzled out pretty much right after her new husband slid the wedding ring onto her left hand. And even though Ginger said they were both to blame for it not working out, Isabel had painted a fairly vivid picture in her head of the ex-husband as a self-obsessed bully who had once masqueraded—very briefly—as Mr. Right. She didn't have a much better image of Ginger's parents.

Ginger made a face. "No. Jeremy wouldn't come all the way out here to see me. From what I've heard he's already moved on to a tiny little brunette with a button nose and hollow cheekbones. And my mother would absolutely lose it out here with all the bugs, so no chance of that."

And yet, Isabel noted, Ginger's cheeks were growing more flushed in the empty space between sentences.

"His name is Connor. Connor MacKenzie. His grandparents own Poplar Cove. He thought he was going to be moving in today. Until he found me on the porch. He's here now, in the diner. Sitting at the counter."

Isabel heard her own sudden intake of breath and had to ask herself why it felt like her world had just been rocked, why she was reaching for the hood of the nearest car with a death grip.

So one of the grandkids next door was in town for a visit. So what?

"Do you know why Connor came back to the lake?"

"He wants to fix up the cabin for his brother's wedding."

Isabel felt the rock sink deeper into her gut. Weddings meant family. Mothers.

And fathers.

"When's the wedding?"

"July thirty-first."

Four weeks away. Long enough, Isabel reckoned, to get a new haircut. No, a complete makeover. To make sure she blew Andrew away when she saw him.

If she saw him.

God, what was wrong with her? She hadn't seen Connor's father in thirty years. Ancient history. She had a full, wonderful life; a thriving business, lots of friends, and a great son.

"Connor told me the house is unsafe. That it's a fire hazard and he needs to work on it. But even though he's probably right, I'm freaking out about having a guy all up in my space. Especially him."

"Why?" Isabel asked, feeling very protective of her friend. "What did he do? Did he try something?"

Ginger blushed. "Oh God, no. Of course not. It's just that . . ."

"What? You can tell me." And then Isabel would head back into the restaurant and kill him.

The last thing she was prepared for was Ginger saying, "Oh Isabel, there's just something about him. Not just that he's big and strong and gorgeous, but it's like there's this weird connection between us. Like we're supposed to be . . ."

Isabel tried to think how she would have normally responded if she didn't know the MacKenzies. Probably would have encouraged Ginger to break her year of celibacy with the guy.

Fortunately, Ginger was already laughing at herself. "Listen to me. You'd think I was fifteen again with a crush on the quarterback. Talking about how the stars are aligning to bring us together. Could we both forget I said any of that?"

But the thing was, Isabel remembered what good-looking kids the MacKenzie boys were. There was a reason for Ginger's bright eyes and flushed skin. MacKenzie men were a force to be reckoned with. As a teenager, Isabel had half wondered if their father did indeed hold the strings to the stars.

"Hey, your family has lived next door to the MacKenzies for a long time. Is there something I should know about them? Some sort of warning you should be giving me about him?"

Isabel shook her head no, but she put too much force

in it and ended up feeling dizzy. "Well, Helen and George are great. But you already know that from dealing with them over the phone."

She should stop there, shut her mouth. But somehow, she couldn't.

"I knew Connor's father, Andrew. We dated for a while. A very long time ago."

Seeing the interest on Ginger's face, Isabel moved to quickly stamp it out. "We were just kids. Like Josh and the girl he went to the movies with. I haven't thought about him in years. I probably wouldn't even recognize him if he walked into the diner."

Too late she realized it sounded like she was trying way too hard to convince Ginger about just how no-big-deal it was. A clear case of "she who doth protest too much."

Fortunately, Ginger was too wrapped up in her own problems to pay much attention. "Guess I'd better get back out there before the customers start a mutiny."

Isabel said "Sure" in an easy voice. But when she went back into the kitchen and picked up her knife, her hands were shaking.

This was usually the time of day she liked best, when the dinner crush had erupted in organized chaos; but it was hard to focus on her job, impossible to stop her brain from rewinding, from retracing the steps that had brought her here. To this diner on the lake.

Ten years had passed since the day she'd bought the run-down building on Blue Mountain Lake's small main street. At that time, the town had barely been more than a grocery store, a post office, a liquor store, and a gas station. Lately, though, she'd step outside to mail a letter and surprise would catch her at just how far the small town had come.

A bustling café that often housed live music occupied an old white post-and-beam house on the corner. Anderson's Market, a grocery store that had been around since her grandparents had built their cabin on the lake, had done major upgrades in the past couple of years, going so far as to stock organic fruits and vegetables all year long, rather than just July and August to appease the summer folks. And the Inn now had huge plantings of bright flowers all along the fence that bordered the street.

Only the knitting store was showing signs of wear and tear. Isabel remembered learning to knit on the comfortable couches in the middle of the store one summer when Josh was still an infant—mostly for the help of extra hands to take her baby, less because she had any affinity whatsoever for yarn.

After her divorce, the only thing that had made sense was to leave the city and settle in Blue Mountain Lake permanently. Her heart had always been there, waiting September through May for June fifteenth to roll around again. By the time she and Brian split, she'd been a full-time mom for five years, but everything changed once she took off her wedding ring. It wasn't okay to let her ex support them anymore.

Josh had made it through his childhood and early teens relatively unscathed, in large part, she believed, because Blue Mountain Lake was a world apart from the fast-moving city she'd grown up in. It helped a great deal that cell phones hadn't made their way into town until recently. Because of the thick forests throughout the Adirondacks—and a blanket unwillingness to rent out land for cell towers on the part of the locals—cell reception had been little to none in most parts of town.

Over the years, as cell phones had become increasingly popular, Isabel often had to swallow a laugh at summer visitors standing in the middle of a canoe on the lake waving their cell phones in the air trying desperately to stay connected to their fast-paced lives back home.

Wasn't that the whole point of coming to Blue Mountain Lake? To get away from everything they needed to get away from?

It was what she'd done.

Her first day back in town she'd seen the FOR SALE sign on the old diner and the lightbulb had gone on. Cooking had always been her passion, the best way to settle her nerves at the end of a long, irritating day.

Fortunately, living full-time in the lakefront cabin had given her the freedom to use her savings to lease and fix up the old diner. And in the end, having to figure out how to cook, day in and day out, for paying customers, learning how to hire other cooks and waitstaff and be a good boss to them, was the perfect way to get over her divorce. To get past it.

Long hours behind the stove or hunched over her computer in the office going over payroll helped her turn down the volume on the things she and Brian had said to each other at the end, the horrible accusations he'd made.

"Did you ever really love me, Isabel?" he'd asked. *"Was there ever enough room in your heart for both me and him?"*

Dampness crept between her breasts, across her forehead. The Big M was creeping up on her. More and more often she found herself tangled up in sweaty sheets in the middle of the night. She didn't mind at all the thought of not having a period anymore. That had never been her best week of the month.

What got to her was the sense that she wasn't going to be a real woman anymore. That forty-eight would turn to fifty in the blink of an eye and she'd be nothing more than a dried-up old woman. That her best years would be far behind her.

As she moved through the kitchen and into the blissfully cool walk-in refrigerator to check the stock, she knew it wasn't fair to paint the past as bad. As a kid, she'd spent many happy rainy afternoons at the original diner's counter, sipping milkshakes and malts, giggling with her friends over the cute boys. Thirty-five years later, the picture hadn't changed much. Every summer, girls on the verge of becoming full-blown women came in through her doors in cutoff shorts and flip-flops and giggled with their friends over the boys they'd seen that day on the beach.

Sometimes in her dreams she still felt like one of those girls. Unlike Ginger, fifteen hadn't been bad for Isabel. Just the opposite, in fact.

Fifteen was when she'd met . . . well, there was no point in going back there.

Caitlyn, a lovely twenty-two-year-old who had a way

with greens, poked her head in. "Oh, Isabel, you're in here. Just making sure the door hadn't been left open."

Isabel knew she must look like a crazy lady standing in the refrigerator staring at nothing. Grabbing a couple of eggplants and a fistful of carrots from a metal shelf, she took them over to the sink and washed them. She was drying her hands on a brightly printed dish towel when Ginger came back into the kitchen carrying a special.

"Is there something wrong with the food?" Isabel asked.

"No. It was Connor's. But he's gone."

Just then, Isabel heard a loud crack from behind her. She turned around just in time to see the upper hinge on the back kitchen door finally pull free from the wall, leaving a rusty hole on the white door.

As they stood there watching the door swing back and forth haphazardly on its remaining hinge, Isabel couldn't help but feel that it was a bad omen.

The horror movie had sucked. Big-time. But Josh Wilcox didn't care. He couldn't have concentrated on it anyway. Not with Hannah sitting right next to him. She'd grabbed his arm during one scene where the doll's head spun off and blood spurted everywhere. It had been awesome.

Everyone else had to get home after the movie, but Josh knew his mother would be at the diner until eleven at least. He had plenty of time before he needed to get home.

"It's pretty dark out," Hannah said when their friends dropped them off on Main Street.

He wasn't sure if she was hinting, but he dared a, "Want me to walk you home?" anyway.

She smiled at him and they headed down to the beach. Hannah's house wasn't far from Main, unlike his, which was halfway around the lake. He could bike the route into town in his sleep.

There were several campfires going and Hannah said, "Can you believe that I've never had a s'more?"

He turned around and tried not to stare at her like a total dork. "Seriously?"

"Weird, huh?" she said, looking a little embarrassed. "Maybe you could show me how to make one sometime?"

His heartbeat kicked up as he nodded in a way that he already knew was a little too enthusiastic. But he couldn't help himself. Not when this was his chance to shine. Because everyone knew that he was a master s'more maker.

"Sure." They were nearly at her house now. "How about tonight?" Then it occurred to him. "You probably don't have the stuff for it, though."

But she nodded, and said, "Actually, I do." He sat on her dock as she ran up to her house and came back with graham crackers and marshmallows and chocolate and matches.

"Follow me." Walking over toward some trees, he pointed to the ground. "First, you've got to find the perfect stick. Not too fat, not too thin, not too short, not too long. And it needs to have a narrow tip so that you can slide the marshmallow on to it.

She picked up a stick. "What about this one?"

He looked at it and grinned. "Talk about beginner's luck. It's perfect."

She blushed at his compliment. "Thanks. Now what?"

"Now we start a fire."

He'd been building campfires his whole life and liked the pyramid technique best. Minutes later, the fire was blazing. He quickly grabbed a stick of his own.

"Pretty much the most important part of a s'more is how you cook the marshmallow. It should be crispy and golden brown on the outside, but completely gooey and melted on the inside. That way the chocolate melts on contact. The worst thing is to accidentally light your marshmallow on fire because it only chars the outside, but the rest is still raw." He made a face. "Little kids tend to do it like that a lot."

"Wow," she said, "this sounds sort of complicated. Maybe you should just make me one."

"Nah," he said with a shrug, "it's pretty easy. Once you get a feel for the fire, you'll be a total pro."

Popping a marshmallow on the end of each of their sticks, he squatted down on the outside of the large bonfire. "It's best to slow roast it by the coals. Takes a little longer, but it's worth it."

As Hannah knelt down beside him, he felt his stomach unclench. They roasted in silence until their marshmallows had hit that perfect brown, bubbly look on the outside.

"I think we're good to go," he said. They walked back

over to the tray of graham crackers and chocolate. Breaking a cracker in half, he put a block of chocolate on it and said, "Here's how you put it all together. Hold out your stick."

Using the graham cracker halves, he slowly pulled her marshmallow off her stick, being careful not to drop the chocolate. "Go ahead, try it."

He watched carefully as she took a bite. Her eyes closed and she had a look of complete ecstasy on her face. He'd never felt this way about a girl before. Never wanted to see the pleasure on her face as she did something totally boring like eat a s'more. But he could have sat there and watched Hannah forever.

"How is it?" he asked, his words coming out a little scratchy.

She opened her eyes and smiled at him. "Totally amazing."

And then, just as he was trying to figure out if he should try to kiss her, she said, "I can't believe you've always grown up here. You're so lucky. And it's great that your mom owns the diner. You must know everyone."

"Ugh. That's what I like about the city. Total anonymity. Not like here, when every time I go to the post office Mrs. Hendricks asks me if I've grown some more."

Hannah giggled. "Have you?"

"A couple of inches maybe." She laughed again. "But seriously, it's so boring here."

She stopped laughing and he quickly said, "I mean, not with you or anything. It's just I've done the lake thing for so long. And my mom is constantly on me."

"Me and my parents ate at the diner when we were looking at buying a camp here and your mom came out and talked to us for a while about what it's like to live here. She was really cool. Really nice to us."

He shrugged. "Yeah, she's all right, I guess."

"Does she have a boyfriend?"

"No."

"Really? But she's really pretty. Does she date at least?"

He thought about it, tried to see his mom in any other light than as his mother. "Nope. She doesn't date."

Maybe that was the problem. His mom had no life of her own. No wonder she had to get all up in his business and was always asking him to go out in the rowboat or for a hike.

The fire was starting to go out when Hannah's mom called to her from their porch. "I've got to go," she said. "Thanks for the s'mores lesson."

As he walked down the beach back to where he'd left his bike that afternoon, he walked past a couple of shady looking guys. "Got fireworks?"

He almost kept walking and ignored them, but then he stopped. Hannah would be seriously impressed if he invited her over on the Fourth and he had his own personal stash of fireworks. Pulling out his wallet, he handed over a wad of the money his father had given him.

CHAPTER FIVE

AFTER GRABBING his bag from the Inn and leaving a short note for Stu, Connor headed back to Poplar Cove. A part of him felt bad about letting Ginger think he was going to have to ship all the way off to Piseco when Stu's couch was his for the taking. But he quickly quashed that.

Poplar Cove was his. He belonged here, not crammed onto a couch at the Inn.

He stood on the porch looking out at the dark water for several minutes. After twelve years in Lake Tahoe he hadn't expected Poplar Cove to feel so much like home. Maybe it was that he could feel his grandparents' presence all around him.

The chair covers his grandmother had made, the way she'd freak if he or Sam got mud on them. The bookshelves he'd built with his grandfather when he was ten, the same year his grandfather had finally let him use the electric table saw. Somehow he'd managed to keep all of his fingers.

His gaze moved to Ginger's painting, half-finished on the easel on the far end of the porch. He'd never been a museum kind of guy, never had the urge to capture a scene for posterity, not when he'd rather be out in trees and dirt and water. And yet, something in the painting resonated within him.

Heading up to the second floor, he automatically turned into the first door on the left, the room that had always been his.

Her scent hit him first, the faint hint of vanilla mixed with something earthy, sexy. Color barreled into him next. Bright clothes were hanging from the pegs on the wall and vivid canvases were crowding each other for space on all four walls. The top of the antique pine dresser was covered with bottles and jewelry and postcards propped up against the mirror.

His old bedroom had been transformed into a vibrant rainbow and the energy was palpable. The bed, now covered with a bright printed quilt rather than the serviceable blue denim he'd had forever, was unmade. Just looking at the rumpled sheets stirred him as if she were there in the room with him, naked and beckoning.

His grandparents' old bedroom was the farthest away, at the end of the hall. But he didn't feel right taking their room. Instead he moved to the guest room, which shared a wall with Ginger's.

He needed to get outside, grab a kayak, get out on the

lake and paddle hard against the driving wind. Running his body into the ground would be his only chance for sleep . . . and the only way to up the odds that he'd sleep hard enough to hold back his nightmares while he and Ginger shared the same roof.

At ten, Ginger untied her apron and hung it up in her locker. She'd already spent far longer cleaning up than she usually did. Most weeknights, after the dinner shift, she was home by now. Tonight, she'd tried to work off her careening thoughts with a mop and sponge.

Isabel emerged from the office where she'd been working on the computer and looked at the gleaming floors and stainless steel counters.

"Wow. These could be photographed for a magazine." She shot Ginger a look. "Having second thoughts about letting Connor stay at your house for a couple of nights?"

Ginger sighed. The log cabin really did feel like home. Which was exactly her problem. Somewhere along the way she'd forgotten that Poplar Cove was only a temporary respite from her normal life. As much as she wanted to pretend that the log cabin was hers—and that she could live there in blissful peace forever without having to face life's usual stresses—it wasn't.

"When my lease is up, he'll probably want the cabin back."

"Is that what's really bothering you? That you're going to have to look for a new place to live in a few months? I'm sure you could find another lakefront cabin to rent by then."

"You're right," Ginger admitted. "It's just that . . ." She tried to figure out how to put her feelings into words. "This might sound weird, but for the first time in my life I felt like I could be myself."

Her parents weren't here telling her how to behave. Her ex-husband wasn't here criticizing her. She'd found a place where people were getting to know her for her and not because of who her father was or how much money she had.

"And in so many ways Connor reminds me of my ex-husband."

There was that same initial attraction. That same alpha-male-coming-to-take-what's-mine act.

"Having Connor in the cabin, I'll have to watch how I look. What I wear. What I say."

It had already started. Look at her, doing anything she could think of to avoid going home.

"Why do you think you need to do any of that?" Isabel argued. "Why can't you just go on exactly as you have been and if he doesn't like it, who cares? You've really come into your own here. I find it hard to believe that one guy could make you forget that."

"You know what?" Ginger said slowly, as Isabel's words seeped in. "I think you're right. It'll be fine."

If there was one thing she'd learned during the past eight months, it was that she needed to live a life that made her happy. Wear whatever she wanted. Do whatever she wanted. Say whatever she wanted.

So Connor was going to be moving in and out of her space over the next few weeks, so he was going to be sleeping in one of the empty bedrooms for a couple of nights. So what?

The wind was blowing even harder as Ginger went out to her car. As she drove back to the cabin, Isabel's words ran on repeat in her head, working to set her straight right when she'd been about to veer off course.

Getting out of the car behind the log cabin, she crossed over the patch of grass beside the house onto the beach. Standing under the huge clump of old poplar trees that shaded the house most of the day, she stretched out her arms to let the frenzied wind whip her hair and clothes around.

She loved it here, loved the raw and wild weather that blew in and out almost at random. Living in the log cabin made her feel the same way, as if she were constantly surrounded by a forest rather than four walls.

All of a sudden there was a loud screeching sound right above her head. Connor's warnings about how unsafe the cabin was shot through her brain just as she heard an ear-splitting crack. She tried to move, to run, but she didn't know which way to go, could barely seem to pick up her feet.

Suddenly, strong hands and arms came around her rib cage, picking her up and throwing her across the sand.

Connor.

She landed hard on her side a split second before he leaped onto her, covering her with his body.

She felt it then, the force of something hitting them

hard. Her stomach lurched like she was in an elevator on a free fall, and the back of her arm behind her elbow stung, but even as her brain worked to process the last thirty seconds, she knew it was Connor who had taken the brunt of . . . whatever had just hit them.

"What just happened?" she rasped against his collarbone.

Connor's breathing was just as ragged as hers. She could feel every beat of his heart as it thumped hard against hers.

He didn't answer her question, just ground out a rough, "Are you hurt?"

In the dark, his fingers ran across her face, from her forehead, to her cheekbones, down to her mouth as if he needed to check for himself that everything was still intact.

"No," she said, shivering at his touch even as she asked again, "What hit us?"

His words rumbled from his chest to hers as he told her, "It was a widow maker. It almost fell right on you. Almost crushed you."

"A widow maker?"

He shifted them slightly, but still kept her cradled in his arms. No one had ever held her like that, like he would protect her with his last breath. Not even the man she'd married.

Despite the cold wind, the press of Connor's hard muscles against her had heat pooling at her breasts. Between her legs.

She'd known he would be hard, but she didn't realize

just how small she'd feel pressed up against him, that her curves would almost melt into his strength.

Her head, her insides spun and swirled as he pointed up to the large grove of poplar trees. "A widow maker is a dead branch or limb resting on live ones. Every year hundreds of people die beneath them when they fall."

In the dim moonlight peeking out between the clouds, she saw an enormous limb lying on the beach not more than a foot away from them. At its biggest point it was at least a foot thick. She could only guess how much it weighed, how close she had been to becoming another casualty.

"If you hadn't seen it, if you hadn't moved so quickly—" She started shaking at the realization of what might have happened if not for Connor. "Thank you for saving my life."

"I saw it this afternoon. I should have taken it down right away." He cursed, drew her closer. "What the hell was I waiting for?"

Wait a minute, was he blaming himself for this?

"It was an accident."

"You could have been hurt. So badly."

"I swear, I wasn't. Just a scratch, that's all," she said, showing him her arm, wanting him to know it wasn't his fault.

She wasn't prepared for his fingers to move to her elbow, for him to gently stroke her bruised skin.

"Where else does it hurt?"

She found herself saying, "My knee," even though it was barely throbbing, simply because she wanted him to tend to her again. And when he did, when he gently caressed her leg, she couldn't repress a low moan of pleasure.

His hand stilled on her knee. "Are you sure you're okay?"

Her arms and legs were fine. It was every other part of her that ached. For more of him.

She said, "Yes, I'm okay," and then the next thing she knew he was hauling her to her feet and moving away. The wind rushed between them as he said, "What were you doing out here so late?"

Thrown by his abrupt question, and by the loss of his heat and rock-hard strength against her limbs, her mind went blank for a moment.

"Sometimes I'm wound up after working the dinner shift." Especially tonight after going several rounds with him across the counter. "And I love the lake on nights like this when a storm is rolling in."

It hit her, how had he been there to save her at all? "Why were you outside? How did you see me?"

"I was in the kayak, paddling back to shore when I saw you walk out on the beach and stop under the tree. That was when I heard the limb shift."

"You were kayaking at night? Why?"

He took another step away from her. "I haven't been back here in twelve years. I wanted to get out on the water."

"You couldn't wait until morning?" was her first question and when he didn't answer she asked another, "Twelve years is a long time to stay away. Did you come to the lake a lot before then? As a kid?"

"Every summer."

It didn't add up. "It's so beautiful here. How could you have stayed away for so long?"

"Fighting fire was more important."

A puzzle piece clicked into place. "That's how you got burned, isn't it?"

He didn't answer, then, just backed completely out of the moonlight so that his face went into shadows.

"Good night, Ginger."

Great. She'd done it again. Let curiosity get the best of her, about his scars. He probably thought they were the only thing she'd noticed about him.

She walked back into the cabin and went upstairs, took a shower to clean the smell of grease from her hair and skin, brushed her teeth and slid into bed. But all the while, she could still feel the heavy beat of his heart against her chest, the way he'd run his fingers so gently over her face and her limbs when he thought she'd been hurt.

After ten years as a hotshot, Connor knew his limits. He'd pushed himself hard today, harder than he usually did and his muscles were screaming for rest, for a few hours to rebuild what he'd broken down.

But it was hell trying to sleep one wall away from Ginger. Especially now that he knew how it felt to hold her.

He couldn't stop replaying the scene in his head. Watching Ginger stop under the trees. Hearing the shifting and cracking of the limb, knowing it was going to crush her. Jumping out of his kayak and running through the water praying he'd get to her in time.

Sweating again at the thought of how close it had been, he kicked off the thin blanket covering his naked body. Finally, as the wind blew rain hard on the roof, Connor slept.

Ginger was wrapped deep in a dark and swirling dream where she was running through a forest full of falling widow makers when a cross between a scream and a roar woke her. Sitting up in bed, her hand on her heart, it took only a second to realize it was coming from Connor's room.

Her stomach clenched with fear as she threw on a flimsy robe and shot out of her room. My God, what could possibly be happening to him? She shoved his door open.

From the dim light in the hall she could see that he wasn't on the bed, but on his feet now, swinging at the air like a tortured beast, his eyes closed, his beautiful face taken over by rage. And deep, deep pain. His fists were closed so tightly the scars on his knuckles stood in out sharp relief and her heart broke into a million pieces as she watched this big, strong man fighting like hell against some demon in his head.

A voice in the back of her mind told her to leave him. That she should let him fight his battles alone. That he would probably break her in two if she got involved and he didn't wake up.

But she couldn't do that.

Not after he'd rushed in to save her from the falling limb tonight. Not after he'd taken the full force of the hit on his own back.

Not after he'd been so gentle, so protective of her out on the beach just hours before.

She ran over to Connor, any thoughts of fear gone. She put her hand on his arm and as soon as he felt her touch, he grabbed her forearm in a vice grip and pulled her against him, her robe opening and falling off her shoulders.

Oh God, he was squeezing her so tight, she cried out with whatever breath she could find.

"Connor! It's me. Ginger. You're having a bad dream. It's just a dream. Please wake up."

His eyes opened but she could tell he didn't see her, that he was still trapped in his own personal hell. And then, in a flash, his eyes cleared and he came back to her, to his bedroom, to Poplar Cove.

His chest was rising and falling hard against hers and as their bare skin rubbed together, in the back of her mind it registered that he was naked and she nearly was. But it didn't matter. Not when she'd just seen him go through something so horrible, not when she was so worried about him.

"What are you doing in here?" His words were as gruff and hard as he'd been when she'd first met him on the porch.

"I had to come, when I heard the—" She cut herself

off as she realized just how much he was going to hate her having seen him like this. "I had to help you."

His hands that had been so tightly gripping her shoulders moved, slightly at first, down over her shoulder blades, then farther down her spine, to her hips. His next words were so low she almost couldn't make them out.

"And you thought this was how you could help me?"

She could hardly breathe, certainly couldn't move, not when he was still holding her so tightly. Not when leaving his arms was the very last thing her body wanted. And then one of his hands curled into her hair and her head was tilting back and he was kissing her. Every part of her that was woman wanted to take this moment and give in to it. Give in to him.

Connor needed healing more than anyone she'd ever met, and imprisoned in his arms, with his mouth ravaging hers, while his hands cupped her ass as if he owned her, she wanted to be the woman to heal him.

All the while knowing that it wasn't just giving, it was taking, that she was seeking her own pleasure too.

And then his hands were moving up from her hips to cup her breasts and she didn't recognize herself anymore, this woman who was moaning as his fingertips brushed against her nipples. His skin felt deliciously rough and jagged against her, and her sound of pleasure came straight from the center of her.

Oh yes, please, more. She hadn't been this close to coming apart in a man's arms in years and she wanted it so badly that when he abruptly cursed and pushed away from her, it came as a total shock.

She sat down hard on his bed. What had just happened? One minute his hands were everywhere, the next he didn't want to touch her.

It was so tempting to go to the place where her feelings were hurt, where she could tell herself that he didn't like big girls like her. Every last one of her instincts tried to take her there, but she fought hard against them all.

It just didn't make sense. He'd wanted her, she knew he did. What had been about to happen was elemental. Completely out of control for both of them.

He couldn't have just up and changed his mind. Not without a damn good reason. So, for once, instead of running off with her tail between her legs, she wrapped her robe around her and stayed where she was.

"What happened? What's wrong?"

It was like looking at a rock, he was so devoid of emotion as he stood against the window. Almost as if he refused to let himself feel anything at all.

"I told myself I wasn't going to touch you. Jesus, I was completely out of control. I could have hurt you."

It was scary, but she had to say it, had to tell him the truth. "I wanted it just as much as you did." She'd been just as out of control as he had.

Giving in to her desire for Connor was the most reckless and impulsive thing she'd ever done. She knew she should be relieved that he'd stopped her, that they hadn't made any bigger of a mistake than this.

But she wasn't. She wasn't relieved at all.

He still wasn't looking at her. He continued staring at the wall behind her head as he said, "I couldn't feel you."

He couldn't feel her?

"Of course you could. It was—" The word incredible was on the tip of her tongue, but before she could say anything more, his eyes locked onto hers.

"My hands. They went numb."

There was so much darkness in his blue depths it took her breath away.

"I couldn't feel you."

CHAPTER SIX

CONNOR COULDN'T believe he'd just told her that. No one knew about his hands going numb except for the doctors he'd secretly visited. He'd gotten so good at faking it these past couple of years, made sure not to grab anything if he wasn't absolutely certain he'd hang on to it, but just now, when he couldn't resist touching her bare skin, he'd lost all sensation.

Fuck.

He wanted to be left alone. To get the hell out of here. To find some alternate reality where this shit would stop happening. Where he'd be normal—hell, where he'd be sane—again.

"What were you dreaming about? When I came in?"

Shit. How could he have forgotten? That's why she was in his room in the first place. Because he'd been stuck in a flashback.

His pride pricked at his insides, made his words rough and mean. "You don't know me. I don't know you."

He let his eyes move across her thighs peeking out from her robe, made damn sure she could see that he was still completely naked—and that his body still wanted her despite everything.

"Don't confuse wanting sex with something more."

Okay. Any moment now she'd get off his bed and run back to her room. But as the seconds ticked down she stayed right where she was. Frustration ate away at him, even as sensation came back into his hands, the worst case of pins and needles he'd had yet.

"You need to leave. Now."

But she didn't so much as flinch. Instead, her gaze was steady.

"If you're done with your whole big bad wolf thing, I really think you'll feel better if we talk about what just happened."

She licked her lips. Her beautiful, full lips that had tasted like heaven.

"No one knows about your nightmares, do they?"

He didn't answer, but that was only because he knew he didn't need to. This woman sitting on his bed saw too much, her big green eyes taking in everything he didn't want her to. Everything other people didn't.

"You were dreaming about the fire, weren't you? The fire that did that to your hands."

The next thing he knew, she was getting off the bed and coming over to him. She picked up one of his hands, turning it over in her own small hands.

"Are they still numb?" she asked softly. "Or can you feel this now?"

She ran her finger lightly down the worst of the scars, the one that cut his palm in two.

"I can feel that."

Her smile was big. Beautiful. Like a ray of sunshine was shooting in through the roof.

She said, "Good. I'm glad," and then, "What happened? Not tonight, but two years ago. When you got burned."

There was no reason to tell her about the fire. For two years he'd kept the story tightly locked inside. Had told himself that talking about it wouldn't help a damn thing.

But no one else had ever witnessed one of his nightmares. Only Ginger. She'd seen him at his worst.

Fine. He'd give her the answers she was looking for. And he wouldn't bother to spare her the gory details. When he was done, she'd regret that she ever asked.

"Firefighters get burned all the time. Fire is a finicky bitch," he said, not bothering to watch his mouth. If she didn't like it, she could leave.

"I wouldn't think that makes it hurt any less, though."

A vision of the fire in Desolation rammed into him like an out of control train. Fire rolling over the mountain like a wave. Thick, dark smoke rising up into the sky, taking over the blue so completely that he could hardly see the narrow trail beneath his feet.

"We were out in Desolation Wilderness, where my crew is based. I've hiked that trail a hundred times. My brother and squad boss were out clearing brush. The fire was nothing. We wanted a real fire, something to really sink our axes into."

But there hadn't been another fire. Not for him, anyway. Whereas Sam had gotten right back out there. Connor would have done the same thing if it had been Sam lying there on a stretcher. He would have headed straight back in to get his revenge. To strangle the fire with his bare hands for taking down his own blood.

"What happened? How did the fire change into something worse?"

It was the question he'd asked himself a thousand times. "The wind must have shifted. Dropped a spark. Logan saw it first, realized we were on top of the fire. First thing you teach a rookie, fire goes up. Ninety-nine percent of the time it'll outrun you. Logan should have saved himself. Instead he hiked down the hill to get me and Sam. Told us to drop everything and start running."

Jesus, he still remembered that moment so well. He was running his chain saw through a huge clump of dry brush, his entire focus on blade cutting through wood. From the corner of his eyes he thought he saw Sam waving his arms and cut his engine. Sam put his chain saw down and said two words. *"A blowup?"* Logan nodded and without saying anything more, the three of them started running straight up a near-vertical slope.

"We were swallowing dirt and sparks, running through piles of white ash. I started coughing and they slowed to make sure we stayed together, but even then we still thought we were going to sit around with the guys and laugh about it at the bar that night."

His breath came fast. Sweat started to drip between his pecs.

Ginger was squeezing his hand, now, and the feel of her soft skin against his helped to calm him, to bring him back into the cabin, into the bedroom where he'd almost lost control with her.

She'd been so silent he'd forgotten she was there. But now that he remembered, he knew that if he pulled her against him and kissed her again he could stop talking, could make her forget all about his story, could maybe even forget for a few minutes himself.

He took in her soft skin, her luscious curves, her curls falling around her shoulders, and was tempted, so incredibly tempted to taste her again. Sex would be easier than talking, so much more direct and to the point, so much less dangerous than this spark of deeper connection.

But the part of his mind that could still think straight—the part that wasn't completely hypnotized by her scent, by the feel of her hand on his—knew it would only be a temporary respite.

Because as soon as they were done, as soon as they'd had their fill, she'd come at him with her questions again.

"The wind whipped up and it was like looking straight into a wall of fire."

"I can't imagine," she whispered.

"No. You couldn't. And then the flames reached out and grabbed me, pulled me down."

His name came out of Ginger's lips in a rush of emotion, her hand tightened on his.

"Sam and Logan were way out in front. They heard me

fall. They came back for me." He still couldn't believe they'd done it. "They came back for me."

"Of course they did."

"No." The word was practically a roar. "They almost died. They should have gone on. Left me." Instead they'd picked him up between them and run like hell. "Logan spotted a rock face just big enough for us to get over. In the end, the fire hit the rock and turned back on itself."

He didn't remember much after that, knew he'd passed out, but he'd heard the nurses talking about him in the hospital as he went in and out of consciousness that first day.

"My turnouts had melted into my arms. The doctors ended up taking off most of it in sheets." From his elbows down, his skin had been stripped away. He pointed to the tops of his thighs. "They took most of the new skin from my legs, just peeled it off like an apple."

She looked down at the scars on his thighs. "I—" She stopped, swallowed hard enough that he could hear it. "I hadn't noticed those scars."

His mouth twisted. "Everything they say about skin grafts is true. Hurts like a bitch."

His arms and hands hurt less, probably due to the nerve damage. But his thighs where they'd harvested the new skin—that had been a bad couple of months. Anytime he moved or fabric brushed against his limbs he'd wanted to cry like a baby from the pain. The doctors had tried to get him to take the drugs, the painkillers, but he hated feeling foggy, like everything was in slow motion.

That was when the nightmares had started.

"Most people don't have the courage to consider being a firefighter in the first place," Ginger said softly, "let alone go back to it after something like that."

Used to be, he'd eaten up people's admiration. Especially from beautiful women. He wasn't that guy anymore.

He shook her hand off. "You can save your praise. I haven't been out there in two years. The Forest Service has made sure of that."

She took a step back in surprise. "But I thought you said—"

"I'm on my last appeal."

Oh fuck, he hadn't believed it himself. Not until he'd just said the words aloud. This was his final chance to do the job he was born to do. And if they took it away from him, then what?

"They're afraid I'm going to freeze out there. Possibly kill myself, or worse, take out a civilian too."

"But surely they can see how committed you are? How much you want it?"

It was the same thing he'd been telling himself, the reason he got up every morning at five and ran ten miles every goddamned day.

"Do they know about your nightmares? About your hands?"

He reached into his bag on the dresser, pulled on a pair of shorts. "What do you think?"

"No, I don't suppose I would tell them either if I wanted to get back on the job." There was no judgment in her words, no pity either. Just understanding. "When are you supposed to hear about your appeal?"

He watched her tighten her robe around her waist, wanting her despite all the reasons to stay away. One more kiss. That was all it would take. And then they'd be on his bed and he'd be over her, sliding against her, into her, until they were both completely lost in each other's skin, and sweat, and sex, his nightmare forgotten for a few blessed seconds.

But after the way she'd listened to him, the comfort she'd given, she deserved better than a night of hot sex with some out-of-work firefighter who had random night terrors and hands that went from too much sensation to none at all.

"This summer."

She stared at him for a long moment before turning and walking to the door. Over her shoulder she softly said, "I really hope you get what you want. Good night, Connor."

Dropping to the floor he did one push-up. And then another and another to drive away the swirling emptiness that was there, still waiting for him to drop back into it.

He'd gotten all the sleep he was going to get tonight.

CHAPTER SEVEN

THROUGHOUT THE rest of the night as Ginger fell in and out of sleep, Connor's story ran through her brain. All the pictures he'd painted. All the ones he hadn't that she could so easily imagine on her own.

Endless hospital visits. Not knowing if he was going to be able to use his hands again. And then having to fight with the Forest Service to get his job back after he'd already sacrificed so much.

His agonizing story had touched her deeply. Every word had pierced the core of who she was. She'd ached for him as he talked. She'd had to reach out for his hand, to let him know that he wasn't alone, to try to absorb some of his pain, if only for a second. Waking up throughout the night, she found herself worrying about him, wondering if he'd managed to sleep, hoping another nightmare wouldn't come for him as soon as he let his guard down.

For the first time in years she was awakened by her alarm, rather than with the first rays of the sun. At six a.m., she'd assumed Connor would still be asleep, but his door was wide open. Where could he be? Could he have decided he'd had enough of her probing questions and packed up his things to head back to California?

Her stomach twisted at the thought of it—even though his leaving had been exactly what she'd wanted the previous afternoon—and she had to go to his room to see if his things were still there.

Seeing his bag on the dresser sent relief washing over her. He wasn't gone. Not yet. And even though she didn't have a clue about where things could possibly go between them after what had happened last night, she was glad.

Quickly showering and dressing, she went downstairs to guzzle a cup of coffee before she headed back to the diner. And that was when she looked out the kitchen window and saw him on the beach, putting himself through what looked to be an intense workout. He was doing pull-ups on one of the trees at the edge of the white-gold sand in front of the cabin.

Watching him brought back the sensation of his body against hers, the hard warmth of his muscles, the slide of his fingers against her breasts. She'd never been so physically drawn to any man, had never wanted to be *possessed.*

In the sunlight his scars stood out in sharp relief. And as she watched him, she saw the horrible fire in Lake Tahoe play out in her mind, almost as if she'd been there with him.

How hard, she wondered, had it been for him to get to

this point, where he could withstand the pressure of wrapping his scarred hands around a tree limb and pull himself up?

And how hard must it continue to be?

Although she'd trained in many different disciplines of art, she'd never been particularly drawn to sculpture until this very moment. If only she had clay at her fingertips, she felt that she could make something truly great. Simply because she was wholly inspired by her subject.

Whenever she worked the breakfast-into-lunch shift Ginger was amazed by how quickly seven hours could disappear.

"So," Isabel finally said when they were the last two in the restaurant. "How'd it go last night with Connor?"

Ginger knew Isabel had been dying to ask all day. Just as she'd been dying to confess, "The only word I can think of is gravity."

Isabel grabbed her arm and pulled her down into one of the chairs in the empty dining room. "What are you talking about?"

"We talked last night." *Among other things.* "For quite a while."

All she had to do was close her eyes and she was right there again, in his bedroom, watching him try to fight back his pain as he told her about the fire.

"He's gone through so much, has worked so hard to get to where he is today. He's really an extraordinary man."

"I thought he reminded you of your ex-husband."

Oh yeah, she had said that, hadn't she?

"Do you think first impressions can be wrong? That once you learn more about someone, once you've had a chance to go deeper, that everything can change?"

"Maybe. Or maybe it's just our way of trying to convince ourselves that we can have the one thing we know we should stay away from," Isabel said pointedly. "Besides, how deep could you possibly have gone in one night?"

Ginger instantly gave herself away with a deep flush.

"Are you telling me that you slept with him? The same guy you didn't want anything to do with yesterday?"

"No," she said, glad to be able to tell her friend the truth. "He saved me from a falling tree branch and then later we kissed but—"

"Oh Ginger." Isabel ran one hand over her face. "I didn't want to say anything to you last night. I hoped I wouldn't have to, not when you were so clear about keeping your distance. But I really think you should watch it with Connor."

"Why?" Isabel was the one who'd been pushing her to get out there and date. "Did you know him well as a kid?"

"No. Actually, I hardly ever saw him or his brother. Only when they were having bonfires out on the beach or they were water skiing. I'm just trying to make sure you don't get hurt."

"I appreciate that," Ginger said slowly, and she did, but Isabel's warning didn't sit quite right with her. If Connor were anyone else, wouldn't her friend be encouraging her to live a little? To stop clinging to safety and take a risk for once in her life?

Another possibility struck her. "How serious were you and his father? A couple of dates? Or was it something more?"

Pain flickered across Isabel's face so quickly she instantly regretted her question. Ginger had been such a shrinking flower for so many years that she sometimes had the sense that she was overcompensating. First with Connor and now with Isabel, pushing and pushing until she forced them to tell her things they'd much rather keep buried.

But before Ginger could tell her friend to forget it, that her probing question was way out of bounds and she was grateful to know Isabel was looking out for her well-being, Isabel said, "We were pretty serious. Very serious, actually."

And just like that, Isabel started telling her about Connor's father.

Fifteen years old, her limbs long and slim and tanned in a sundress, Isabel waited on the curb at the corner of Main Street and First.

She'd ridden her bike into town from her parents' cabin. Her friend Judy was supposed to meet her here, but even though she'd been standing on the curb outside the diner for a half hour, Judy hadn't shown up yet. But Isabel hadn't been upset with her friend, whose parents could be uptight about Judy riding into town by herself. After all, it was another perfect summer day, and she'd been wanting to go into the small general store on the corner and try on some sandals she'd seen in the window.

Maybe, she thought with a smile, her parents would buy her a pair for her birthday, which was coming up in a few weeks. As working musicians, they didn't have much money to spare, but she'd never felt like they were poor. How could they be, when they had an amazing cabin to come to every summer on Blue Mountain Lake? Her grandfather had built it in the teens and all of her five much older siblings—she was the baby of the family, a "wonderful surprise" was what her mother said—had spent their summers on the beach just outside the front door. The whole summer stretched before her. No school. No lessons. Nothing but fun in the sun.

Smiling to herself, she left her bike propped up against the diner's brick wall and headed down the street. In previous years, she'd brought friends from the city up for a week or two at a time, but none of them ever appreciated it as much as she did. They called Blue Mountain Lake "the middle of nowhere" and bemoaned the lack of shops and boys.

But as far as Isabel was concerned, there were plenty of places to window-shop back in the city the other nine months of the year. June, July, and August were all about being outdoors, family time, and having fun.

And as for cute boys, there was only one that mattered to Isabel.

His name was Andrew. He lived next door. And he didn't seem to notice she was alive.

Seventeen years old, he was built more like a man than a boy, with broad shoulders and light brown hair that picked up the sunlight in blond streaks with every passing week of summer. She'd fallen in love with him when she was ten. Five years of looking. Five years of dreaming. Five years of planning exactly what she'd say to impress him the first time he talked to her.

Andrew was her Prince Charming, she was absolutely positive of it. One day he'd finally turn around and notice her. One day he'd kiss her—she blushed just thinking about—and then when he realized he couldn't live without her, they'd get married and live happily ever after.

Looking both ways before she ran across the street, Isabel was panting as she reached for the front door of the general store. A two-story house that had been turned into a store when she was just a baby, it was the only place in town to go if you needed underwear or flip-flops or dishes.

Her hand still on the door, she stopped to read a sign that said, PART TIME CASHIER HELP WANTED. *Pondering whether it might be fun to spend a few hours a week ringing up purchases, thereby earning a few more dollars for milkshakes and Popsicles on the beach with her friends, she was surprised when a strong, tanned arm reached around her and opened up the door.*

Her breath caught in her throat as she looked up into Andrew's eyes. "Oh, sorry, I shouldn't be standing here blocking traffic," she babbled, her words tripping over one another to her increasing mortification.

But the boy she'd always loved from afar didn't seem the least bit impatient. Instead, he smiled, his green eyes crinkling up at the corners, his white teeth a beautiful contrast to his deeply tanned skin.

"Don't worry," he said, his low voice sending shivers of excitement through her. "I'm not in any rush. Are you?"

Her cheeks felt so hot she was afraid her head was going to burst into flames.

"No," she finally said, her voice sounding too loud, far too excited for their simple conversation. Realizing he was still holding the door for her, she rushed inside, the cool air in the store a welcome change to the heat coursing through her. Maybe by tonight, her heart would stop pounding like a snare drum. But instead of moving past her, he simply stood beside her, the same smile on his lips.

His eyes scanned her face for a long moment and she forgot to breathe until he said, "We live next door, don't we?"

Her ponytail bobbed up and down as she nodded. So many times she'd played out this moment. She'd planned on being alluring, yet coy, pleased that she had his attention, yet aloof enough to keep his interest.

Instead, she was acting like a little puppy, desperate for a pat on the head.

But even though she was inexperienced with the opposite sex—no kisses, no hand-holding, not even a trip to the movies—on the verge of becoming a woman, some inner voice she'd never heard before told her to slow down, to let him make the first move.

Taking a deep breath, she found a small smile to mirror his. "Yes, we do. I'm Isabel."

"Andrew," he said, holding out his hand.

She loved how he said it, as if she didn't know his name, as if she hadn't been drooling over him for the past five years.

Using every spare ounce of willpower she possessed, she shook his hand, then said, "See you around," and breezed past him up the stairs to the women's clothing department.

Grabbing a random sweater off the nearest rack, she rushed into a changing room, pulled the door closed, and sat down on the floor, utterly dazed. Her heart was still racing and when she looked up into the mirror, she saw that her cheeks were flushed a bright pink. Thankfully, it wasn't an unflattering look, but she was certain that despite her cool good-bye, Andrew knew exactly how big of a crush she had on him.

Which was why she was going to stay in this dressing room until she could be absolutely certain that he was gone.

After several minutes had passed, a knock came at the door. "Excuse me, miss, are you all right in there?"

Isabel quickly stood up, ran her hands over her hair and opened the door. "Yes, thanks." Holding up the sweater, she said, "I'm afraid this doesn't look quite right on me, however."

Handing the sales clerk the sweater, Isabel saw for the first time that it was embroidered with eight leaping reindeers, Santa Claus beaming from the center. It was a sweater even her grandmother wouldn't be caught dead in.

Again, a quick exit seemed best. Deciding to try on the flip-flops another day, she left the store and was running back across the street to get her bike when the first drops of rain started falling. A loud clap of thunder came next and she knew she'd better look for cover. Too embarrassed to go back into the store, she headed for the covered boathouse at the end of the public dock. She'd wait out the storm there.

Sitting down on the painted wooden planks, she leaned against a wall and looked out at the whitecaps blowing across the lake, the hard rain leaving momentary divots across the surface of the water. She breathed in the fresh mountain air, the sweet smell of the rain, and finally relaxed again.

A part of her wanted to replay, to savor, her encounter with Andrew. But another part of her wished she could forget it entirely. Best case, he simply thought of her as a little girl. Worst case, he would laugh with his friends about the huge crush she had on him.

Curling her knees up to her chin, she wrapped her hands around her legs and sighed. No wonder why singers were always going on about love hurting. It did. It really did.

Especially when it was wholly and completely unrequited.

"Mind if I join you?"

The low voice startled her and she spun her head around with a gasp.

Andrew's smile was warm, maybe even a little apologetic. "I didn't mean to surprise you." He held out an ice-cream cone. "Maybe I can make it up to you with this?"

His hair was all wet and there was rain dripping down his cheeks. Isabel couldn't hold back the huge smile that took over her face. How could she, when every one of her dreams was coming true? But as she took the dripping ice cream, sudden shyness tied her tongue again, making it impossible to speak.

"Nice place to wait out a thunderstorm," he said as he sat down beside her, kicking his long, tanned legs out in front of him.

She licked her ice cream and nodded, still too unsure of herself to say a word. Why, she wondered, had he sought her out? Was it because he felt sorry for her, the red-faced girl from the store whose world he'd totally rocked just by speaking to her? Or, could there be another reason?

Was there some slim chance that he actually liked her too?

"So," he said casually, "what grade are you going into next year?"

She swallowed a bite of her vanilla cone so fast it went straight to her forehead and she winced at the sudden ice-cream headache. "Eleventh." She looked at him out of the corner of her eyes, but he was so good-looking all it did was make her head spin. Turning her gaze back to the water, she asked, "What about you?"

"I'll be starting NYU in the fall."

She didn't live far from campus. "Congratulations," she said. "That's a great school." Screwing up her nerve some more, she asked, "Do you know what you want to study?"

"Industrial engineering. But not for buildings. For boats. I'm going to build a boat and sail around the world."

She found herself nodding, smiling at him. "Oh, I love to sail. There's nothing like it."

He looked into her eyes. "Sounds like we'd make a pretty good team, doesn't it?"

Midlick, she almost dropped her cone. She'd had a crush on him for so long, she knew she was reading volumes into everything he said.

But he was looking at her so intently, she didn't know what to think, until he said, "You've got a little ice cream right here," and then his fingers were on her cheek and he was brushing at her skin, and her entire body erupted in goose bumps at his touch.

She felt her mouth drop open just in time to clamp it shut.

Not only had he talked to her, but he'd touched her.

And then, just as quickly as the storm began, it ended. Soon, the sun was shining off the water, steam rising from the lake's surface.

"Looks like it's safe to head home now," he said as he stood

up. Helping her up, he asked, "Can I give you a ride back home?"

She pointed to her bike, sad to have to turn down the best offer she'd ever had.

"It'll fit in my trunk, no problem."

Walking together to get her bike from the front of the Blue Mountain Diner, she followed him to an amazing-looking classic car.

He opened the trunk, trying to sound nonchalant. "I fixed it up myself. Wanted to have it ready by summer."

Easily lifting her bike up, he slid it into the huge trunk, then walked around to the passenger side of the car and opened the door for her.

"You're my first passenger."

Beyond thrilled, Isabel slid onto the cool leather seats, tightly clasping her hands on her lap so they wouldn't give her nerves away by shaking. But instead of getting in behind the wheel, Andrew leaned into the car and found a crank beside the backseat. Moments later, the roof was coming down.

Sensing his pride, she said, "Wow. What a car!"

Again, he smiled at her, the pleasure in his green eyes taking her breath away. "I'm glad you like it. And I'm glad you're the one helping me christen it."

For the first time since running into him on the steps of the general store, she forgot to be nervous. How could she be scared when he was looking at her that way, like she was the most beautiful girl in the world? No one had ever looked at her like that before. It was beyond thrilling.

Andrew pulled out and as they slowly drove down Main Street, she noticed more than one person admiring his car. As they took the lakeside road out of town toward their cabins, she pulled out her ponytail and closed her eyes as the wind rushed through her hair. She'd never been so happy. Never felt so alive.

The five-mile drive went far too quickly and before she was ready for her time with Andrew to end, he was parking his car in the small gravel lot behind his parents' log cabin.

"I'll walk you back to your cabin," he offered and even though she could easily traverse the two hundred yards on her own, she didn't turn him down. He wheeled her bike between them as they walked through the thick grove of trees that separated the two cabins.

"Thanks for the ride," she said softly as the poplar trees thinned out and her parents' cabin came into view. "And the ice-cream cone."

For the first time, he was the one who looked nervous. Isabel was surprised to feel the shift between them, even more surprised when she realized he was about to ask her out.

On the verge of screaming, "Yes!" before he could even ask the question, she bit down on the inside of her cheek to let him make the first move.

"I'd, uh," he cleared his throat, "I'd love to see you again, Isabel."

"I'd like that too," she said softly, then before she could stop herself, went up on her tippy toes and brushed a kiss against his lips.

She ran through the forest the rest of the way to her house, leaving Andrew standing alone, still holding her bike.

* * *

The reproduction Coke-bottle clock behind the bar chimed loudly, three times, pulling Isabel from her memories.

"I can't believe I've kept you here for an hour, talking your ears off about ancient history."

Ginger protested, saying no, of course she wanted to hear it, but Isabel could see the dark smudges beneath her eyes. Whatever had or hadn't happened with Connor the previous night, Ginger clearly hadn't gotten much sleep.

Pushing back her chair, Isabel said, "Let's get out of here."

"But you haven't told me what happened yet, why the two of you broke up," Ginger said. "I mean, it sounded like true love, like the two of you were meant to be together."

"How about I give it to you in ten words or less?"

"Okay."

"He cheated on me. She got pregnant. He married her."

"Wow," Ginger said. "Ten words exactly."

All Isabel could do was laugh. She'd long ago decided it was so much better than crying.

CHAPTER EIGHT

THERE WAS nothing quite like swimming for an hour in the crystal clear lake and yet Connor didn't feel nearly as loose and relaxed as he should have. Not after last night, after the things he'd said to Ginger, the fact that he'd practically had to chain her door shut to stay the hell away from her.

Thank God she was at work. It would give him a few hours to get a grip. To try to convince himself that just holding her hand hadn't rocked his world more than sex with any other woman would have.

He didn't have anything to give anyone else right now. Maybe if he'd met her two years ago they could have—

Fuck. Why was he even going there? He'd never been a believer in love and marriage, not after watching his parents rip each other to shreds his whole life. He liked everything about women—the way they moved, smelled, came—but he'd never even come close to finding a woman special enough to make him want to rethink his take on relationships.

A beach towel around his hips as he walked up the stairs, his feet lightly dusted with sand, instead of continuing past Ginger's room, he stopped, absently rubbed one of the scarves hanging over her door between his thumb and forefinger.

He could still feel her, soft and warm, as he'd held her. And he could still remember the way she'd looked at him as she'd pulled his story from him, as if she'd experienced enough of her own darkness to understand his. No one, not his brother, not the rest of his crew—certainly not the psychologists hired by the Forest Service—had ever listened to him the way she had. Really listened without judgment, without any agenda of her own.

Wrenching himself away from her doorway, he shoved on some dry clothes and forcefully pushed Ginger out of his head. For the next hour, he walked through the house and made a long list of everything that needed to be done to get the place up to code.

With thousands of fires under his belt, he saw everything through a firefighter's eyes. His first task would be to redo the ancient electrical wiring and get a new stove in to replace the old two-burner stove and oven unit his grandmother had been so proud of when he was a kid. They needed fire alarms in every single room along with a fire extinguisher and escape ladders in the upstairs bedrooms and bathroom.

He needed to head to the hardware store to start buying supplies, but first it was time to get rid of the rental car. For the work he was going to be doing, especially when he got around to replacing the rotten logs around the living room, he needed a truck.

Picking up the phone, he called over to the only place in town where you could get a car. He was surprised when Tim Carlson picked up the phone.

Damn it, his old friends kept popping up around every corner. And he was even less in the mood for a round of catch-up today. Still, he needed a truck and ten minutes later he was pulling up outside a newly painted white farmhouse.

He was barely out of the car when a pretty little toddler with pigtails ran out to greet him.

"Hi!" she yelled, her chubby hand waving up and down.

Squatting down to her level, as he took in her one-toothed smile and big brown eyes, a smile won out over his dark mood.

"Hey there, pretty lady. I'm Connor."

The toddler babbled something that he assumed was her name just as his friend, Tim, came and swooped her up into his arms. She giggled as he lifted her above his head, then handed her off to her mother who had just come outside to join them.

"Great to see you again," Tim said, giving Connor a one-armed hug before introducing him to his wife. "Kelsey, this is Connor." As they shook hands, his friend added, "Now you see why I waited until we were married to introduce you to this guy. Connor and his brother Sam made the rest of us look like sorry alternatives."

Laughing, she shifted the baby to her other hip. "This is Holly." Holly yawned and rubbed her eyes. "I'm going to put her down for her morning nap. When you boys are done playing with trucks, brunch will be ready."

Connor quickly learned that Tim ran Carlson Construction and was now one of the main home builders in town. Five years ago he'd gotten married, chucked in his life in the city and started up the small-town business. On the side, he fixed up old trucks and when he'd gotten to about a dozen, his wife had told him he might as well buy the car lot too. So he did.

Considering the mood he'd been in when he'd gotten out of the car, Connor was surprised to realize he was almost relaxed as they walked across a newly mowed field where a trio of horses were feeding. It had been a long time since he'd hung out with a guy who wasn't a firefighter, who didn't constantly remind him of everything he wasn't doing.

"Nice looking family you've got there," Connor said.

"Thanks. We're happy. And I'm glad Holly's playing outside in the grass and dirt, rather than on sidewalks and chain-link-fenced parks." He shot Connor a speculative glance. "What the hell happened to your hands, man?"

Connor was starting to think he should get a shirt made that said, WILDFIRES ARE A BITCH on it.

"Gotta learn to run faster."

"Sure," Tim said, "you don't need to go into the whole deal. You must be sick of talking about it."

But the truth was, he really hadn't talked about it to anyone. Not until last night with Ginger. Suddenly, Connor realized he was sick of acting like it hadn't happened when anyone with working eyes could see that it had.

"The quick version is that it was a really bad day on the mountain. I got stuck in a place I shouldn't have been." He held up his hands. "And I paid the price."

"And now?"

"I should be hearing from the Forest Service about getting back to my hotshot crew soon. Until then, I'll be here working on Poplar Cove for Sam's wedding. Make sure to keep July thirty-first open."

"Any chance you'd consider moving out here full time?" Tim asked. "You know, joining up with the local firefighting crew. My business is growing fast and you were always a whiz at building things. I could certainly use the help."

Connor didn't even have to think about it. "My life is back in Tahoe." He couldn't imagine leaving the Tahoe Pines hotshot crew for good. He'd never pictured anything else for himself, never wanted to.

Then again, he'd never pictured meeting a woman like Ginger out here, either.

"Yeah," Tim agreed, "it's so wet in the Adirondacks, I'm sure the action you'd see out here is nothing compared to what you get out in the West. I can't think of the last time a cabin burned on the lake."

They turned into a big workshop and Connor whistled low between his teeth at the half-dozen old Ford trucks currently in process. "Quite a setup you've got here."

Walking up to the nearest, a dented and scratched cherry-red Ford with duct-taped seats, Tim said, "Do you think this one would work for the summer? It's already beat to all hell, so you won't have to worry about chucking scraps and tools into it. Besides, I don't have time to work on it until fall."

"I was going to offer to pay you for it, but now I think I'm going to keep my money."

"You're welcome," Tim said, clearly grinning at the thought of Connor riding around town in the old jalopy. "Now let's get back to the kitchen before Kelsey's blueberry pancakes get cold." He rubbed his slightly rounding belly. "There's one big reason to get married. Great cooking."

But talking about his Forest Service appeal had brought the agitation back. "Thanks, but I'm good grabbing something in town."

There was a threat in his friend's eyes. "Kelsey's feelings will be hurt if you leave now."

Minutes later Connor was sitting down at the breakfast bar digging into the plates of food set out across the tiled counter. Still eating long after Tim and his wife were finished, his friend frowned and said, "How the hell do you eat like that and not gain weight?"

Kelsey teased her husband. "My guess is he does more exercise than walking the dog to the nearest tree before bed."

"So if you're fixing up Poplar Cove for Sam's wedding," Tim asked, "then where's Ginger staying?"

"Poplar Cove."

Kelsey and Tim shot each other a loaded look. "Hey, Connor," Kelsey asked, "tell me, is there a pretty little thing back home pining away for you?"

"No."

Hell no. Connor figured that was his cue to leave before they went all matchmaker on his ass.

"Thanks for the great food." He held up the keys. "And the truck. I'll do my best not to wrap it around a tree."

"I'll follow you to drop off the rental car," Tim offered.

As they drove tandem into town, Connor noted that all around him, people were paired off. His friends, Tim and Stu. His brother, Sam. His squad boss, Logan.

From out of the blue, a picture of Ginger holding his hand in his bedroom hit him straight in the gut.

He could still remember how good it had felt to have her small fingers softly stroking his scars.

Soothing him.

Heading into the grocery store after work, Ginger bypassed the stack of blue plastic baskets to grab one of the carts on wheels. She was halfway through the produce aisle when she asked herself what in heck was she doing buying all this food? She certainly didn't need an entire bag of apples or a big bunch of bananas.

Five minutes with a man under her roof and she'd turned into Old Mother Hubbard.

Connor wasn't a real houseguest. She didn't have to feed him. Or clean up after him. He was a big boy. He could take care of himself. Find his own food. Cook his own meals.

But as she started to put the bananas back on the pile she couldn't help but feel like a total bitch.

She needed to feed herself anyway. So, really, what was the big deal of making enough for two? She'd feel horrible sitting in the dining room eating while he starved. Especially given how much he worked out. If it had been a woman who'd shown up on her porch yesterday, would she have made such a big stinking deal about the whole thing?

No, of course not.

Really, she told herself as she put the bananas back in her cart and continued through the meat aisle, picking up a roast and some ground turkey, she'd always liked to cook. And meals for one could get kind of boring, unless you didn't mind tons of leftovers. For the next few days, she'd get a chance to make a few of the new recipes she'd ripped out of *Cooking Light* magazine. That'd be fun.

And then he'd leave and she'd get back to her normal life. Cabin all to herself. Free to do what she wanted, when she wanted, with no input from anyone else.

Funny how it no longer sounded quite as good as it once had.

Thirty minutes later she pulled up at Poplar Cove beside a classic Ford truck. Quickly guessing that Connor had traded in his rental, she was pleasantly surprised by his choice. She would have figured a firefighter would choose one of those monster trucks on huge tires, the ones you needed a ladder to climb into. Not something with dents and scratches. She couldn't help but smile as she looked in the window and saw duct tape all over the seats.

It all went back to first impressions and how incorrect they could be. Because here was more proof that Connor was nothing like her ex-husband. Jeremy wouldn't have been caught dead in a beat-up old truck.

Grocery bags in hand, Ginger walked up the porch stairs to the sounds of hammering. Her heart skipped a beat at the thought of a man who actually knew how to do more than screw in a lightbulb. Telling herself there were plenty of things sexier than a guy who knew how to use hand tools—although right at this moment she couldn't think of any—she took a deep breath and headed for the kitchen.

He didn't notice her at first and for good reason. He'd pulled the old stove out from the wall and was kneeling in front of a panel of very confusing-looking wires. Not wanting him to electrocute himself on her account, she was about to turn around and leave when he looked up.

And then, before she realized what he was doing, he took the grocery bags from her and started emptying out the contents on the Formica countertops. Her ex had never done that. He'd been very clear about what was women's work and what was men's work.

Then again, Jeremy hadn't known how to hammer in a nail or rewire an electrical system either. Why, she wondered, had she let him get away with doing so little outside of the office? Why hadn't she ever thought to ask for what she wanted?

"I should have checked with you before I started tearing apart the kitchen," Connor said, and she appreciated the apology behind his words. "Fortunately, the refrigerator is on a different breaker."

Realizing she was standing there like an idiot, she moved next to him to start putting the meat and cheese away. In the small kitchen, she caught the heady scent of him, the clean smell of a man hard at work making things safe. Opening up the fridge, she was glad for the cool rush of air.

Between the two of them, the task of putting everything away was quickly done, leaving her feeling awkward. He picked up a screwdriver and squatted down over the electrical box when she jerked her thumb over her shoulder.

"I'll get out of your way. I was just going to head out to the porch to paint."

Out on the porch, she set up her paints and canvas. Usually, within seconds, she was hard at work. Today, however, a good five minutes passed before she realized she was still mixing red and orange, the colors having gone an ugly brown.

She turned and looked over her shoulder toward the kitchen. It was quiet back there now as he redid the wires, and she supposed she could pretend that things were back to normal, that she was alone and content in the lakefront cabin. But Connor's presence was so big, so overwhelming, her thoughts kept shifting back to him.

Maybe she should pack up her things and head out of the cabin to paint, find even ground to stand on and get back into her groove. But she couldn't run from him all summer. If that was her plan, she might as well move out.

Closing her eyes, she was trying to relax by taking several deep breaths when she heard Connor kick the stove and mutter a curse. Opening her eyes, a smile on her lips, she picked up her paintbrush and it started moving, almost on its own accord, great wide strokes of vibrant color across the canvas.

Connor's stomach growled, but he wanted to finish rewiring the kitchen's electrical panel before quitting for the day. Tomorrow, he'd junk the old stove and go into town to pick up a new one. Every thirty minutes or so, when he stood up to stretch his legs and back, his eyes were drawn to the porch.

To Ginger.

Her hands moved quickly as she painted, deft strokes of color. She was incredibly talented, anyone could see that, even a guy like him who didn't know the first thing about art.

He watched her pile her curls up on top of her head as the late afternoon heat kicked in and rays of sun moved across the porch. He couldn't bring himself to step away before she noticed him standing in the doorway behind her.

She tried to cover the canvas with her arms as if to hide it from him. "It isn't done. I'm not sure it's any good yet."

"It's good."

Color rushed to her cheeks at his compliment. “Thanks.”

Staring at her painting, he realized he finally saw the stillness he’d been looking for out on the dock that first night.

“How’d you do it?”

“Do what?”

He looked away from the painting, caught Ginger’s bewildered gaze, realized he’d spoken out loud.

“Never mind.”

“No,” she said, “you were going to say something about my painting.”

He held up his hands. “I don’t know anything about art.”

“Just spit it out already,” she said, clearly frustrated. “What were you going to say?”

“The lake. The mountains.” He hated this, feeling like an idiot. Every time he was with her, something happened. His hands went numb. He said too much. “I didn’t know anyone else saw them like that.”

“Like what?” she pressed.

Why couldn’t she just leave well enough alone?

“Alive,” he ground out. “They look alive.”

Her eyes went wide as she moved one hand over her heart. “You can see it? What I’m painting?”

“I told you. I don’t know what I’m talking about.”

His breath caught in his throat as she smiled back at him; her cheeks were a rosy pink, her hair piled on her head exposing her long, slender neck.

“No. I mean, yes, you do. You’re right. I’m painting the

lake. The energy that's within it and around it every single day. And no one has ever really seen—" She shook her head. "With abstract art, most people think it's just a bunch of random colors."

Oh shit. This conversation, these smiles, were the opposite of what he should be doing. "I'll clean up my tools and get out of your hair for a while."

She blinked at the abrupt switch, before saying, "Don't go." Looking flustered, she added, "I'm going to make some ground-turkey tacos. Are you hungry?"

"Starved," he admitted, "but I can grab something in town."

She was already moving past him into the kitchen, pulling out peppers and salsa and black olives. "It's not a problem. I'd end up with leftovers anyway."

Thinking of how Tim had said Kelsey would be insulted if he didn't eat the breakfast she'd made, Connor told himself he didn't have any choice but to accept.

He banged his knuckles against the stove. "You probably need this, right?"

"A stove would certainly be handy."

Sweet Lord, the kitchen was so small that they were practically right on top of each other. Clamping his fingers around the edge of the stove hard enough to turn his knuckles white, he shoved the stove back into place against the wall.

"I'll go clean up and come back down to help."

Turning the water on, he stepped into the ice-cold spray before the old pipes had a chance to heat up and decided to leave it cold. This dinner was going to be a lesson in self-control. Or purgatory.

The green farmhouse dining table on the porch was set and full of food by the time he made it back downstairs, a beer in front of each plate. Sitting down on opposite sides of the narrow table, neither of them spoke as they concentrated on assembling their tacos.

After taking a bite, Connor had to tell her, "This is great, Ginger."

Waving away his praise she said, "It's nothing. Just tacos."

He finished the first taco, started another. "You should be in the kitchen, not waiting tables."

"Waiting tables is just for money. I'd rather paint."

Watching as she sucked her lower lip beneath her upper teeth made not only Connor's groin react, but also something in his chest. And even though he'd told himself over and over to keep his distance, he found that he wanted to know more about her, wanted to try to solve the mystery of her.

Maybe then she'd stop being so damn intriguing.

"Why are you here?"

She blinked, clearly thrown off by his abrupt question.

"Most people have never heard of Blue Mountain Lake."

She put down her half-eaten taco. "I got a divorce. And just to be clear, I'm the one who wanted out. But once it was all done I knew I couldn't stay there anymore."

"Where's there?"

"New York City."

The picture was growing clearer. "You didn't wait tables in the city, did you?"

"No. I did a lot of fund-raising." She raised her eyebrows. "More than you'd think was humanly possible, actually."

Another puzzle piece slid into place. She didn't dress like a rich girl, but there was a sophistication in the way she moved.

"Most people don't walk away from money."

She took a long drink from her bottle of beer, then said, "I know this is going to sound like I'm a poor little rich girl, but I love how different Blue Mountain Lake is from my previous life. My parents think I'm crazy to want to be out here, can't believe I'm waiting tables for nothing, but it's my decision. I waited thirty-three years for this, for something all my own, to use my own hands and brain rather than have everything handed to me on a silver platter." She paused, looked him straight in the eye. "I came here to finally get it right."

Any other time, any other person, he would have let it be. But the way Ginger had pushed him to talk last night about the fire, about his hands, still grated. He'd call it retribution, and work like hell to believe that's all it was.

Rather than out-and-out fascination.

"Why'd your marriage fall apart?"

Instead of flinching at his pointed question, she came right back at him. "What is this, twenty questions?"

"Last night you got to ask the questions. Now it's my turn."

She seemed to consider it before nodding once in

agreement. "Fine. But I'm not going to spare you the gory details."

Jesus, he'd already felt that she'd understood him last night, but now it seemed that she'd almost been in his head too.

"I'd get them out of you anyway."

Loaded tension swung back around to heat, back to the sensual chemistry they couldn't push down.

"It was lust at first sight. Jeremy and I met at a dinner party given by a family friend. We left early to have sex at his frat house."

Lust? Jealous sparks shot through him.

Looked like she was right. He didn't want the gory details after all.

"I was twenty-two. A virgin in her senior year of college, the good girl who'd been saving herself for Mr. Perfect. So naive you wouldn't believe it. Within weeks his ring was on my finger. My parents fought it, told me to slow down, but I just thought they were being their usual rich, cautious selves, that they were snobs because he didn't have a huge bank account. So I ripped up the prenup they wanted him to sign and when he wanted money to start a company I gave it to him without doing any due diligence. I was so blindly, stupidly in love." Her mouth twisted. "And then one day I realized it hadn't been love at all. Just pretty good sex that left as quickly as it had come."

Pretty good grated, but not as much as great or fantastic would have. Connor did the math.

"You must have been with him ten years."

"Don't remind me. What a waste. Ten years I spent trying to pretend everything was fine, trying to convince myself that I hadn't made the wrong choice, that I hadn't failed."

"Why did you finally leave?"

Her eyes closed tight. "I'd rather not talk about it."

A nice guy would have dropped it. But he'd lost that guy in the fire. "I talked last night. Fair is fair."

Without opening her eyes, she said, "We were at one of the auctions I'd organized. Jeremy liked to be the auctioneer, was pretty good at it actually. Except that night, he'd been drinking. And when he drank he got sort of . . . mean."

Connor's fists clenched. "Did he hurt you?"

Her eyes flew open. "No." She shook her head. "Yes. It was one of those 'buy a date' auctions and I was one of the last women to be auctioned off. He made a joke."

"A joke."

"About a cow." Two bright spots of color spread across her cheeks. "About how if we lived in India I would be the prize for the night. That there must be some guy out there who liked," she lifted her hands to make quote marks around the words, "big girls like me. And then he grimaced to show just how disgusting he thought I was."

Connor had never met the guy, but he wanted to rip him apart with his bare hands.

"My father yanked him off the stage. I don't remember exactly how I got to him through all the tables and chairs." She smiled then, a bitter twist of her lips. "But I'll never forget how good it felt to slap him. The sound it made when my palm hit his jaw. And then he swung at me with both fists, would have hit me if one of my father's friends hadn't pulled me out of the way in time."

She took a breath, seemed to come back to the porch, the dining table. "It was the final straw. What was the point of pretending anymore? Everyone could already see what a mess my marriage was. So I filed. And got the hell out of there."

"Your husband was an asshole."

She smiled, almost seeming surprised by it. "You're right. He was. Is."

"And he was wrong. About you, about how you look."

"Connor, you don't have to. It's taken me a long time, but I'm finally starting to come to terms with my body. With my shape." Another smile, this time more sad than happy. "I spent a lot of summers at fat camp."

"Whoa. You're joking, right?"

"Every summer I got to hang out with fifty of my best overweight friends. I could quote the calorie handbook to you verbatim."

He hated everything about the idea of fat camp. Especially when there was nothing wrong with Ginger. Nothing at all.

"I still don't get it. Why would they have sent you to—"

No, he wasn't going to say the words. Not when they didn't fit her.

On the surface Ginger seemed so strong. She hadn't taken any of his bull, had come right back at him every time. But now, for the first time, he saw a hint of the fragility she'd been hiding.

"I guess my parents thought life would be easier for me if I were prettier, if I could wear the same things everyone else did. But like I said, I'm over it." She held out her arms. "After my divorce, I figured it was time for a new approach. To say this is me. Take it or leave it."

Jesus, she didn't get it, how badly he wanted to take it. Take her. Rage rushed through him at what that prick of an ex-husband had said to her, at the way her parents had belittled her beauty; he forgot his vow to stay in neutral territory.

"The first moment I saw you standing on the porch in your cutoff shorts and tight little shirt, I wanted you."

Ginger pushed her chair back so fast the loud scrape of the chair echoed all through the porch. She grabbed their plates.

"I'll clear this up."

But the kitchen wasn't far enough away, didn't give her the space she needed to pull herself back together.

She'd been about to throw herself at him, about to beg him to make love to her, to shove the plates and food off the dining table and pull him down over her as a thank-you not just for saying something so incredibly sweet, but for getting her art in a way few other people ever had.

Only, she'd just told him her whole sob story. If anything had happened just then she would feel like it was out of pity.

He walked into the kitchen holding the rest of the

dishes, his large presence seeming to suck up all the air in the room.

"I was out of line. Right now and last night."

Knowing they were both trying to stay above the waterline tonight, she simply said, "Don't worry about it, Connor. Not any of it."

Pulling from a past that involved plenty of small talk, she purposefully shifted to a more innocuous subject. "I'd love to know what the lake was like when you were a kid. I always dreamed of coming to a place like this."

He moved over to the sink, turned it on to wash the dishes by hand. "I learned to swim when I was three and my brother shoved me off the end of the dock." At her gasp, he said, "Don't worry. He wouldn't have let me drown. That's what he says, anyway. The rest of the summer I barely came out of the lake at all, except to crew with my grandfather in his *Sun Fish*."

"What about when you were a teenager, was it still as much fun?"

"Sure," he said, his voice more easy than she'd yet to hear. "Sam and I spent one summer rebuilding a busted-up party boat from scratch with some buddies. Did donuts in the middle of the lake until the ranger came out to give us a ticket for reckless driving."

"How could you stay away for so long?" she asked "You obviously love it here."

His hands stilled in the soapy water. "I already told you. I had a job to do."

"Of course firefighting is important," she agreed, "but what about the rest of your life? You can't be a superhero twenty-four-seven. Surely the Forest Service doesn't expect you to give up everything for the job."

"No one forced me to keep going out there." He was defensive now, the sponge scraping at the already clean plate. "It was my choice. I've never wanted another life. Never wanted anything else."

"Seriously? There's nothing else you want? Nothing?"

After last night, she'd told herself she wasn't going to push him so hard again, but she couldn't help it. Not when she couldn't fully grasp what he was saying.

"You don't want a family? Kids? Something beyond your job?"

"After the fire I saw how fast it could all go up in smoke. How damn easy it would be for me to walk out the door one morning and not come back. I would never want to leave a family behind. And I can't live without fire. So, yeah, I've made my choice."

Now it was her turn to apologize. "It's very commendable. Choosing firefighting over everything else. I didn't mean to make it sound like your choice is wrong. I'm just not sure I could make the same one."

He slammed a plate into the drying rack. "Don't you think I've gone over this a hundred times? That maybe if I'd taken some time off, gotten more sleep, spent some time with someone who wasn't also living and breathing fire, that I could have outrun the flames?"

"What happened in Lake Tahoe wasn't your fault, Connor."

"One of our guys died in that fire. Jamie. He was just a

kid. A rookie thrilled to be working his first couple of fires for the summer."

She wanted to put her arms around him, but after last night touching him seemed like the worst possible option. Not unless she wanted to end up in his arms again.

Which she did.

She gripped the dish towel tightly. "I'm sure you and your crew did everything you could to save him."

"They were down one man. Me. I should have been out there with Jamie when the bomb went off. Maybe I could have seen that something wasn't right and got him out in time. Instead he was out there all alone, without a chance in hell. I should be grateful to be able to stand here and wash the dishes. I can run and swim, get back out in the woods whenever I want to. But all I can do is complain about my hands, about not being allowed to do my job."

He left the room and she wanted to go after him, to force him to see that he was doing the best he could, better than most, and that he needed to stop beating up on himself for being human.

But something told her he wouldn't hear her. Not tonight.

Not yet. Maybe not ever.

She wasn't surprised when she heard him start up his truck and drive away.

The phone rang and she'd been so deep in her thoughts she nearly dropped the plate she'd been holding. "I'm sorry to disturb you tonight," a man said, "but I was wondering if my son was there by any chance?"

Isabel's story instantly came back to her along with the unhappy ending, *He cheated on me. She got pregnant. He married her.*

"You must be Andrew."

"Yes. I didn't realize my parents were renting out the cabin. How have you enjoyed being there?"

Strange how different this conversation with Connor's father was from any she'd had with his son. Connor didn't waste words, whereas his father struck her as extremely smooth. And yet, neither of them knew Helen and George had decided to rent out the log cabin. Not the closest family in the world.

"Poplar Cove is wonderful, thank you. And, yes Connor's staying here, but he just went out."

Somewhere, anywhere to get away from her. Because everything she'd said reminded him of his own pain.

"Could you tell Connor I called? That I'd very much like to speak with him?"

She wondered if she were hearing things that weren't there, the hint of desperation in Andrew's voice. "Of course. I'll tell him."

After hanging up, she pulled a sticky note off the fridge and wrote, "Your father called," on it. Quickly deciding he might not find it on the fridge, she headed upstairs with the note and down the hall to his bedroom.

She paused at the threshold, thinking of what had happened in the room not twenty-four hours ago, her body responding with a flood of desire. Of longing.

She wasn't blind to all the reasons not to fall for Connor. She wanted kids and family. He didn't. She was looking for balance. He'd given his whole focus to fire and only fire. But every time she was with him, she couldn't help but see not only how different Connor was from her shallow ex-husband, but how different he was from anyone she'd ever met before.

He was a hero and yet he couldn't forgive himself for not being the man he once was. Everything in her ached to heal his pain. His regret. To pull him into her arms and hold on tight until he could finally let it all go.

As she put the note on his pillow, even as she tried, one more time, to remind herself that she hadn't come to the lake to get involved with an off-limits man, she felt as if she were watching a crash about to happen in her rearview mirror. And there was nothing she could do to stop it.

Because she wasn't sure she wanted to.

CHAPTER NINE

GINGER RAN all the next day from back-to-back shifts at the diner, to a private art lesson at the home of one of her favorite students, and finally to the Thursday Night knitting group at Lake Yarns on Main.

Her friends were there already. Rebecca and Sue from the Inn. Kelsey taking a few hours away from her little girl. A couple of mothers she was on the school art board with, one of whom was complaining about being pregnant for the fourth time.

"I actually cried when I found out," the woman confessed. "Here I thought I was out of diapers, that they were all going to be in school during the day, and *bam!* Those dreams all went up in smoke."

Ginger was glad everyone else was talking at once, alternately consoling and congratulating the woman, because she simply couldn't speak around the bitter lump in her throat.

God, it shouldn't sting so much to watch someone else get everything she wanted. Not just one child, but four.

But any way she tried to reframe it, it still stung like crazy.

Once the wine had been poured, the brownies passed around, and they'd all finally pulled out their various works in progress, Rebecca turned to her on the small couch the two of them were sharing with Kelsey.

"Did you do something with your hair, Ginger? You look different."

It was funny, when she'd looked in the mirror that morning, she'd done a double take herself. She fumbled her needles, one of them clacking to the floor.

"No. Everything's just the same as always."

Only it wasn't. Not at all.

Kelsey glanced up from the scarf she was working on, a knowing sparkle in her eyes. "Really? Exactly the same? Even with Connor staying with you?"

Ginger couldn't control the flush that hit her smack in the middle of her cheeks. "How do you know about Connor?"

"He picked up one of Tim's cars."

"And I met him at the Inn," Rebecca added.

Ginger had a crazy urge to stick each of her friends with a needle.

"Stu was going to give him the couch in his room until the bride from hell left, but—"

Kelsey finished her sentence, "I guess he got a better offer."

"He didn't tell me about Stu's couch," Ginger said. "He made it sound like he was going to have to go all the way to Piseco."

Rebecca's grin grew bigger. "Can't blame a guy for stretching the truth a bit."

"Not when he looks like that, anyway," Kelsey joked.

This time, Ginger couldn't resist a jab in each of their arms.

"Ow!" they chorused.

"You're testy," Rebecca said. "Something's definitely up."

Thirty-three years of feeling one thing and saying another had her on the verge of holding her friends at bay again with a *Really. Nothing's up, nothing at all.*

But this wasn't her old life, these weren't her old friends where everything was supposed to stay on the surface. These were women that she'd bonded with over too many margaritas in a party boat. They'd shed tears together over their past mistakes, which was how she knew Rebecca's past hadn't exactly been rosy either.

Her friends wouldn't judge her. And maybe, if she talked through what she was feeling with them, they could help her get her head back on straight.

Still, she didn't want everyone else in the yarn shop to know her business, so she lowered her voice and kept her head down over a half-finished sweater.

"You're right. Something has changed."

She'd been thinking all day about this, yet it was still

hard to figure out how to put it into words. "All my life I've done the safest thing, followed everyone else's rules. The only impulsive thing I've ever done was marry Jeremy, but that was just a weird blip on the radar screen, something I think I did more to piss off my parents, to show them I could make my own decisions. And then it was ten more years of safe. Of boring."

"Safe doesn't always work out, does it?" Rebecca murmured, her fingers flying over wool and wood tips as she asked the question.

"No," Ginger said. "It's never gotten me anywhere. The best thing I ever did was chucking it all in and coming here."

She looked at the needles and yarn in her hands, realized she hadn't done so much as one knit or purl stitch yet.

"Are you saying what I think you're saying?" Kelsey asked, not bothering to hide the excitement in her voice.

Of course all her friends saw was Connor the gorgeous firefighter. But it was so much more complicated than that.

Knowing she had to be honest, not just with her friends, but with herself most of all, Ginger said, "The odds of anything working out long-term with Connor are slim to none. He's going back to California soon and he's already made it perfectly clear that he's not the least bit interested in a wife and kids. But—"

Her friends had both stopped knitting now, too, all smiles gone as they listened intently.

"I'm sick of trying so hard to make the right decisions

all the time." She nodded at the four-times-pregnant woman across the room. "She has everything I want. I thought if I followed all the rules, I'd get it too." Bitterness came at her again. "I'm thirty-three years old. I'm sick of waiting for the perfect moment, for the perfect situation, for the perfect man. All I know is that I've never felt an attraction like this before."

She took a deep breath. And then another.

"All I keep thinking is that even if it all ends up being a huge mistake, at least I'll know I really lived, for once in my life. Because damn it, this time I want to leap."

Not to piss anyone off this time. Not to prove anything to anyone. But simply because everything in her head, heart, and body was drawn to Connor. Because she'd pleased everyone else for so long.

And this time, she wanted something for herself.

Rebecca grabbed her right hand. "Then I say you should leap."

Kelsey took her left hand. "And know that we'll be here to catch you if you need us."

The next morning, Connor slid his saw into the soft wood of the log he'd punched a hole in that first day on the porch and began the painstaking process of cutting off the rotted parts. He'd finished most of the rewiring the night before and relished digging into the grueling job of cutting into the logs by hand, just as he'd always enjoyed working as a hotshot in a forest cutting down brush and dead trees.

If he couldn't fight fire, he wanted to be sweating in other ways.

After only four days of working on the cabin, he was impressed with the work his great-grandparents had put into building this house. If renovation took this much sweat-equity, he was certain building from scratch—without the help of carpenters and architects—was a thousand times harder. And all that more satisfying.

One day, he'd started to think, he'd like to build his own log cabin out in Lake Tahoe. Working on Poplar Cove was like taking a hands-on class, the best possible way to learn what needed to be done.

Working on the cabin gave him plenty of time to think. Enough time to come up with a plan for dealing with Ginger.

During the day he was going to keep his head down in the cabin, focus on the work that he needed to get done. No more shared meals. No more cozy chats. And at night, when a full day of pent-up desire had him bursting at the seams, he'd get the hell out of Poplar Cove and stay away until he was sure Ginger was safely tucked into bed.

Last night, he'd headed into the local watering hole at the end of Main. Fourth of July preparations were heavily under way along Main Street with large groups of kids and parents working to decorate floats. He'd been one of those kids once, had looked forward to the parade and fireworks all year.

Becoming a hotshot had changed fireworks for him. Even before he'd gotten burned, the first two weeks of July were rough. Constant fires, both accidental and intentional. He hadn't enjoyed watching a Fourth of July show in years. But last summer had been the worst, knowing there would be fires and that he wouldn't be out there to put them out. He wasn't looking forward to tonight's show, was already thinking about getting out on the roof and dock and watering them down.

He tensed as he heard the screen door open, knew it was time to put his plan into action. To stay on his side of the room. Looking up at the clock he saw that it was only 11 a.m. Ginger must only be working breakfast today.

What was he doing following her schedule so closely?

She put her bag down on the nearest chair and smiled. "Hi."

The tightness in his chest opened up when he saw her. He drank her in, forgetting everything for the moment but the pleasure of being in the same room.

She moved closer, looked at the new hole in the wall. "Wow, you really are going to replace the logs, aren't you?"

A strand of hair was in her mouth and the next thing he knew he was hooking a finger on it, his knuckle sliding against her cheek.

He made himself move away from her. "I told myself I wasn't going to touch you."

"No," she said softly, "this is good. We need to talk about this. What's between us."

"There can't be anything between us."

She nodded, but said, "Why not?"

Before he could remember any of the reasons, she was moving closer to him, saying, "No, don't answer that. I already know why we shouldn't do this. But do you really think we can stop it?"

He couldn't look away from her mouth, from the soft, pink flesh. There wasn't enough self-control in the world to stay away from her, but just before he gave in to the thing he most wanted, he heard her voice in his head from last night.

"I wasted thirty-three years. I came here to finally get it right."

Getting involved with him would be getting it all wrong.

"We've got to stop it."

Hurt flashed in her eyes so quickly that he almost missed it. But not quite. He couldn't let her think she wasn't desirable like her dickhead of a husband had.

"Don't think that I don't want you, Ginger. I've wanted you from the first moment. You know that."

He watched her swallow, lick her lips. "I do know it. But I don't know why you have to be so hell-bent on doing the right thing. Most guys would just take what they could get and not worry about consequences."

"I like you," he said slowly, knowing he was trying to remind himself as much as her of his reasons. "If we had met in a bar, if I knew I was never going to see you again, if we weren't sharing this cabin for the next month, if I didn't know about your marriage, then things would be different. But we both know I'm heading back to Tahoe soon. We both know that this isn't going to work."

But even as he said it, he was getting lost in her eyes, could feel his fingertips start to burn with the need to touch her.

It would be so easy to get lost in Ginger.

Again and again she pulled things out of him he'd never said to anyone, was forcing him to look at things he'd thought he knew for sure in a new light. And when he'd tried to turn the tables on her by making her confess her own secrets, instead of closing the intriguing circle, learning more about her had blown the mystery wide open.

Sure, she'd had money. But it hadn't made her life any easier. It hadn't made her husband any less of an asshole.

All his life he'd been a master of control. There was no reason Ginger should be any different. He just needed to take the reins back.

"You have my word that I won't touch you again."

He'd never been a liar. And until this moment he hadn't thought he'd ever become one. But he was very much afraid he just had. Because after only the smallest taste of her sweetness, he could see keeping his word might very well be impossible.

She was so easy to read, her expressive face telling him she was disappointed. But after their discussion last night, staying away from her had turned into more than just keeping his focus on firefighting, on getting back on his crew. He liked her too much to use her, to give in to the urge to take her when he barely had one foot in the door. Liked her too much to be one more dickhead in her life.

He watched her pull in a shaky breath, look at the floor, say in a low voice, "So much for taking chances."

When she looked back up at him, her once bright eyes

had dimmed. "So what else is on the agenda with the cabin after you replace the logs?"

He hated to see the life go out of her, but knew it was for the best, that they had to stay in neutral territory.

"I'll have to rechink between the logs, then strip off the soot and age so that I can revarnish them. I'd been hoping to get to the furniture too, see what I could do to fix it up as a surprise for my grandmother. Now I don't know if that will happen."

She made a sound of pleasure that set off another inextinguishable spark behind his breastbone.

"Actually, I've been dying to get my hands on some of the old furniture. It's all so classic and beautiful and I know with a light sanding and coat of fresh paint, I can probably make some of the side tables and dressers look like new." Her words were coming out in a rush. "And I've seen some really gorgeous retro fabric in town that would look great on the cushions. It isn't hard to do and probably wouldn't take me much time at all."

The furniture really needed refurbishing, but something told him this was a bad idea. That once Ginger had put her permanent mark on his family's things, it would be like she was a part of the family. And that would only make it harder to leave her behind when he went back to Lake Tahoe.

"Thanks for the offer, but I wouldn't feel right asking you to do that. You're already paying to live here."

"Please, Connor," she said softly, her eyes shining again at the thought of refinishing the furniture his great-grandfather had built by hand. "I'd like to help."

"What about your painting?"

"Actually, I'm kind of in the thinking and planning stage with a couple of them right now. Might be nice to work on something else for a few hours. How about if I start to strip and repaint the dresser in my bedroom?"

It was the best idea of the day, sending her out to the workshop in the woods. Far away from the cabin.

Far away from him.

"I'll go upstairs and grab it right now. Put it in the workshop for you to work on."

"The workshop? Oh, do you mean the red barn in the woods?" When he nodded, she said, "I've walked by it so many times, and even though I longed to go inside and look around, it felt too much like trespassing."

He was glad for the heavy weight of the four-drawer dresser, for the fact that carrying it down the stairs and through the woods was making his hands hurt like hell. Anything to distract him from what being around Ginger made him feel.

The workshop was a good quarter mile back from the house and the smell of sawdust and oil was strong as they entered the large dark barn. Connor put the dresser down outside the big doors, his palms burning. After opening one, he found the light switch on the wall and flicked it on to illuminate the rows of lights that hung from the open beamed ceiling.

"Wow, this place is incredible," she said as she slowly walked around the large space. "Every time I walked by I sensed that there was magic inside."

"Sam and I were always begging to come out here

when we were kids," he told her, trying not to wince as he picked the dresser back up to bring it inside. "That was the lathe my grandfather used to turn all of the legs on the chairs and tables and beds. He taught me how to use it when I was five."

Her eyes widened. "Five? Wasn't he afraid you'd hurt yourself?"

"He believed in having us learn from our mistakes. Knowing we could slice open a hand was a pretty big motivator not to goof around while using his tools. Plus," he said, running his hand over the dusty tool, "I wanted to be just like him."

"What did he do the rest of the year?"

"High school principal. My grandmother taught French and German. The past couple of years they've both been pleased to have me follow in their footsteps. Finally."

She cocked her head to the side. "You're also a teacher?"

"Since the accident, that's what I've been doing. Teaching rookies the ropes, leading safety seminars. My scars scare them enough to make sure they really pay attention. Same principle my grandfather worked off of, I guess."

She came to a stop in front of a half-built sailboat that was flipped upside down in the middle of the room. "What's this?"

"A boat my grandfather never finished building. It was always just there. Sam and I offered to finish building it for him a couple of times, but he said no, he'd do it himself. Guess he never got around to it."

He walked over to a large rolling toolbox pushed up against the wall and yanked out several drawers, the rusty metal protesting his rough touch.

"Here's some sandpaper to get started. Let me know if you need more. I can pick up some paint at the hardware store when you're ready for it."

And then he got the hell out before he could come up with an excuse to be near her a little while longer.

Over the course of his career, he'd been called a hero countless times, but this was the first time Connor had ever wondered if he had it in him to do the right thing.

CHAPTER TEN

GINGER PULLED out the top drawer and began the painstaking job of sanding off the rough edges of peeling paint, making sure to scuff up every inch of the surface so that the new primer and paint would dry. One by one, she worked through the drawers.

It was good, hard work. The perfect project to take her mind off Connor.

She supposed she should have been embarrassed by what she'd said to him about her frustration over all of his respect for her, but she wasn't.

Yet again, it had felt surprisingly good to put voice to what she wanted. Even if being turned down flat had been a pretty crushing blow.

Then again, she suddenly realized, hadn't she'd known all along that she was safe? That Connor was so damned noble there was no way he'd ever take advantage of her.

In the same way the wood had revealed itself beneath the cracking paint, her hours of sanding had slowly uncovered the truth: She hadn't risked much at all.

Not when she'd known all along that Connor would be a hero.

Beyond irritated with the train of her thoughts, she yanked hard at the stuck bottom drawer. She heard a sharp crack.

"Oh no," she cried, instantly assuming she'd snapped off a hunk of old wood. But when she pulled the drawer all the way out and put it on the floor, she was surprised to see a stack of letters tied together with a string sitting at the bottom of the dresser's now-empty shell.

A secret romantic who'd always had a stash of romance novels tucked away in a bag in her closet to read when no one was home, Ginger's fingers trembled with excitement as she reached for the bundle.

Love letters. They had to be love letters. Otherwise why would someone keep them, hide them away?

The papers looked water-stained and crispy, the rope hard and brittle. Although she picked up the package carefully, the white binding crumbled in her hands. One opened in her hands and, unable to help herself, she started reading the neat cursive.

Andrew,

These have been the worst two weeks of my entire life. I can't sleep. I can't eat. All I want is to be with you.

Last night when I called home, I begged my parents to let me come back to the lake early. It's not like I'm good enough to go pro or anything, so why do I have to go away to tennis camp for three weeks? I told them I'd much rather be out at the lake spending time with them. They didn't buy it and said no.

I think they're suspicious about us. Even though we've been so careful. I don't know what they'd do if they found out we're spending so much time together.

Every night I lay awake in bed thinking about when I snuck out and we drove up to the pond. Can you believe I've spent fifteen summers at Blue Mountain Lake and never knew it was there? I'm so glad you showed it to me. I loved night swimming with you. And I loved everything else we did that night too.

Especially the way you kissed me and said I'd be yours forever.

Love, Isabel

Oh my God. She'd accidentally found love letters her friend Isabel had written to Connor's father.

Ginger felt a shocked little thrill run through her. She should stop reading right now, especially given that she knew she was invading her friend's privacy. But her hands and eyes seemed to have a will of their own.

Andrew,

Last night I had a dream that we were already on our boat, that were were halfway around the world. Drinking out of coconuts, the warm salty breeze on our skin.

It was heaven.

Sometimes I think we should just pack a couple of bags and leave now. Forget about college. Forget about everything but going out there and living our dream. Together.

I love you,

Isabel

Ginger didn't know how many letters she'd read by the time she got to,

Andrew,

I love you. I love you. I love you. I love you. I love you. I love you. I love you. I love you. I love you. I love you. I love you. I love you. I love you. I love you. I love you.

Isabel

She heard Connor's voice behind her. "It's getting dark. And I heard in town there's been a lot of bear sightings this summer in these woods. I didn't want you walking back alone."

She looked up from where she'd been sitting cross-legged, the letters on the floor all around her.

Uh oh. She hadn't thought about getting caught reading them. Hadn't been able to think about anything other than Isabel's love affair with Connor's father.

"What are those?"

"They fell out of the back of the dresser." Quickly picking up the pages, stacking them on top of each other, she held out the bundle. "I didn't mean to read them, but one fell open and . . . I couldn't help myself. They're so beautiful that I lost all track of time. No wonder your father kept them."

"My father?"

He grabbed the letters from her, started scanning the one on top that said I love you over and over, his posture, his face, growing harder with every passing second.

"I knew he and Isabel had dated for a while," she said, "that it was pretty serious, but—"

His eyes lifted from the letters. "What are you talking about?"

"You didn't know about your father and Isabel?"

"Hell no."

"They met as teenagers. It was love at first sight. These must be letters she wrote him when she was a teenager."

She suddenly realized what she'd said, that she'd made a huge deal out of Connor's father loving a woman his son hadn't known anything about. It had to sting.

"My ex always said I had a bad habit of blurting out every thought that passed through my head," she said by way of an apology. "It must be weird to read love letters written to your father by someone other than your mother. Almost like a betrayal."

The man of cold, hard stone she'd seen in his bedroom that first night was back.

"Whatever he did before he married my mom is none of my business."

But she didn't buy that. Not for a single second. If it were true, he wouldn't be acting like this.

"I can understand why the letters would bother you."

"Didn't you hear what I just said? *I don't care.*"

She took a step toward him. She'd let him keep his hands to himself, but she wouldn't let him lie to her.

"You sure look angry for a man who doesn't care."

He came toward her, then, closing the rest of the space between them, his lips so close to hers that she could almost taste them.

"What the hell makes you think you know me so well?"

He was right. It shouldn't make any sense. They'd only just met, not even a week ago, and yet . . .

"I'm right, aren't I?"

His eyes were on her mouth again, his eyes dark and intense, and she felt it coming, another kiss like the one in his bedroom, violent, all-consuming. And in that moment as his heat seeped into her pores, she wanted nothing else.

But instead of kissing her, he turned away and walked over to the half-built boat. She found herself fighting back another strong wave of disappointment as he said, "I've never met anyone like you, Ginger."

It didn't sound like a compliment, but she quickly decided that was okay. Because she knew she'd just stumbled over a really important chapter of Connor's story. And she couldn't have stopped turning the pages if her life depended on it.

"What's your father like?"

Running a hand over a golden red board, Connor said, "Uptight. I can't imagine anyone writing a letter like that to him."

She remembered how smooth Andrew had seemed over the phone. She searched for the right occupation.

"Surgeon? Professor?"

"Lawyer."

"How'd he feel about you becoming a hotshot?"

He laughed, but it was a hollow sound. "I can honestly say he didn't give a damn."

"Impossible. He's your father. He had to care."

"When I was five, my mother had to go away to help her sister with a new baby. He was supposed to pick me and Sam up from school. Every single day that week, he forgot. When I was ten the soccer league called to see if he could fill in for the regular coach for a practice. He asked if they had any idea how much two hours of his afternoon were worth. By the time he missed my high school graduation, I'd already learned to accept who he was. And who he was never going to be."

"But surely after your accident, he must have tried harder."

"Sure. A few phone calls. Couple of beers."

That reminded her. "You got the message that he called, right? I put in on your pillow."

"Couldn't miss it."

He didn't say anything more about it and the crazy thing was, Ginger got the sense he was even more shut down about his father than he had been about the wildfire that had burned his hands.

"What are you going to do with the letters?"

"I'm sure someone's going to need kindling tonight for a Fourth of July bonfire."

The thought of the love letters going up in flames horrified her. She pounced on the old papers, safely cradling them against her chest.

"You can't do that! What if your father wants them back?"

"He left them here for over thirty years. What does he care?"

"The fact that he kept them in the first place shows how much he cared."

"Yeah, he cared all right. About Isabel."

Okay, so he had a point. Still, Ginger couldn't reconcile the man from the letters, the man Isabel had loved so deeply, so passionately, with the father Connor spoke of. His father must have had—at least in his youth—some redeeming qualities.

The big question was, what happened once he married his wife and became a father?

And then she realized Connor hadn't read enough to know, "That was your father's boat. He and Isabel were building it together."

He pushed away from the sailboat. "Something else for the fire pit."

"Connor!"

He shot her a hard look. "You want to keep the letters, be my guest. I don't care what happens to them."

But everything about the rigid lines of his body, the way he was repeatedly clenching and opening his fists, told her that he did.

CHAPTER ELEVEN

CONNOR WAS irritated. Not with Ginger for her usual rounds of endless questions. With himself.

So his father had gotten letters from some girl. So what? Sure, Connor was protective of his mother, but she'd taken control of her own life a couple of years ago when she'd filed for divorce. She was dating a nice guy who wanted her to move with him to Florida. She was fine.

But it grated at him, reading the lovey-dovey words Isabel had written. He couldn't imagine anyone feeling that way about Andrew. Didn't, frankly, know his father well enough to see who he might have been when he was nineteen years old.

Knowing it was long past time to change the subject, he gestured to the dresser. "I'm impressed that you sanded almost all of the drawers already. That's a big job."

Her eyes held his and he could almost see her weighing the pros and cons of keeping after him about his father or backing off.

Finally, she stretched her arms over her head, tilted her head from one side to the other, and it was crazy but he was almost disappointed by her choice to let it go.

He'd gotten used to having her dig around, challenge him at every turn.

"I'm tired. A good kind of tired. But you're right, I should probably get back to work at the easel. My first art show is coming up soon. Right before your brother's wedding. I may have to start painting round the clock soon if I don't finish a couple of big ones this week."

They headed out of the workshop and back through the woods, every step he took beside Ginger confirming to Connor that he should be keeping his distance. Staying the hell out of her business.

Only, he couldn't help wanting to know more about what made her tick. He was still reeling from how upfront she'd been about her desire for him. But it was more than that, more than just the way their bodies inevitably responded to each other.

Somehow, she seemed to know when he was lying, not just to her, but to himself too.

"Did you always want to paint?"

"Always."

"But you didn't, not until you moved here?"

"No. Not really."

"Why not?"

"I don't know."

She wouldn't let him lie to her. He wouldn't stand for it either.

"You know."

She stopped beside a tree trunk, wrapped her arms around it, leaned into it. "I was afraid I wasn't good enough. I thought everyone else knew more than I did. I thought I needed to listen to their advice, that I had to believe them when they told me I was doing it all wrong. I let them mold me, even when the voices in the back of my head were screaming no. In the end, I didn't pick up my paintbrushes for three years."

"That's a long time to stay away from something you love." He knew firsthand.

"It wasn't until I arrived here last October, when I unpacked my easel and put it on your grandparents' porch, that I realized I had it in me all along."

Ginger's words dug in right behind his solar plexus. It was just what the Forest Service had been telling him for so long. That he wasn't good enough anymore. That he needed to listen to their advice and train for something else.

"Ginger," he said, unable to keep from closing the gap between them despite his best intentions, "I—"

The rest of his sentence was cut off by a loud explosion from the beach.

"Someone must be lighting off fireworks in front of the cabin."

He ran through the rest of the trees and found the kids just off to the right of Poplar Cove's beach.

Isabel's property. The woman who'd been his father's girlfriend.

"Those fireworks are illegal."

The two teenage boys barely looked up at him. "Dude, it's July Fourth. We're just having a little fun." The girl, however, looked a little worried.

He held out one hand. "Give me the rest. I'll get rid of them for you."

But instead of giving them to him, the dark-haired kid flicked open a lighter and started to light one.

Connor had the back of the kid's neck in a death grip so fast, the kid dropped the almost-lit firework to the sand.

"Anyone ever told you why these are illegal?"

The kid shrugged, still trying to act brave. "Let go of me."

"This one," Connor said, not letting go of the boy as he picked up the charred remains of one of the fireworks, "usually blows off a finger or two." He picked up another wrapping. "But this one." He whistled low. "This one is a real beauty. Has a tendency to pop open from the back and explode in your face. Usually blinds you, although sometimes, after enough surgeries, if you're lucky you don't go completely blind."

"Shit, man," the scared kid said to his friend, "you said these were safe."

Deciding he'd done all he could to scare them, Connor let the bolder kid wriggle away.

"This old dude is just trying to scare us. He's probably making this stuff up."

Connor shrugged and said, "It's up to you if you want to find out for yourself," but the kids were already running up the beach, leaving the fireworks behind.

He picked up the wrappers, then turned around and crashed into Ginger. He had to drop the fireworks to grab her rib cage to keep her from falling. They stood like that for several seconds, both of them breathing hard.

She looked mad as hell. "You scared Josh and his friends half to death, Connor."

"Good."

"They're just kids."

"Doesn't mean they can get away with acting stupid."

"That's what kids do, Connor! They make mistakes and they learn from them."

"Since you already know everything, why don't you tell me what happens if the mistake is too big? If one of these fireworks takes something away from them, something they'd never thought to lose? What then?"

Her hands moved to his face, holding him still, calming him as she would a wild animal.

"I know how bad it must have hurt. How bad it still does. But it's going to be okay, Connor. One day soon. It has to be."

A violent boom of thunder in the dark sky above them was their only warning as rain began to pour down on them.

"At least now you don't have to worry about fireworks anymore."

"Not that kind, anyway," he said, then bent his head down to hers.

Her lips were soft, so damn soft that he wanted to devour her, starting with her mouth and running down to her breasts, but even so, he was working like hell to get hold of himself, to stop before things got really out of control.

And then, her tongue moved against his, and he was a goner.

Sparks of heat worked through him as she threaded her fingers through his hair and pulled his head down closer to kiss him, her tongue moving in time with his, her breasts pressed against his chest. She moaned softly against his mouth and all he could think was that she felt so good in his hands, just the way a woman should feel, soft warmth instead of sharp bones and harsh angles.

As his hands moved over her hips, to her waist, you would have thought four days was four years, he wanted her so bad. She gasped when his fingers found bare skin at the base of her shirt and he wanted to forget his vow to stay away from her, wanted to forget everything but pleasure.

But even as his extreme passion for her threatened to take over everything else, he knew he needed to give her one last chance to walk away.

"We shouldn't do this. I don't have anything to give to you, Ginger. Nothing at all."

Ginger couldn't catch her breath. Connor seemed to know her body better than she did. He knew just where she wanted to be stroked, just how she wanted to be kissed. Four days of pent-up longing overflowed inside of her as she breathed in his scent, earthy from the wood he'd been working with, as clean and fresh as the cold rain on his warm skin.

Somewhere through the fog she'd heard him say they should stop, that he couldn't make her any promises. But she didn't believe him. Not way down deep in her heart.

He needed her. Needed her to wrap her arms around him and show him someone cared. She couldn't run, couldn't turn her back on him.

"Take me back to your room. To your bed."

But instead of doing what she'd asked him to, he simply brushed the pad of his thumb against her lower lip. She realized his hands were shaking—my God, had anyone ever wanted her this much?—and she pressed a kiss onto the scarred skin covering the tip, her tongue swirling as she sucked him in between her lips.

"I promised you I wouldn't do this," he said, his voice hoarse. Rough with desire.

"I don't want your noble vow, Connor. I want this. I want you. I've never felt this way with anyone else. I want to explore it. Please, just for one night, don't be the hero."

He groaned, said, "Only you would ask me to do that," and then he was kissing her again. She threaded her fingers through his to pull him through the driving rain, up the stairs. On the porch, he picked her up, carrying her through the living room, up the stairs and kicking open his bedroom door. He put her down on the floor, making sure there was a slow slide of her body against his the entire way.

He reached for the hem of her shirt and with painstaking slowness he raised the thin, wet cotton up over her stomach, then her rib cage, and finally, over her breasts. Her pants came off next, just as slowly, and she relished every single sensation.

The roughness of the fabric against her sensitive skin.

The gentleness of his hands.

The heat from his body, which singed her in the most delicious way.

And then she was standing in front of him in nothing but her bra and panties and even though she'd been practically naked that first night, this felt different. More real, somehow. Real enough that all the insecurities that had been chasing her for thirty-three years decided to take that moment to race into the bedroom and wind themselves around her, whispering vicious things about wrinkles and cellulite.

She thought she'd outrun her past, the years of self-hatred. She was stunned to realize she'd been wrong.

She wanted to push away from him, hide herself behind a thick cover, but then he said, "God, you're beautiful," and the reverence in his words worked like magic to strip away her fears, the conviction in Connor's voice making Ginger believe, for the very first time in her life, that she truly was beautiful.

He swept his thumbs across the upper curve of her breasts, where they swelled over her bra cups. "You're so soft."

Pleasure rippling through her at his gentle touch, Ginger closed her eyes and arched her back slightly into his hands, her own hands finding his hips so that she could hold herself steady on increasingly unsteady ground. He slid one strap off and then the other. With nothing to hold up the lace, her nipples popped over the edge, into his waiting hands.

"So perfect."

His thumbs circled the tight buds, tightening further at his teasing caress. Her entire being was focused on two square inches of skin. She'd never felt pleasure so exquisite, never knew her breasts could be so incredibly sensitive. Connor's erection pressed hard against her belly and she felt an answering warmth between her legs.

"For four days I've had your taste on my tongue. And I've wanted more. So much more."

A thrill shot through her in the same moment his mouth came down over her nipples. Cupping her breasts, he pushed them together so that he could easily move from one to the next, laving them with long, soft strokes of his tongue.

"Connor," she moaned as she arched herself even closer to his incredible mouth.

At the sound of his name, he took one of her nipples between his lips and sucked it into his mouth, his teeth gently scoring the sensitive flesh. One hand still cupping her breasts, the other moved to her backside, splaying one butt cheek and dragging her tighter against his shaft as he slipped one thigh between hers.

As he moved his attention to the other nipple, her arousal grew so intense that she couldn't help but grind herself against the hard column of his leg. He encouraged her with his arm, helping her move in perfect rhythm to his tongue and lips on her breasts. And then, his fingers were on her belly, moving swiftly toward her wetness.

And then, sweet Lord, his fingers found her clitoris. She opened up her legs for him as she rocked against his fingers, wanting desperately for him to keep touching her, just like that, right there, where it felt so good. She was so close, just on the verge of breaking apart into a million little pieces, when he pulled his hand away and took a step backward. Away from her.

The loss of his heat, of his touch, felt like ramming straight into an iceberg.

But then, it hit her what must have happened. She reached out to him. "Did it happen again? Your hands, did they go numb?"

He looked down at his hands, clenched into fists. "No. I could feel you. Too well." He winced. "I can't control myself around you, Ginger. I'm too rough. I'm going to hurt you. God, I don't want to hurt you."

She could barely believe what she was hearing. Was he really apologizing for wanting to make love to her so badly that he was losing control?

"I'm tougher than I look."

She needed to let Connor know how much she wanted this, that she was desperate for his fingers and hands and mouth on her. Fast or slow, she didn't care. All she cared about was the pleasure of touching and being touched by him.

Reaching behind her back, she undid her bra and let it fall to the floor between them. "I loved what you were doing to my breasts," she said in a hoarse voice before stepping back from him and stripping off her panties.

Boldly taking his hand, she placed it onto her mound, trembling as his rough fingers made contact with her heavily aroused skin, full with desire.

"I loved what you were doing right here too. Do it again, Connor. Take me higher, take me all the way over the edge." She went on her tippy toes and whispered into his ear, "And don't worry about me. I can handle you."

He moved her so fast from standing in the middle of the room to flat on her back on the bed that she lost her breath. A heartbeat later, his head was between her legs, his mouth replacing his hand. Crying out, she arched up into his lips as his tongue slid into her wetness, then up to her clitoris, then back down the length of her labia. His hands held her hips steady as she forgot how to breathe, how to think, how to do anything but feel.

And then, oh God, there it was, a higher peak than she'd ever climbed before, and she was exploding beneath him, her body wracked with spasms of ecstasy. Through it all, he continued licking and sucking and plunging with his tongue, never letting up, not until he'd wrung every ounce of pleasure from her body.

Tears pricked her eyes, not just from the pleasure, but from the intense emotions that Connor's care with her body stirred up. The way he touched her, kissed her, stroked her, made her feel beautiful.

Special.

"I didn't know," she said when she could finally speak. "I didn't know it could be like that."

Running kisses along the insides of her thighs, then up her belly and her rib cage, he found her breasts again with his hands and mouth.

"I need to be inside you." His eyes held hers in the near darkness. "Now. Before I explode."

Together they yanked off his pants and pulled off his shirt until he was levered over her, completely naked.

Ginger was sure that nothing and no one had ever felt this good. She wanted to touch and kiss every inch of him, take her time exploring his perfection. But those explorations would have to wait, because he was pushing her thighs apart with one knee and lifting himself up her body so that the head of his penis was pressed up against her open folds. And then, before she could take her next breath, he was inside her, in one long stroke.

"You're so tight," he groaned, going completely still as her body stretched to accept his thick member. "So wet."

She could feel him throbbing against her womb, her body answering with more wetness and fluttering way down deep in her belly.

"Please, Connor," she begged, not knowing the right words to ask for what she wanted, but knowing it was waiting for her just the same.

But those two simple words were magic, because a moment later, he began the long, slow slide out, then back in. Out. In. Out. In. Over and over again until she was delirious with desire and the peak that she'd crested only minutes earlier was, amazingly, back within reach.

She pulled his face down to hers so that she could show him with her kisses how much this lovemaking meant to her. That it was everything she'd been waiting for. That being with him was so much more than anything she'd ever felt before.

And as they kissed, he grew bigger still inside her until that moment when she felt her hold on her body give way again to another mind-blowing orgasm and he was throbbing and pulsing inside of her, pushing harder, higher, deeper as they both came.

Panting hard, her skin still slick from the rain, but mostly from the intense heat they'd generated, Connor shifted their weight so that his back was on the mattress and her head was cradled against his chest.

One of his arms over her hip, one leg wound against her, exhaustion swept over her, the perfect kind of tiredness that came from having given all of herself. It was similar to how she felt after an all-day painting marathon, but far more special.

Because she wasn't alone.

Connor breathed her in, the delicious scent that was so unique to Ginger. Her name said it all; sweet and spicy mingling together in the perfect package.

He hadn't meant to attack her like that. Hadn't meant to bury his face in her breasts, between her legs. Hadn't meant to pound her hard into the mattress. But he hadn't been able to help himself.

It was the first time he'd ever completely lost control with a woman.

And yet, as he lay there with Ginger warm in his arms,

he knew it had been about more than just making her come, more than loving the feel of her soft flesh in his hands.

She was so incredibly beautiful, inside and out. He'd felt her surprise when he'd said as much to her, and he'd wanted so badly to erase all those years of fat camps, all the horrible things her husband had done to her. He knew he'd never find the words, but here in his bed, in the dark, he could show her how special she was.

Closing his eyes, he took several deep breaths to try to steady his heartbeat, counting backward from one hundred to let her fall asleep, but somewhere around thirty, he was kissing her again and she was responding by rubbing her breasts against his chest. Wanting to go slower this time, he kissed her along her forehead, her cheekbones, her chin, then her neck and collarbones. His hands ran softly over her breasts, to her waist and hips.

Rolling her over so that she was lying on top of him, he said, "You make me crazy, Ginger," his voice rough with desire, and then she was grinding against him, bringing him back in record time.

"You. These." He cupped her breasts together, then closed his eyes and tilted his face up to rub himself on her like a lion would his mate. "There are no words," he finally said a moment before he sucked one taut nipple in between his lips.

She arched her back to give him better access to her breasts and he was laving both breasts at once, his tongue darting, his teeth lightly scoring her nipples, his stubble brushing against her flushed skin.

He could feel how ready she was as she rocked into his erection and then he was pushing up into her again, sounds coming out of their mouths that they couldn't control, and everything was connected, his mouth on her breasts, his hands on her hips as she rode him faster, harder, his desire for her growing bigger, stronger than anything he'd known was possible. And then, she was crying out, slamming herself against him as she reached the pinnacle and started to fall.

Her orgasm was so sweet he swore he could hear the angels sing as she came, and then he stopped trying to hold on to his self-control and gave himself up completely to pure pleasure.

Minutes later, with Ginger's curves pressed up tight into him, her breathing soft and even as the storm raged above them, Connor fell into the deepest sleep he'd had in two years.

CHAPTER TWELVE

SNIPPETS OF the previous night slowly came to Ginger as she woke up. Remembrances of intense pleasure. Connor's mouth on her. Moaning—screaming—his name as she came. And then as she grew more fully awake she realized that she was in his bed, and he was still there with her, his large arms holding her tightly against him.

He was running the tip of his fingers over her hips, the small of her back, the side of her breasts. But she hadn't yet tasted him with her lips, her tongue, and now it was what she most wanted, so she put her hands on his chest and said, "I want to give you pleasure."

He groaned and shook his head. "Sweetheart, I don't know if I can let you—"

This time she finished his sentence with a kiss, pushing him flat on his back on the bed.

"You're so beautiful," she whispered as she ran kisses

down his face, his shoulders, his chest. The deeply ridged muscles on his stomach rippled and tightened as she brushed her fingertips over the peaks and valleys.

His erection bumped into her forearm and she shifted her attention lower, to his impressive penis. Her mouth watered and she didn't think, she just did what was natural and bent over to taste him. Her hair brushing against him made him groan again and then she was pressing her lips to the soft, hot skin stretched across the head of his cock. She'd never thought the word before, but it was the perfect description for his magnificent erection.

His hands threaded into her hair, helping her take him deeper. She was amazed by how sexy this was, how good it felt to give him such deep pleasure. She moved her mouth slowly back up, then down him, once, then twice. With every stroke of her tongue, he grew bigger, harder. And then, she was on her back on the bed and he was driving in between her thighs, and she was crying out his name.

They lay together in silence for several minutes as sunlight streamed in through his window. To say that Ginger had rocked his world wasn't even cutting into the surface. Still, a warning light went off behind his breastbone, one he wanted to ignore but couldn't.

He'd promised himself that he'd keep his distance. The last thing he wanted to do was hurt her. Instead, not only had he been all over her last night, but they'd been in such a hurry all three times, they hadn't used a condom. Hadn't done a single thing to prevent diseases. Or pregnancy.

"Ginger, we need to talk."

She scooted away from him slightly, pulled the sheet up to cover her gorgeous curves. "I knew you were going to say that."

That was when he saw the faint scar on her shoulder. "Right there," he said, running two fingers over the slightly discolored skin, from her collarbone all the way to the underside of her left breast. "That's where you were burned."

She nodded and he leaned closer to run kisses down her skin. "I'm sorry you had to feel that."

Her fingers threaded into his hair. "I'm okay now," she said. "Perfectly okay."

The taste of her still on his tongue, somehow he managed, "We didn't use anything. I haven't been with a woman in a while. But the last time the fire station tested us, I was clean."

"Me too."

"What about—"

Jesus, he was breaking out in a sweat just thinking about the odds of becoming a father like this. All because he couldn't keep his hands off her.

"Is this the right time of the month for—"

But she was already shaking her head and saying, "No. I don't think I'm ovulating."

She hadn't blushed when she'd been taking him into her mouth, but now that they were talking about the repercussions of the mind-blowing sex they'd just had, both of them were uncomfortable.

"My cycle is pretty wonky, but I seriously doubt we're in danger of anything like that."

Relief shot through him and he finally let himself smile. "Good."

"Yeah," she said, even though she wasn't smiling back. "It's great."

"We'll have to be more careful next time."

Her eyes flew to his. "Next time?"

"I told myself I was going to stay the hell away from you, but it was a lie, Ginger. Every last thing about you blows my mind. I don't think I could keep my hands off you if I tried."

She shivered, reached for him. "I don't want you to."

God, he hated the need to lay it all out like this. But there was no other way. Because if they were going to go forward, he had to make absolutely sure they were on the same page.

"You know I'm going back to Lake Tahoe after the summer to rejoin my crew, right?"

"Of course you will. They're going to be lucky to have you back."

She was so damn sweet, it seemed that she almost wanted his career as a hotshot back for him as much as he did. The warning light behind his breastbone shifted as it was shoved to the side by something else entirely.

Something he couldn't possibly acknowledge.

He knew he shouldn't reach for her until they were

done talking, but he couldn't help himself and slid her onto his lap anyway.

"Could we enjoy each other for the summer and agree to stay friends when we both go our separate ways?"

She didn't say anything for several moments, confirming that he was asking for too much. Ginger should be saving herself for a good man, for someone who could give her a future.

Not wasting time on a dead end.

But then, when she smiled at him and said, "It sounds perfect," he was so glad that he lifted her up and carried her into the bathroom to seal the deal, barely remembering at the last minute to reach into his dresser to grab a condom.

Turning on the shower with his free hand, he ran his hands over her hips, her waist, her breasts.

She reached over his shoulder. "How about I soap you up?"

She moved around behind him and started running the soap between his shoulder blades, down his back, along his arms. Sure, they'd made love repeatedly. She'd held his hands, stroked them, but to take the time to run a bar of soap over the parts of him that were so damaged, well, he wouldn't ask that of anyone. Especially not when he knew damn well how sickened other women had been doing far less.

"You don't have to do that."

Her hands stilled. "Why wouldn't I want to, Connor?"

His throat tightened, making it hard to say, "I know what my skin looks like. How bad it is."

She moved back around the front of him. "How bad do you think it is?"

"It's a mess," he rasped out. "You don't have to prove anything to me. What we've done is already enough."

It had to be.

But she didn't seem to be listening, because she had already dropped the soap to the floor and was lifting both of his hands to her lips. She kissed his knuckles and then the silvery gray skin where they'd stitched it together, the raised and bumpy patches where it had simply pulled away with his melted gloves.

And then she was putting his scarred hands against her chest, pressing his palms flat so that he could feel her heart beat beneath her breastbone.

"Don't you dare try to tell me what I shouldn't do, Connor. I'm a big girl. And I'm not scared of you. Not one single thing about you. Even if you think I should be."

He kissed her then, and as he took her one more time, he couldn't help but wonder where a woman this incredible could have come from.

And just what the hell he was going to do about her when it came time to head back to California. Without her.

Ginger couldn't remember ever feeling this exhausted. Or this exhilarated.

Connor was her fantasy lover come to life. Big and strong, almost ruthless in his passion. She'd come violently every single time, and even when she hadn't thought it could get better, it had.

He was wrapping a towel around her, his mouth on her neck, sending thrill bumps running across the surface of her body, when she realized the phone was ringing. Whoever it was, she'd just ignore it. Whatever they wanted, she'd deal with it later.

But instead of stopping, the phone kept ringing and ringing. Over and over until Connor finally lifted his head from that spot right between her breasts where he could run his tongue over both at once.

"Sounds like you'd better get that."

More than a little irritated by the interruption, she tucked the towel under her arms and headed into her bedroom to pick up the cordless.

"Hello."

An unfamiliar male voice greeted her on the other end. "Hi. Sorry to bother you, but this is Sam MacKenzie. Any chance my brother is there?"

Connor was just walking past her door to his bedroom, a towel slung low around his narrow hips. "Yes, he is. I'll put him right on." To Connor she said, "It's Sam."

Connor lifted an eyebrow in surprise as he took the phone. "What's up?"

She couldn't hear what Sam was saying, but as she watched Connor's expression change back into that ice-cold rock she'd seen more than once, her concern morphed into full-on fear.

"Got it," he finally said. "Nope. It's fine. Talk to you later."

"Connor?" She moved closer. "Did something happen?"

He didn't say anything for quite a while, just stood there. His face was turned away from her so she couldn't get a read on him as he said, "The Forest Service has been trying to get hold of me. They called Thursday, left a couple of messages at my house and on my cell. When they didn't hear back, a friend of ours called Sam to make sure I was handling the news okay."

Oh God, she knew what he was going to say. "What was the news?"

"I'm out. For good."

His fingertips were numb as he dialed his voice mail to listen to the Forest Service director's message.

"After reviewing your case again the Forest Service has decided not to put you back out in the field. And, as I'm sure you're aware, you are at the end of the appeal process. A member of our reorganization program will be contacting you in a few days to discuss your new options within the Forest Service family. Again, we hope you'll decide to stay on with the Forest Service in some capacity. You have been a great asset to our organization during the past decade and we are confident that you will be just as great of an asset in the future in whatever new role you take."

New options?

Future?

From the day he'd graduated high school, Connor had been up in the mountains chasing wildfires. What the hell was he supposed to do with himself now? Teach from a book for the rest of his life? Wear a suit and get a paunch and tell the same stories over and over again about the "good old days" to the rookies?

He felt the bomb that had been building inside of him during the past two years start to detonate, slowly but surely. Blackness was swirling up from deep in his gut—a blackness that he hadn't wanted to face, not even in the darkest days of his burns and skin grafts—like thick ink soaking straight into his cells.

Two years ago, everything had happened so fast he hadn't had a chance to brace himself for the hit. Whereas this loss of everything he was, his world falling literally off its axis, was almost coming in slow motion.

But at the same time that the agony was prolonged, it gave him time to try to find something to hold on to, anything, just as long as it would keep his head above water for a little while longer.

Ginger's arms came around him, then, and as she murmured how sorry she was, he realized the answer was right here.

As long as he could keep losing himself in Ginger, he might be able to keep the demons at bay.

CHAPTER THIRTEEN

GINGER HAD never felt the need to comfort someone as much as she did in that moment after Connor heard the bad news. She tried to think what she would want him to do if their positions were reversed, if an all-controlling organization took her paints and canvases away for good. She would have wanted to bury herself in his warmth, let her tears pour down onto his chest while he stroked her and told her everything was going to be all right.

So she'd taken one step and then another toward him and put her arms around him. Tears pricked at her eyes as she held him and although his arms came around her too, even though he didn't push her away, after a few moments she realized he wasn't letting loose at all, wasn't giving in to the inner turmoil that had to be ripping him apart.

He probably just needed some time to digest the news

was what she told herself as they went about their day. She drew sketches for some new paintings out on the porch; he worked on the cabin. By noon the storm had blown out of town, leaving behind brilliant blue skies and blinding sparkles across the surface of the water. But the underlying tension in the cabin was suffocating.

Even after lunch, when he'd said it was time for dessert and then lifted her up on the indoor dining table and made love to her, while the pleasure was just as intense as it had been all night long and into the morning, she couldn't help but feel like what was between them had changed.

On the one hand, it was obvious that he needed her more than ever. His constant caresses and kisses in the hours after the phone call were testament to that. But at the same time, she felt that he'd begun to hold pieces of himself back.

She tried to tell herself that she'd only known him five days, but no matter how she spun it, any way she looked at it, his behavior didn't make sense.

He should be yelling. Lashing out.

She still remembered how she felt that night at the auction when Jeremy had said those horrible things, how she'd finally let go of everything she'd been holding back for so long. Her smiles gave way to rage. And, oh, it had felt so good to just let it all come spilling out. Not to worry about the mess she left behind, because she was already gone. Already starting over.

And it was because Connor's situation felt so similar—and because she already cared so deeply for him—that she wanted to call him on it, wanted to force him to grieve, to truly face what had happened, to start to come to terms with his new future.

Whatever that future held.

There had to be plenty of other people hurting for him today. His brother obviously was. And his parents, when they finally found out, would probably be devastated as well.

Thinking of Connor's parents made her finally remember.

The love letters.

Everything had happened so fast after they'd left the workshop the night before. The kids lighting fireworks. Kissing Connor in the rain. Thoughts of him had used up every last brain cell until now.

She needed to see Isabel. Give the stack of letters to her friend. And maybe, while she was gone, Connor might start to come to terms with the about-face his life had taken and he might be more ready to talk to her about it when she got back.

Thankfully she'd stashed the letters back in the dresser in the workshop. If she'd had them with her when they left the workshop they would have gotten soaked.

Connor saw her grab her keys and purse. "Heading out?"

"I just remembered an errand I've got to run."

It almost felt like lying, not telling him that she was going to give Isabel the letters, but she didn't think mentioning those right now would make his day any better and, at least for today, it seemed more important to protect him from any further pain.

"Come here first."

The command in his voice, along with the sensual promise in his eyes, had her walking over to him in a semi-daze. And then, when she was barely within reaching distance, he pulled her into his arms, his fingers threading into her hair, his mouth coming down over hers. His kiss consumed her and she felt herself falling, heading further and further beneath his spell.

Finally, he let her up for air. "You sure your errand can't wait?"

And even though a voice in her head told her that making love with him again was only helping him hide out from everything he needed to face, she couldn't walk away. Not only because giving herself to him like this was the best—and only—way she could think of right now to provide the comfort he desperately needed.

But, on a less altruistic note, because stealing every hour that she possibly could with him was what she most wanted for herself.

By the time Ginger walked into the diner, the old letters safe in her large purse, Isabel was just turning the sign to CLOSED.

"This is a nice surprise. I didn't expect to see you here today. Hungry?"

"No. I've already had lunch." And then some.

"What's up?" Isabel stopped fiddling with the blinds

on the windows, looked more carefully at Ginger's face. "Is it Connor? Did something else happen since I last saw you?"

Ginger hadn't come here to talk about Connor, but now that her friend was asking she just couldn't hold it in. "We . . . he . . . and then . . ."

Isabel grabbed her arm, pulled her over to a bar stool. "Coffee. That's what you need. And then you can tell me everything."

"But what about how you said I should stay away from him?"

"I'm not sure that's exactly what I said, but you were right. Just because I have a past with his father, doesn't mean I have anything against Connor. If you say he's great, I'm sure he is." She put a cup down in front of Ginger. "So how great is he?"

Ginger blushed, tried to buy herself time by taking a sip.

"Never mind. I think I get the gist of it already, just looking at you."

But Ginger wanted to try to put what she was feeling into words. Maybe then she'd understand it better.

"It's like something in him just pulls at me. And every second we're together, I just . . ." She put her hand over her heart. "Right here. I feel him here."

Isabel came around the counter, sat down next to Ginger. "You're in deep already, aren't you?"

There was no point in lying to herself about it. "Yes. And I don't know how to stop it."

"That only matters if you want to stop it."

"It's just a summer fling." It was all they'd agreed on.

"No reason summer can't turn to fall," Isabel suggested.

Suddenly, Ginger realized they'd made that agreement when they thought he was going to be heading back to work for the Forest Service in California. But now that everything had changed for him, she realized that every day she spent with Connor was going to start and end with her hoping for one more day. For more of him.

Even after he'd told her flat-out that he had nothing to give.

"You're scared, aren't you?"

Ginger looked at her friend, saw love and concern in her eyes, and knew she could confess, "More scared than I've ever been. And at the same time, I'm so incredibly happy. Almost as if I could burst from it."

Isabel leaned her head on Ginger's shoulder, two friends sitting in an empty diner, sharing confidences. "I wish I knew the right thing to say to you. The perfect advice to give to make it less confusing. But I'm afraid you're talking to someone who doesn't know the first thing about making relationships work."

Damn it, Ginger thought. She'd forgotten about the letters again.

"Actually, I came here to give you something." Ginger reached into her purse and pulled them out. "I found these stuck behind one of my dresser drawers."

Isabel's face went white with shock. "My letters to Andrew." She rubbed her fingers over the papers. "He kept them."

"Isabel, I'm sorry," Ginger blurted, "but one fell open and then once I started reading, I couldn't help myself."

But Isabel didn't seem to hear her. "I was so young," she said so quietly it was almost a whisper. "Sitting here, just like you are now. So in love with him that I could hardly see straight."

Isabel's words nearly knocked Ginger off of her stool. She didn't think Isabel had even heard what she'd just said, she was so wrapped up in poring through the letters. But now that it was there—love, oh God, could that be what this pull was?—Ginger couldn't look away from it.

"I can't believe I wrote these things," Isabel was saying. "I had the future all planned out." She pressed her lips together. Sighed. "Stupid girl."

"I still don't get it," Ginger said, working like crazy to focus on what her friend was saying, rather than the swirling mass of emotions pushing around inside her. "How could all of that," she gestured to the letters, "have become ten terrible words?"

Isabel shrugged. "Who the hell knows. Andrew and I were just kids who didn't know any better, I guess."

"Is it going to be weird to see him when he comes out for Sam's wedding?"

"Very," Isabel admitted. "But at least I have a few weeks to prepare myself for it, right? Not," she said with a rueful grin, "that I should be wasting too much time on that." Pushing off the stool, she said, "I know you have a lot of painting to get done. Thanks for bringing these to me."

Understanding that her friend wanted to be alone

with the letters, and glad to have some time on her own to think, Ginger headed out.

Was it possible for her to have fallen in love with Connor already? During her short drive home, her brain insisted on playing out a montage of images.

Protecting her from the falling branch, his heart beating wildly against her back, even harder than hers because he'd been so afraid of something happening to her.

Connor's anguish the night in his bedroom when his fingers had gone numb as he stroked her. Holding his hand but feeling she was really holding his heart.

The way he'd looked at her paintings and seen straightaway what she was trying to get down on the canvas, understanding her in a way few people ever had.

And, of course, all those precious, sweet hours in his arms.

A sharp sense of relief shot through her when she came home and saw that the red truck was gone. She couldn't face him yet. Not when the possibility of being in love was still so new to her, when she felt as if she were strapped into a runaway train that she couldn't even remember getting on.

Walking over to stand in front of her canvas, she stared at the painting she'd been working on.

"Before Love" was how it seemed now. How, she wondered, was she seeing things so differently after such a short time with Connor? After only one incredible night in his arms?

And yet, there was no denying that even the colors in her palette were richer now. Deeper.

A voice in her head told her she should be looking at falling in love with Connor as a disaster, the biggest one of her life. But that scared voice sounded so much like the one that had told her for so many years that she didn't know how to paint, that she couldn't possibly follow her own heart and create something beautiful.

She picked up her brush and then, before she could possibly get ready for it, all hell was breaking loose, her fingers and hands and arms all pushing her to paint as fast as she could.

The images came to her as quickly as she could put them onto the canvases, one after the other. And while there was similar motion and color and energy to the paintings she'd made since coming to Poplar Cove eight months ago, there was something more to these paintings.

More emotion.

More tenderness.

When she finally stepped back to catch her breath, she realized what she was doing. She was painting Connor in all the ways she saw him. Swimming across the lake, doing sit-ups on the beach, but also naked and levered above her in bed, his eyes full of desire as he told her she was beautiful. She was painting him as a hero, saving the world single-handedly. And then, standing in the middle of flames, melting down inside, but doing everything he could to hide it.

She jumped as a sharp sound knocked her out of the zone. Realizing it was the phone, she dropped her brush and ran to get it.

After this morning, the phone felt like the bearer of

bad news. What news could be coming now? She prayed it wasn't anything that would hurt Connor more.

"Ginger, darling, it's me."

Ah, her mother. She plopped down on one of the nearby kitchen chairs. Alexandra liked to tell her all the gossip. And even though Ginger wasn't at all interested in the comings and goings of a bunch of her mother's friends, she was glad for the growing connection with her mother. Amazingly, in the eight months since she'd left the city, they'd spoken more on the phone than they had in person during her whole marriage when they lived just down the street.

"I'm sorry I haven't been in touch since last week. It's been so busy with fund-raising for the upcoming opera season, as you know."

Her mother cleared her throat and Ginger had the strangest sense that she was uncomfortable.

Alexandra Sinclair was never uncomfortable and it sent a flicker of unease down Ginger's spine.

"In any case, dear, I needed to call and tell you the news. Before you hear it from anyone else."

Ginger could hear her father saying something in the background.

"No, I can't just hang up without telling her now," her mother hissed at him, before saying to Ginger, "Honey, when I was at lunch today I heard that Jeremy and his new girlfriend . . ."

It wasn't hard for Ginger to fill in the blanks. "They're getting married."

Honestly, she was glad if her ex could find happiness with someone else. Everyone deserved a chance at love. Including her. And Connor, too.

"Yes, they're getting married." Her mother made a small sound of distress. "Because they're having a baby."

Connor walked into the kitchen as she said, "Oh. I see. A baby." She could feel her limbs shaking, her eyes starting to water. "But he never wanted—"

"Oh honey, you're better off without him. You always were."

"Mmm," was all Ginger could manage around the lump in her throat.

Fortunately, her mother wasn't a big fan of emotional scenes. "If I were you I wouldn't give it another thought."

"No. I won't," Ginger lied. "I'll talk to you soon, Mom."

"Ginger," Connor asked, his eyes dark with concern as he came to kneel in front of her. "What's wrong?"

"My mother called. My ex-husband is having a—"

The final word got lost on her tongue, refused to come, but he'd obviously heard enough of the conversation to guess.

"A baby?"

She nodded, hating the tear that rolled down her cheek.

"You want a baby," he said again and overpowering longing hit her before she could brace herself.

"More than anything."

"Did he shoot blanks? Was that the problem? Is that why you don't have any already?"

Laughter was the last thing she'd expected, but his

question was so perfectly timed—so perfectly Connor—that she couldn't help but choke one out.

"No," she said, a split second before her smile fell away. "That wasn't the problem."

"Then what was?"

"Our marriage sucked for one."

"Plenty of people have kids when their marriages suck. Take my parents. It was the only thing they did well together."

"Jeremy didn't want a baby." No, that wasn't true anymore. "Not with me, anyway."

"I know I've said this before, but he sounds like a stupid fuck. Why the hell did you marry him?"

She matched the anger of his words with hers. "Because I thought he was the best I could do. Because I couldn't believe he actually wanted me. That he'd chosen me instead of one of the perfect sorority girls throwing themselves at him. It's why I didn't leave for so long. Because I thought I'd never do any better."

"And you actually wanted to have a kid with this guy? Jesus, Ginger, don't you have any sense at all? What the hell do you see when you look in the mirror? Who do you think you are?"

The answer was easy. *A girl who had never been good enough for anyone, no matter how hard she tried.*

"You're coming with me."

Grabbing her hand, he pulled her out of the kitchen, up the stairs, into her bedroom, not stopping until they were standing in front of the full-length mirror, her back to his front.

"I've never admitted this to anyone before," he said in a soft voice, "but do you know how hard it was for me to look at my burns for the first time?"

She swallowed hard, instinctively covering his hands and arms with her own, gently stroking the raised scars.

"When they unwrapped the bandages that first time and I saw the wreckage of what had once been perfectly good hands, perfectly good skin, I wanted to cry like a baby. But I couldn't. Not with everyone watching. Not when everyone expected me to be the tough firefighter."

She'd never thought about how hard it was on men like Connor to get injured and feel like they couldn't break down, not even once.

Staring at the two of them together in the mirror, Ginger felt that her concerns about her weight were incredibly petty. How could she have spent so much time worrying about her size when her body was, essentially, perfect. Sure, maybe she didn't fit into the current cultural norms of perfection, but she could run and jump and swim and paint. What on earth did she have to complain about?

Connor stroked her hair back from her face. "If you're thinking I just told you all of that to invalidate your feelings, think again."

"But it's true. My issues are nothing compared to what you've been through."

He squeezed her more tightly around the waist, pulling her closer against his rock hard chest and thighs. "Here's how I see it. I've had a couple of rough years with my body, but before that everyone told me how great I looked, how strong I was, how well-built. Crazy as it seems to me, I get the feeling no one has ever said those things to you before now." Holding her eyes in the mirror, he asked, "What do you see?"

Ginger's chest was clenched and tight. "Just me."

"Really? Is that all you can see, sweetheart? There isn't anything else?"

To have such a big, strong man be so gentle with her . . . she could feel herself melting in his arms.

"I don't know," she whispered. "I don't know what I see."

His hands and arms still wrapped tightly around her, he whispered, "Then how about I tell you what I see? You're strong." Her breath came faster as he pressed a kiss just above her left ear. "You're beautiful." He spun her around to face him and cupped her face in his large hands. She blinked up at him and got lost in his blue eyes. "And every time I look at you, you completely take my breath away."

He slowly undressed her and she drank in every touch, every caress, every path of his fingers across her skin. He ran his lips, his tongue, his fingertips over every inch of her skin reverently as her clothes seemed to disappear and she trembled everywhere he'd touched.

When she was finally naked, he said, "Turn around, sweetheart."

She couldn't do it. Not with years of self-hatred coming at her. She was stunned. She'd thought she'd beaten down the beast within, had been so confident of her triumph.

But he was already turning her in his strong hands, forcing her to see something she wished she could hide from forever—just as she'd forced him to see it in himself the night before.

God, how she hated this fear. So she forced herself to look.

And lost her breath.

"I look so small compared to you," she whispered.

With Connor behind her, all six-feet-plus of him, she looked tiny. She'd never before thought that word in relation to herself. But he was so big, so broad, that instead of taking note of her bumps and lumps, she saw her breasts, heavy with arousal, the way her skin glowed from the afternoon sun that covered her on the porch as she painted, the fact that her lush curves were the perfect contrast to Connor's hard muscles.

"Tell me what else you see."

"A woman I don't think I've ever seen before."

"She's beautiful, isn't she?"

Looking herself straight in the eye, she tried out the word in her head first to make sure it was really true.

"Yes."

"Let me show you just how beautiful you are, Ginger. Let me love you."

The four-letter word exploded in her head, filled her completely.

There was no longer any room for doubt. Not with Connor seeing her beauty like no one else ever had. Not when he wanted so desperately to make her see it too.

It would be easy, so much easier just to tell herself that

she was confusing sex with love like she had with her ex-husband. But she wasn't that naive young girl anymore.

She was a woman who knew her own mind, a woman who knew her own heart.

And yes, oh yes, she loved him.

Turning back around in his arms, she pulled him against her and then she was on the bed and he was sliding into her in one thick stroke, working to heal her with his body as she'd tried to heal him with hers.

His name on her lips as they rocked together, she got lost in the slip and slide of their bodies, the delicious friction of his skin on hers, the way he filled her so completely.

And when he sent her reeling over the edge it was the most natural thing in the world for her to take him with her.

She'd fallen asleep in his arms, utterly content to listen to his heart beat beneath her ear as her eyes closed and she let exhaustion take her. Now she woke up alone in the bed as the sun was setting to the sound of the phone ringing again, alone in the bed again.

In the end she spent a good hour fielding phone calls from not only Connor's brother, but a dozen of his friends on his hotshot crew. So many people who cared about him. So many people who wanted to be there for him.

For every call she picked up, another voice mail came in. His mother sounded like she'd been crying and Ginger was selfishly glad that call hadn't come through. She wouldn't have known what to say. Just when she thought the lull in calls might mean that the rush was over, the phone rang one more time.

"Hi, I'm sorry to bother you again. This is Connor's father. Is he there?"

She thought about everything Connor had told her about his father, flashing next to the letters Isabel had written him and the way she'd reacted to seeing the faded pages again on the bar stool in the diner. Ginger hadn't even met the man, and yet, strangely, she felt that she knew him so well already.

"I'm so sorry, Mr. MacKenzie. He's out, but I promise to let him know the minute he walks in that you called."

"Please," Connor's father said, "just tell him I'm coming. I'm taking the red-eye out of San Francisco."

He abruptly hung up and she held on to the phone for several moments before realizing she was staring blankly out at the sun setting over the lake through the kitchen window, the receiver still in her hand. How, she wondered, was Connor going to react to his father's arrival?

No question, Isabel was going to freak. Instead of three weeks to prepare she'd have eight hours.

Ginger called the diner, but when no one picked up she knew they must be running like crazy tonight.

She was about to leave a message telling her friend to call. Tonight. Whenever. But just as she was about to hang up, she decided, no, it wasn't fair not to just spit it out.

"Andrew's coming, Isabel. He's taking the red-eye out tonight. I figured you'd want to know."

She left the same message on Isabel's home phone, and

then, as she hung up the phone for what felt like the millionth time, she saw a flash of light out on the beach in front of the house.

Someone was out there with a flashlight. Looking out the window, she recognized the dark figure as Connor, but couldn't figure out what he was dragging behind him. A hose, she quickly guessed, although she couldn't figure out why.

A couple of minutes later when she got down to the sand she had to speak loudly to be heard over the sound of water spraying out of the hose.

"Connor? Why are you hosing down the boat?

"They're shooting the fireworks off tonight."

She knew July fifth was the makeup day for fireworks if it rained on the Fourth. Still, she didn't understand what any of that had to do with what he was doing right now.

"But everything is still wet from the storm. It didn't stop raining until late this morning."

"You can never be too careful."

Finally, she got it. For all that he was trying to pretend everything was fine, that he could roll with the punches, no problem, he couldn't let go.

Fire hadn't just burned his hands. It was as if it were burning him up from the inside too.

She knew exactly what she needed to do to help him, had known all along that he needed her to help him accept what had happened. "You got a lot of phone calls while you were gone."

"Who from?"

As easy as his voice seemed, she couldn't miss the slight change in the tenor of his voice.

"Your brother called again, wanted to let you know your friends from the crew would be calling soon. And they did call, Connor. So many of them I can't keep track of their names, but I wrote them down. Your mother left a message too." She paused. "And your father, he called again too."

She waited for him to respond, but when all he did was nod and continue spraying water over the already soaked wood and canvas, she said, "He wanted me to tell you he's coming here. On the red-eye. He'll be here tomorrow."

"You've got to be kidding me?"

Finally, a reaction. "Turn the hose off, Connor. Talk to me. Please."

He did put the hose down, and she was filled with hope that maybe, just maybe, he was finally ready to take his first step toward healing.

"Come swimming with me, Ginger."

Her head spun at the abrupt switch, but also from being pulled back into his arms. Because now that she knew she loved him everything felt so different.

Bigger. Sweeter. A hundred times more intense.

A thousand times more frightening.

"Swimming?" she asked stupidly.

"Night swimming. Right now. Here. In the dark, beneath the fireworks."

She tried to shake her head, tried to put voice to the word no. Sex wouldn't solve anything for him. But his hands were already on her body, stripping her down, and his mouth was on hers, taking, giving, and she couldn't help but go with him. And then her fingers were moving too, pulling at his clothes, wanting them off faster, wanting nothing between them, to be as close to him as she could possibly be.

Sliding his fingers through hers, he took her over to the edge of the dock.

"Ready to jump, sweetheart?"

It was the sweetheart that did her in, that took any chance of protest away from her. And then they were jumping through the warm evening air before splashing in and and going under, the cool water taking what was left of her breath away.

And still, the water had nothing on Connor who had taken her breath away from the first moment she'd met him.

Connor was doing everything he could to drown in her, to keeping losing himself in the softness of her skin, the taste of her mouth, the feel of her tongue against his.

And still, minute by minute, he could feel himself spiraling out of control, like a rope that was unwinding from the inside out, strangling his guts in the threads as it spun faster and faster.

It was taking everything he had to keep it together.

All his life, his instincts had been to get moving, to use blood and sweat to work through the kinks. But this was one hell of a kink. And right now, the only thing that made sense was to go to a place where all that mattered was sensation. Where his only goal was to take Ginger higher, to use his hands and mouth to make her soft and yielding beneath him, to hear her crying out his name as she came.

He pulled her out deep enough in the lake where he could stand, but she had to wrap her legs around him to stay above the water. She wrapped her arms around his neck and he didn't kiss her hard, not this time. He wanted this moment to last forever, wanted the rest of the world to stay the hell away.

Only here, with Ginger, as her tongue slipped and slid against his, did he feel the deep ache inside begin to recede.

Only here, as her hands moved to cup his face, did he let himself accept that being with her was more than just great sex, that he was shaking from the power of their connection.

Only here, in the dark, cold water, as Ginger took him inside in a gasp of pleasure, and he let himself fall completely into her, could he see any light at all.

CHAPTER FOURTEEN

ISABEL WALKED in her front door just as the fireworks had ended. She dropped her keys on the front table, didn't hear any music pumping out of her son's bedroom and worried for a second before she realized he was probably still downtown having fun with his friends.

She went upstairs to her bedroom to get ready for bed, her heart pounding as she brushed her teeth, washed her face, put on her pajamas. All afternoon at the diner, all night as she plated dozens of meals, she'd only been half there. She'd wanted to pull out the letters a hundred times. But she'd had a restaurant to run.

Going to the spot in her closet where she'd dropped her purse, she reached in and pulled out the stack of papers. She still couldn't believe Andrew had kept them all. It meant more to her than it should. Especially since she'd burned all of his.

Slipping beneath her sheets, she turned on her bedside lamp. And as she read one letter after another, two years of young love simply burning up the pages, it all came back to her.

Sailing beside him, capsizing the boat on purpose so that he could pull her against him in the water, kiss her until another boat came around the bend to where they were floating and they were forced to pull away from each other and right their craft.

Hiking through the thick forests, holding his hand at the top of the hill, the whole world at their feet, loving it when he pressed her up against a rough tree trunk, shivering as his fingers moved beneath her shirt, to her bra, crying out as his large palms cupped her, caressed her.

Rowing out to the island and lying in his arms beneath a full moon, listening to the strong, steady beat of his heart as shooting stars fell from the sky.

She nestled deeper beneath her blankets as she read, wishing these sweet memories were all there were, dreading the knowledge that they weren't.

Because she only knew too well the letter she'd find at the bottom of the pile, what it would say.

"You wanted her. You can have her. Forever."

Morning came too fast and Isabel was just taking her first sip of coffee for the day while slipping on her clogs when she saw the light blinking on her old-fashioned message machine. She was leaning into the front door only half listening, when she finally realized what Ginger had said.

"Andrew's coming, Isabel. He's taking the red-eye out tonight. I figured you'd want to know."

No. God no. The only trick was the one her heart was playing on her. She wanted so badly to keep from losing her breath, to stop the room from spinning, but it was already too late, and she had to put a hand out against the front door to hold herself up as her most deeply repressed memory came back to life in brilliant technicolor.

Over the past two years, Isabel had gotten used to sneaking out at night to be with Andrew. During the summers at the lake it was easier when he was right there, just next door and they could meet at the island or out by the old carousel late a night. But the rest of the year, when they were back in the city, while she went to high school and he attended classes at NYU, it was harder to see him without getting endless lectures from her parents.

She wished her parents understood her feelings, wished that they could see how perfect he was for her. Instead they said things like, "You're too young." "You have your whole life ahead of you." And her favorite, "First love doesn't last forever, honey." As if what she felt for Andrew was nothing more than some kid crush.

Fortunately, he'd made sure the little apartment that he shared with a couple of friends was close to her parents' house. Whenever her parents were out—which was often, as they were both heavily involved in the local music scene—she'd stuff her bed with blankets to look like a body before she went down the fire escape out back, just in case they came home early and checked on her.

Andrew was always waiting there for her. It was a safe neighborhood, just mothers with strollers and kids playing ball, businessmen coming home late from work. She would have been fine walking the four blocks to his apartment, but he said he'd never forgive himself if something happened to her. If she got hurt coming to him.

They'd go get coffee sometimes and talk for hours, or comb through used-book stores for old books people had written about sailing, but they'd always end up back at his tiny bedroom, lying together on his small bed. He'd strip her down to her bra and panties and tell her how much loved her. How he couldn't wait for her to turn eighteen so that he could take the promise ring he'd given her, the one she kept buried in her sock drawer, and put it on her finger. How much he wanted to make love to her, to do more than just kiss and stroke her. Sometimes when things got too close, when she wanted to go there with him more than she wanted to breathe, they'd barely pull apart in time. They'd sit on opposite sides of his bed, looking at the nautical maps pinned to his wall and plan their trip around the world until they'd caught their breath.

For all the rules she was breaking every time she snuck out to him, Isabel had heard of several girls in her high school who'd had abortions, and had never wanted to be in that horrible position.

But lately when she pulled away, she'd seen something in Andrew's eyes, a waning of patience. She couldn't blame him, not when they were the same eyes that stared at her in the mirror when she got home from his house.

Aching.

Wanting.

A thousand times, she'd imagined what it would feel like. The long, hard slide of him inside her. Filling her with his heat. With everything he was.

It made her hot all over just thinking about it. Soon, she decided.

Before both of them went crazy.

But she didn't want to be rushed, to have to hurry back into her clothes afterward to get home. She longed to fall asleep in his arms, to spend an entire night with him, to wake up with him in the morning and see the sunlight play across his face. So when her parents told her they'd been invited to play an out-of-town concert, and did she want to come, she made up an excuse about too much homework, needing to get ready for her exams.

She couldn't wait to tell Andrew her plans, to share the delicious anticipation with him. They hadn't planned to see each other that night, but after telling her parents she was going out to meet a girlfriend, she headed for his apartment.

She had to knock hard a couple of times to be heard over the loud music. She'd always thought his roommates were a little strange, but she spent so little time with them it really didn't matter.

James opened the door, his eyes bloodshot, his breath smelling like cheap wine. "Hey baby," he said to her, striking her, as he always did, as slightly lecherous. "Bring any of your hot schoolgirl friends with you?"

"No," she said curtly, looking around the room for Andrew. But he wasn't there. Heading through a haze of smoke, past a couple making out on the ratty couch, another against the kitchen counter, she went into the dark hall.

Andrew's door was closed and she smiled at the thought of finding him in there, hunched over his industrial engineering books while the party raged a hallway away. He'd told her it was the closest thing to getting a degree in boat building and when she'd flipped through his books and saw all the strange equations and graphs, she'd been so impressed.

She didn't knock. Why would she, when she'd spent so many hours in his bedroom? Her heartbeat kicked up again at the thought of what she was about to tell him as she turned the knob and opened the door. She already knew what his reaction would be, that he'd pull her into his arms and kiss her until she was breathless.

But as the door cracked open, instead of finding him at his desk, concentrating on homework, she saw two figures moving together in the semidarkness. The sheet had fallen off and there was so much naked skin, more than she'd ever seen. They were facing backward on the bed, as if they'd been in too much of a rush to figure out which way was up.

Her first thought was that it couldn't be him. But it was—oh God, how could he?—and all she could think around the despair, the betrayal that was rapidly taking over every cell in her body, was that it was supposed to be her beneath him, not some beautiful girl with long dark hair and deeply tanned skin writhing on the bed, calling out his name.

But ultimately it was the expression on his face that she knew she'd never get out of her head. The intense pleasure of release, of all those pent-up years of sexual frustration finally being relieved.

With another girl.

Josh found her there, propped up against the front door, feeling just as nauseous now as she had so many years ago.

"Mom, what are you doing?"

She blinked hard, had to work like hell to push away the vision of Andrew making love to someone else.

"Nothing," she finally managed. "Just getting ready to head off to work."

He looked at her like she was crazy. "Whatever."

Watching him head into the kitchen to get a bowl of cereal, she thought again how much she hated how strained things had been between them since that afternoon at the diner when he'd blown her off.

Forcing a smile, she asked, "Got any fun plans for today?"

He shrugged. "Nope. Just hanging out."

Of course he didn't want to talk to her. He never did anymore. She bit her tongue, knowing better by now than to try to force it. It only made him clam up more.

Her son was growing up. And there was nothing she could do about it. Besides, hadn't she wished her parents would get with the program when she was his age? What went around, she had often discovered over the years as a parent, had a disturbing tendency to come around. The solution was easy. She needed to chill out. Back off a bit.

Still, she couldn't leave without going over and giving him a kiss on his head, even if he pulled away mid smooch.

Grabbing her keys off the counter, she headed into town to open up the diner, working overtime, the entire way, to push memories of Andrew out of her head.

And to convince herself that it wasn't going to hurt like hell to see him again.

* * *

Andrew MacKenzie had planned never to come back to Poplar Cove. And yet he'd just flown into the Albany International airport, picked up a rental car and wound through the same back-country roads he'd driven so many times with his parents when he was a boy.

As a kid, he'd practically held his breath until their log cabin came into view, hurtling out of the car as soon as they parked. Now, just like then, his heart was pounding when he made the turn off the two-lane highway, but for entirely different reasons.

He wasn't a kid with his whole life ahead of him anymore. Instead, he was a man heading toward fifty with a bullet. And all he had to show for it was a failed marriage, forced retirement from the law firm he'd given a hundred twenty hours a week to, and a couple of kids he barely knew.

That was the worst part. Not knowing his sons, having to hear from strangers how heroic they were, that they were two in a million, the best of the best.

He should already know it, damn it, had made God a promise two years ago when his youngest son had ended up in the ICU, unconscious and burned, that if only Connor would be all right, if he would walk out of the hospital in one piece, Andrew would do anything. He would become a better husband. Spend less time at the office. Get close to his sons.

But it hadn't worked out like that at all. Connor was a survivor through and through, thank God, but Elise had served him with the divorce papers practically the same day Connor left the hospital. And although he'd reached out to Sam and Connor again and again, neither of them had wanted anything to do with him. Not until last year, when Sam had fallen in love with the beautiful TV personality from San Francisco. Suddenly, the lines had opened up. Andrew knew he had Dianna to thank for it, that she'd encouraged Sam to return some calls, to accept a couple of dinner invitations.

Connor, on the other hand, was a much tougher nut to crack. Through Sam, Andrew had learned just how much they identified with their jobs. Being a hotshot wasn't just something that paid the bills, it was who they were, all the way to the core. Which was why Andrew had repeatedly offered to help Connor with the Forest Service appeal process, but his son had never taken him up on it.

And then yesterday, Sam had told Andrew the bad news. The Forest Service thought Connor's accident was too extreme. He would never fight fire again.

Andrew picked up the phone and bought the first ticket out to Albany. Connor needed him. For once he wouldn't fail him.

The car drew closer to Poplar Cove and between the cabins, the lake shined so blue he almost thought he was imagining it. Even with sunglasses on he had to squint. Thirty years he'd spent in San Francisco, not once taking a long weekend to go hiking, to throw a fishing pole into the back of his car and find a well-stocked lake.

His chest squeezed. God, how he'd missed this place. He slowed the car so that he could take in the water, the mountains, the familiar old camps.

For a moment, he forgot everything except his intense pleasure at being back at Blue Mountain Lake.

But even as he sat in his car in the middle of the road, it struck him, powerfully, that although he'd been experiencing a major sense of déjà vu since landing in Albany, the fact of the matter was that nothing was the same as it had been thirty years ago.

Sure, the drive was mostly the same. The camps were still just as they always were. The lake was full of boats. But all of Andrew's dreams were buried down so deep that he could no longer say what it was that nineteen-year-old boy he'd once been had really wanted.

All he knew was that he hadn't gotten it.

A car honked behind him and he put his foot on the gas pedal, the gravel lot behind Poplar Cove finally coming into view. Pulling in, he saw a car and a truck. During the short chat he'd had with his parents, they'd told him they were renting the cabin out to a young woman. He assumed the truck belonged to Connor who, evidently, was working on the cabin for Sam's wedding.

Getting out of the car, he took the stairs to the screened porch and knocked on the door. When he looked in he could see a pretty young woman standing in front of an easel. She seemed to be dancing along to something, but he couldn't hear any music.

"Excuse me," he said, but she didn't look over, didn't seem to have heard him. "Excuse me," he said again, louder this time, and this time, she turned just as Connor walked out onto the porch.

"Dad," he said, not exactly looking pleased to see him.

But Andrew couldn't help smiling. To go from where his son had been, lying there under a thin white sheet hooked up to machines to this strong, young man . . . it was a miracle.

"Connor, you're looking great," he said, still standing on the other side of the screen door.

The woman moved past Connor and opened the door. "Hi, I'm Ginger. Why don't you come in?"

He stepped inside and shook her outstretched hand. He thought about walking over to his son and hugging him, but they hadn't hugged since Connor was a little boy. Andrew quickly dismissed the idea as a bad one.

"How was your flight?" Ginger asked him as the silence drew on several beats too long.

"Good." He cleared his throat. "Great."

She shot a glance at Connor, and even from this distance, Andrew could feel a strong connection between the two of them.

"You must be exhausted."

"No, I'm fine. Managed a couple of hours on the plane."

Ginger's wristwatch beeped and she looked down at it in obvious consternation. "I'm sorry, but I've got to head into work." Another quick look at his son. "If you'd like something to eat, Connor knows where all the food is. I'm sure he could heat something up for you."

She turned to head into the house, brushing against Connor as she walked past. Andrew saw his son's reaction, the way his fingers stretched out to brush against hers.

Andrew remembered what it felt like to be with a girl that could take him down with nothing more than a glance, with the soft touch of her fingers on his skin. It had been the greatest feeling in the world.

"Want a Coke?" Connor asked.

"I've had enough caffeine already to last me the week."

Connor raised both eyebrows. "Okay. I'm going to get one."

Had he already put his foot in it, over nothing more than a soda? He should have taken whatever his son offered.

While Connor walked to the kitchen, Andrew looked around the old log cabin. It looked almost identical to the way it had when he was a kid. Some new furniture, a lighter shade of green on the porch, but otherwise like time was standing still.

Ginger came down the stairs, went into the kitchen, said something to Connor that he couldn't make out. Not wanting to be a peeping Tom, he moved back, but not before he caught a glimpse of her going up on her toes to kiss his son.

"I hope to see you later," she said to Andrew as she walked out the screen door.

Connor sat down with his Coke and Andrew dearly wished he had something to do with his hands, even if it was just opening the pop tab.

He'd been like this the day Connor had been born, his hands trembling as he went to pick him up. Newborns scared him. They were so small, so helpless, and every moment they depended on you. And although Connor was a couple of inches taller than him now, Andrew felt just as awkward, just as unsure of himself.

"How's the work on the cabin going?"

"The wiring was a mess. The logs are rotting. The roof is shot."

Andrew nodded, tried to think of what to say next. "Are you staying in town or—"

"Here. I'm staying here."

"That's great. Ginger seems like a beautiful girl."

Shit, another hard stare from his son. He was a lawyer, he should know how to lead a conversation in the direction he wanted it to go.

"Have you run into any of your old friends?"

"Let's cut the bull. Why are you here?"

Andrew bristled at his son's tone, forgot his intention to be the nice guy. "Poplar Cove isn't yours, it's your grandparents'. Which makes it mine too. I have every right to be here."

"Wrong." Connor stood, looked down on him. "This is Ginger's house now. You're only here because she let you in. And that's just because she doesn't know a damn thing about you."

Andrew stood up too, faced off with his son. He wasn't as broad from years of grueling physicality, but they had the same basic build. Apart from the twenty years between them, they were fairly evenly matched.

"How about we cut right to it, then?"

Andrew had thought he needed to tread gently. Fuck that. If Connor was going to come at him full speed ahead, he was going to see that his old man was tough enough to block him.

"Your brother called me. He told me what happened.

That the Forest Service had turned down your final appeal. That's why I'm here. To take care of my own."

"I'm fine."

For the first time in a very long time, Andrew saw himself in his rugged son. He'd done that same thing once, worked like hell to convince everyone—but mostly himself—that the abrupt shift his life had taken was what he'd wanted.

"All my life I've worked on facts and facts alone," he told his son. "Here are the facts. You have always wanted to be a firefighter and nothing else. And now your future has been fucked over by a bunch of suits."

From a legal perspective, Andrew understood why the Forest Service couldn't risk having an injured man in the field who might freeze in a crucial moment.

"That's a brutal blow, Connor. One you're going to have to deal with sooner or later."

"I told you. I'm fine."

"I didn't just fly here on a godforsaken red-eye to hear you spout that denial crap."

Connor's mouth twisted up on one side. "Now that's real suffering. A red-eye flight."

A sound of frustration rippled out from Andrew's throat, two years of rejected invitations to connect with his son all coming at him at once.

"Your IQ tests were off the charts. You could have been anything you wanted to. You're only thirty. It's not too late to go back to school, to become a doctor or professor. Heck, I've heard you've been a hell of a teacher to the rookie hotshots these past couple of years."

"Think how much easier it would have been to tell me that over the phone instead of coming all this way."

"Damn it, Connor, I'm your father. I put aside everything else in my life to come here. To help you."

"Bullshit. You never wanted me and Sam to be firefighters, never got tired of saying it was a dead-end job. Must feel damn good to finally be right."

Andrew needed to call a break, reassess, approach Connor from a different angle, but before he could do any of that, Connor was saying, "Did you cheat on Mom?"

What the hell?

"Cheat on your mom? What are you talking about? I might have done a lot of things, but I never did that."

"I already know about Isabel."

Andrew opened his mouth, closed it hard enough that his teeth clacked together. Now it made sense why Connor had been so pissed off from the moment he'd set foot on the porch.

Through gritted teeth, he said, "I knew Isabel before—"

It was all so intertwined. Andrew was tempted to lie, but something told him that would only come back to bite him in the ass harder.

"We dated before your mom." And he'd desperately wanted Isabel back after. Even though it had been impossible.

"Was Isabel the reason you couldn't make your marriage work?"

"Yes." He shook his head. "No. It was all so long ago.

We tried, Connor. I swear it. Your mother and I tried to make it work."

"She tried." Connor stood up. "You didn't."

Contrition slammed into Andrew as his son moved away, the rewind button in his head taking him through the last several minutes, highlighting every way he'd played it wrong.

Something told him that if he let his son go now, they'd be done. Completely. Which meant he'd have to play his final card. Connor's love for his brother.

"Please, Connor," he said, reaching out to grip his son's scarred arm. "I get that I'm not your favorite person in the world, that you'd love to shove me onto the next plane back to San Francisco. But Sam and Dianna asked if I'd walk her down the aisle and I want to be part of Sam's wedding, do whatever I can to help them get ready for it."

He swallowed everything else. *I want to be a part of your life. Get to finally know the man you've become. Maybe stand up for you one day at your wedding.* Connor didn't want to hear any of that.

The silence dragged on long enough for Andrew to feel rivulets of sweat begin to run down his chest. And then, finally, Connor shrugged.

"Do whatever floats your boat. Doesn't make any difference to me." Connor grabbed his running shoes from the porch. "I'm going to head out for a run."

Andrew stood alone on the cabin's porch, watching his son sprint across the sand, desperate to get away from him.

CHAPTER FIFTEEN

THE SKY was brilliant blue, the lake like glass as Josh untied his mom's speedboat from the dock in front of their house. Five friends—including Hannah Smiley—were already on board, popping soda cans open and talking about the huge flames at last night's bonfire. He'd known all of them, except Hannah, since he was five. Some of them were full-timers like him, others only came during the summer.

Getting behind the wheel, he ignored the five-mile-per-hour courtesy speed in the bay and shot away from the dock, his huge wake quickly washing up on the shore and knocking his neighbor's boats into their docks.

Hannah was the only reason this past week hadn't completely blown. Were it not for her, he would have much rather been back in his father's loft in the city, going to loud, busy restaurants, playing the latest video games on his father's sick gaming system, drinking beer with his father's friends on poker night while betting—and losing—real money on his shitty hands.

Returning to Blue Mountain Lake was like stepping into quicksand. Small. Boring. Could his mother's diner be any more different from his father's buzzing architecture design office downtown? Red and white fifties decor versus glass and steel.

How in hell had his parents ever gotten together? Sure, he loved his mom and everything, but she was so small-town. Whereas his dad had the sharpest suits, the coolest jeans and shoes, even several pairs of funky glasses that he changed throughout the week to match his moods.

He looked back over his shoulder at Hannah in a casual way, not so she'd notice he was checking her out, even though he definitely was. She looked good in her white shorts and yellow T-shirt. Better than good actually. He still couldn't believe she'd wanted to come out on his boat. Not that he was the town loser or anything, but he didn't hang with the partying crowd either. Hannah had the looks to fit in with that crew, but somehow, she'd chosen to hang with him instead.

Cool.

"Man, your boat is sweet," his friend Matt said. "I can't believe your mom lets you take it out without her."

Josh shrugged. Yeah, the boat was fine, but he'd been riding around this lake since he was five. He was almost sixteen. Not a kid anymore.

He was ready for a change, and for the chance to show

Hannah what a badass he really was. Especially after that dude on the beach had freaked about their fireworks.

"Take the wheel," he said, standing up and heading out to the bow.

"Dude, that's illegal," Ben said.

Sure, Josh thought, his mom would shit a brick if she saw him bow riding, but she was always holed up in her diner on the other side of the lake.

"When was the last time a ranger went out on the lake and busted someone?" He looked at Hannah and shook his head as if to say, *"We should have left this loser on shore."*

Crawling across the white fiberglass, he made it to the metal rails on the very tip of the boat. Hooking his legs under them, he yelled back at Matt, "Hit it!"

An evil grin was on Matt's face as his friend punched the engine into overdrive, fast enough that Josh's eyes watered and the skin on his face blew back like he was a basset hound.

Hell yeah, this was more like it.

Adrenaline.

Speed.

Danger.

They whipped in a tight circle to avoid a sailboat and were turning back toward the bay when Matt practically cut the engine cold.

"What the hell—"

The word stalled in his throat when he looked up.

His mom was standing on their beach. And she was clearly yelling.

Fuck. What were the odds? She never left the diner in the middle of the day.

Lucky him, she had to pick the one time he actually had a girl in the boat. Bending his head down so that his hair flopped over his face, he avoided eye contact with Hannah.

He didn't want to see her laughing at him. How the hell was he ever going to live this down?

Feeling suddenly clumsy, he untangled his limbs from the rail and crawled back across the bow. "Give me the wheel," he grunted and Matt jumped out of the way.

"I'm so fucked if my mom finds out I was driving your boat," his friend said. Matt chewed his nails, barely a step up from the thumb sucking he'd done until he was six.

"It was my idea," Josh said. "I'll take all the flack."

Still, even though he didn't want his friends or Hannah to think otherwise, his stomach was twisting and he was fighting the urge to throw up. At the beginning of the summer, his mom had made it really clear to him that driving her boat came with responsibilities. He was pretty sure breaking the law wasn't one of them.

He took extra care to bring the boat into the dock without bumping it, and as soon as he started tying it up, his friends bolted. Getting out last, Hannah stopped beside him.

"Do you need some help?"

Not lifting his face to look at her, he shook his head. "Nope. I'll see you later."

He could see Hannah's feet in her black sandals, her toes painted purple. For a long moment, she stood there silently, almost as if she was waiting for him to say something else. Or, maybe, to look at her again.

He wished she'd leave already and let him die of humiliation alone.

"Um, you're mom's coming, so I guess I'd better go now. I'll see you around."

He swallowed hard past the huge lump in his throat. Why had he decided to go bow riding today? Why couldn't he have just taken everyone out for a cruise on the lake, played it cool?

His mother's footsteps were loud and fast as she walked down the long wooden dock to chew his ass out. Blocking the sun with her shadow as she stood over him, her first words were, "You could have died."

He looked up at his mother, noted the way her voice shook, knew instantly how afraid she'd been of something happening to him. But didn't she get it? He wasn't a little kid anymore. There was no way he would have fallen out, and even if he had, he knew to swim deep to avoid getting chewed up by the propeller.

"I didn't die. I'm fine."

Her expression changed from fear to anger in a heartbeat. "That's all you've got to say to me? No, 'I'm sorry, Mom, I won't do it again.' No, 'Oh gee, I don't know what I was thinking.' Just that you lived through it?"

Knowing he'd better start acting sorry, he said, "I don't know what I was thinking. It won't happen again."

"You scared the shit out of me, kid."

"I know."

She looked at him for a long moment. "Seems like just yesterday you were a little boy."

He stepped away from her and picked up the towels he'd left on the end of the dock. This was exactly what he wanted her to get. Needed her to understand.

"I'm not a kid anymore."

She took a deep breath, then sighed. "I know. And that's why I'm going to have to treat you like a young man instead of a boy." She held out her hand. "Give me the keys."

He stilled, his fingers instinctively closing over the keys.

"I told you, I'm not going to do it again."

"I believe you. But you need to learn a lesson. And since I'm your mom, I'm the one who's going to have to teach it to you." She plucked the keys out of his hand. "The boat is off limits for one week."

Outrage shot through him. "What the hell am I supposed to do in this stupid town without my boat?"

"My boat," she countered. "And now it's two weeks."

First she'd embarrassed the hell out of him in front of Hannah. Now, she was punishing him for one stupid little transgression?

"You suck."

She took a step forward, pushed her index finger into his chest. "Right now, so do you."

Anger caught him, pushed out the words, "I wish I were still in the city with Dad." He wanted her to feel as bad as he did. "No wonder he didn't want to stick around with you. No wonder he divorced you."

But when he finally got what he'd been going for, saw the hurt in his mother's eyes, instead of victory there was only a twisted emptiness. Not knowing how to say he was sorry—not really wanting to either—he ran off the dock.

It would be better for all of them if he started planning his escape to New York City. Only this time, he'd be staying there. For good.

Andrew intended to go back to his rental car, drive into town, find a room at the Inn. Sit down and make a plan to get his son to trust him. But when he got down to the grass at the end of the porch stairs and looked out into the woods that separated his camp from Isabel's, as if pulled by a magnet, his feet started heading that way.

The well-worn path between Poplar Cove and Sunday Morning Camp had grown over and stray branches scratched him through his slacks and long-sleeved button-down shirt. He was dressed all wrong for the lake. As a kid he'd never worn anything other than shorts and T-shirts. He felt like a stuffy old person as he slowly made his way through the woods, the kind of guy he would have made fun of as a kid, a total greenhorn.

He stumbled over a thick dead log and cursed out loud as he caught himself on one of the many poplars his grandparents had named their camp for. His words didn't make much of an impression in the forest, not like they had for three decades in the courtroom.

He thought back two months, when young Douglas Wellings, thirty-five and cocky, called him into the boardroom. There sat the rest of the new guard, a whole host of kids who thought all they needed to win cases was flash and connections. There were a few old guys like him sitting there too, but none of them would meet his eyes. And that's when he'd known. Twenty-five years he'd given to the firm. And it was all gone in an instant.

We all know how bad the economy is. That we've got to make some cuts somewhere. So hard to make this choice. Thanks for your service. Now say good-bye, Grandpa.

For days he made his plans. He'd sue for ageism. For firing him just so they could turn around and hire someone cheaper. He stayed up all night on the Internet, pored through his books, and was just about ready to serve the papers when Sam and Dianna had asked him to meet up in the city.

They were getting married. They wanted him to give Dianna away.

He'd awkwardly blinked back tears on the couch in their living room. Thanked them so profusely for the honor, he knew he'd made them all uncomfortable.

Leaving their house, he realized he wasn't fighting his dismissal so hard because he really wanted his job back. It was simply that he wanted to prove that he was worth something. To someone. To anyone.

He tightened his grip on the tree trunk, not realizing that the bark was digging into his flesh until a moment too late. Another curse left his lips as he saw a streak of blood across his palm. Thirty years away from this place *had* made him a greenhorn with soft hands. First thing tomorrow he'd head up to the general store to get himself a new set of lakeworthy clothes.

Sucking his palm into his mouth, he continued making his way through the trees. The flickers of blue between trunks and branches grew larger and larger until the forest gave way to sand.

The sun was glinting off the water and he was momentarily blinded. And then he saw her.

Isabel.

She was sitting on the edge of her dock, her legs dangling in the water, and his heart stopped in his chest. From where he was standing, time had stood still, and he could have sworn he was looking at the fifteen-year-old girl he'd fallen head over heels in love with.

Her straight blond hair still brushed the edge of her shoulders and her frame was as slim as it had been as a teenager. Without thinking, his feet took him toward her.

A speedboat flew by in the bay and it's sleekly modern lines abruptly catapulted him into the present.

Jesus, what was he thinking? That he could come back to Blue Mountain Lake and rewind thirty years? That he could have everything the way he wished it had been, rather than the way it had actually turned out?

Just then, Isabel shifted on the dock, pushing her feet beneath her to stand up. Andrew worked like hell to find an escape route.

Just turn the fuck around and run, you idiot!

But his feet wouldn't move. Instead, all he could do was stand still as a statue and watch as Isabel turned around.

And saw him.

Isabel closed her eyes hard, forced herself to take a breath. Between last night and this morning, her head had grown fuzzier and fuzzier. And then when Ginger had arrived to work the lunch shift, said she'd just met Andrew, Isabel had been hit by an intense headache.

She would have never dreamed of leaving the diner in the middle of the lunch rush if she hadn't been about to throw up all over the sautéing onions. Scott had assured her again and again that he had the situation well in hand. Ginger had walked her out to her car, told her she'd check in on her later that afternoon, see if she needed anything.

And now, as if things weren't already bad as Isabel reeled from her confrontation with Josh, Andrew had decided to pay her a visit. She still felt nauseous, but dizzy now too.

She'd tried to convince herself that seeing him again wouldn't hurt, that it wouldn't matter.

But when she opened her eyes again and looked at Andrew MacKenzie, the first boy she'd ever loved, the pain was so intense it took her breath away.

Thirty years she'd spent telling herself she was over him. But now . . . now she knew the truth. Knew it as well as she knew her own face in the mirror. As well as she knew the shape of Josh's head beneath her hand as she'd stroked his hair as a child so that he could fall back to sleep in the middle of the night after a bad dream.

She'd never gotten over Andrew MacKenzie. And now, here he was, standing on her beach, staring at her as if he'd seen a ghost.

Her hands went to her throat as she tried to remember how to breathe, a thousand insecurities popping up to the surface at once. The ten pounds she'd put on, mostly from her stomach down after having Josh. The lines on her forehead, beside her eyes, around her mouth and on her neck. The gray hairs that had been waging a war with the blond ones and winning without a fight. The wrinkled jeans and old T-shirt she wore in the kitchen, stained from the farmer's market pesto and tomato sauces she'd made early that morning.

She was tempted to jump into the lake and swim away, but she was going to have to deal with Andrew sometime. Better just to get it over with.

She didn't hurry down the dock, didn't put a smile on her face, didn't have the will for anything so false. But she wouldn't let herself scowl either, opting for no expression whatsoever, a blank face that she hoped told the man on her beach he meant nothing more to her than any stranger.

Just as slowly, he came toward her, his expensive pressed button-down shirt and slacks suiting him to a T, even as they looked ridiculously out of place on the shore.

Thirty years had taken their toll on him too. His light brown hair was mostly gray and he looked like he hadn't slept a full night in a decade, but that was all surface stuff.

As much as she wished otherwise, Isabel could see the magnificent young man he'd once been. Clearly, he was still in good shape and she guessed he put in the hours in the gym to keep up his physique. His hands were still big, his shoulders still broad.

"Isabel."

Hearing her name from his lips again made her feet falter beneath her and she had to dig down deep to keep moving.

She lifted her chin, met his gaze straight on. "Andrew."

"My God, you're still so beautiful."

Her breath left her lungs in shock, her mouth opening, closing with the shock of his words.

"You look exactly the same, Isabel."

"Stop." She held up both hands, saw they were shaking, shoved them into her pockets. "Don't."

She needed to cut him off at the pass before he said anything else, needed to make it clear where the boundaries were.

And that he had no right to any part of her heart.

"I take it you're here to get Poplar Cove ready for your son's wedding."

He didn't answer for a long moment, his gaze growing even more intense. Finally, he nodded. "Yes. And to help Connor too." He cleared his throat. "He's going through a rough patch right now. I need to be here for him."

Listening to Andrew talk about his son with such love mucked around with her insides. He was too close, close enough to set off a thousand butterflies from their cocoons. And, stupidly, she couldn't help but note the absence of a wedding ring on his left hand. As if it mattered whether or not he was married.

"But Sam and Connor aren't the only reason I came back, Izzy."

She hadn't heard that nickname in thirty years. Wouldn't have dreamed of letting anyone call her Izzy. Her ears started ringing, a high-pitched whine. She couldn't listen to any more of this, not now, not on the dock in front of her house, not in the very place he'd told her he loved her for the very first time.

"Don't call me that," she said, but the clouds were drawing a curtain on the sun, turning daylight to night. She felt herself falling, wanted it to be anywhere but into his arms.

CHAPTER SIXTEEN

ANDREW LIFTED Isabel up and rushed up the beach to her house. Seeing her black out like that had scared him and even though her eyelids were already blinking open, her eyes working to focus on his face, he was still shaken.

"I'm fine," she tried, but the words sounded weak, utterly unlike her.

"Shh," he said, instinctively pressing his lips against her forehead. "I've got you," he said as he took the steps up to where he remembered the old master bedroom being as a kid. Pushing the door open with one knee, he saw that Isabel had indeed taken over the room from her parents, had transformed it as her own.

Gently laying her down on the bed, he moved across the room, picked up a blanket from a chest in the corner. He took it back to the bed, covered her with it, sat down on the edge of the mattress and stroked her hair. A thousand emotions rushed through him as he took her in, lying on the bed, her blond hair fanned out on the pillow. There was no point wishing he could have woken up to her like this a thousand times in the past thirty years.

But he wished it anyway.

And then she was shifting beneath the blanket, kicking it off to push away from him and sit up against the thick wood headboard, holding her head in her hands.

"What do you want, Andrew?"

He remembered now, she'd never been a shrinking violet, had never been scared to tell him exactly what she thought. But he was worried about the way she'd dropped on the beach, had to make sure she wasn't ill.

"Are you sick?"

"No." The word was a sharp bullet from her lips.

"You fainted."

She massaged her temples. "I have a headache. I didn't sleep well." She dropped her hands, glared at him. "Why the hell are you here?"

"Izzy—"

"I already told you not to call me that."

He took a breath, found his lungs didn't want to take in—or give—any air.

"I came to say I'm sorry."

She blinked once, twice, almost as if she were trying to figure out just what game he was playing. "Okay."

He was stunned by her response. There had to be more there, didn't there?

But she was already swinging her legs around the opposite side of the bed. He reached out a hand to stop her from leaving.

"No, wait."

He looked down at where they were touching, felt the same strong surge of electricity that had always been between them. He knew he should pull his hand away, but he just couldn't let go of her. Not when he'd waited so long to touch her again.

"Please. I need to say these things."

Her chest was rising and falling fast as she shook off his hand.

"Fine." She shifted farther from him on the bed. "Go ahead."

He hadn't had time to rehearse this, hated trying to win her over without a plan.

"I screwed up, Isabel. I know you already know that, but I've wanted you to hear me say it for so long. I don't know what happened thirty years ago, why I got drunk that night and . . ."

"And slept with someone else," she said, quickly finishing his sentence. "Knocked her up and got married."

He went completely rigid. "You were the one I loved. Always."

"You should have thought of that before you had sex with her."

"I was a stupid kid. Full of hormones. I didn't know what to do with them."

"Really?" she challenged. "You couldn't find any new

excuses in the past thirty years? Couldn't think of anything more interesting than how hard up you were because I wouldn't put out? That's sad, Andrew. Really sad."

"I swear to you, if I had known the way it was going to turn our lives upside down, if I could have seen how it was all going to turn out, I never would have done it."

"You still don't get it, do you? You think we ended because you got her pregnant, don't you? Because you had to do the right thing and marry her? You think if it had just been that one night with no consequences, then I would have eventually forgiven you."

She was up on her knees now on the bed, in the heat of her fury.

"Well you were wrong. You broke my trust, Andrew. I could never have forgiven you, even if there hadn't been a baby involved."

He watched helplessly as she got off the bed, went into her closet and came back with a handful of papers. Shoved them into his chest.

"Here. These are yours." She pointed to the door. "Now get out."

He looked down, realized he was holding the letters she'd written him, the ones he'd kept in the dresser at Poplar Cove. Desperation tore at him. He couldn't let her go so easily. Not now that he was finally with her again.

"Don't you remember how it was for us, Izzy? Don't you remember that we were going to leave everything behind and sail around the world in a boat that I built? Can't you remember how much you loved me?"

"Me, me, me!"

She was yelling now, coming at him from across the room, her fists beating his chest. He had to put his hands on her shoulders to hold them both steady.

"I, I, I! Every single thing you've said so far has been about you. About how much pain you're in. About how badly you need forgiveness. About how much you've changed. About how I should look at the letters as proof of how much I loved you."

"Izzy, I'm sorry, I didn't mean to—"

"No! No more!" She whirled away from him. "I don't want to hear anything else. Do you think I should be impressed that you always loved me more than your wife?"

"She's my ex-wife now."

"Of course she is." She sneered. "Don't you get it that a real man would have accepted the mess he'd made for himself and made the most of it? Don't you see that a real man would have given every ounce of himself to his wife and kids and made damn sure that he forgot all about some girl he left behind?"

Her words were a hundred-mile-an-hour pitch straight to his gut. He'd tried to be that man, to give himself to his wife and kids, but every year it got harder until one day he just couldn't do it anymore.

"How about you and I leave our impromptu little reunion at this: You were a cheating bastard. You screwed up. We moved on with our lives. So if it'll make you feel better, and get you the hell out my life, then I'll say what you so desperately need to hear. I forgive you. In fact, I simply don't care about you at all, about whatever midlife crisis you're having. I've got a great life here in Blue

Mountain. A life that I've built entirely by myself, and I don't need you coming to town trying to get in the middle of it all."

She paused, took a couple of shaky breaths, then clasped her hands together in front of her.

"Now if we're completely done here, I'd very much appreciate if you left."

"I'll go," he said softly, despite the raging drumbeat of his heart at the knowledge of how much she still hated him. "I'll leave you alone. But first I need to say one more thing."

Her eyes were stone cold as he said, "I really am sorry for what I did. If I could change the past, I would. But you're right, I never got over you. And even though I know you think it makes me less of a man, I've spent thirty years missing you, Isabel. Thirty years loving you. And regardless of how you feel about me, I'm going to spend the next thirty feeling exactly the same way."

He walked away, his eyes watering now, a perfect picture of a broken, middle-aged man, as he made his way down the stairs. Ginger came in through Isabel's front door, exclaiming in surprise when she saw him.

"Oh, I didn't expect you to be here. I just came to check on—"

She stopped and he knew she must have read everything he was feeling on his face. Must have seen the embarrassing wetness around the edges of his eyes.

She put her hand on his arm. "Is this the first time you've seen Isabel since—?"

Jesus, even Connor's girlfriend knew what a prick his father was.

"She's upstairs," was all he could say. "Take care of her. For me."

"What just happened?"

Isabel looked up from where she was still standing, frozen, as Ginger rushed through the doorway.

"Why was Andrew here?" Ginger asked. "Why was he on the verge of tears?"

"He was about to cry?"

"Yes."

Isabel was shocked by how close rage was to sorrow. It would be so much easier if she could hold on to to her fury, wrap herself in it like armor.

Time was supposed to heal everything.

Not make it worse.

CHAPTER SEVENTEEN

AFTER TUCKING Isabel into bed with a couple of migraine pills, Ginger walked back to Poplar Cove, incredibly shaken by what she'd just seen.

Andrew and Isabel had obviously loved each other deeply, once upon a time. And then someone had made a mistake, big enough to tear them apart. Before today, Ginger would have assumed thirty years was enough to get over lost love. Now she knew just how wrong she was.

Ginger's thoughts swung back around to Connor, to loving him. To not knowing where that love would go, if he could ever accept it. If he could ever love her back. And how she'd feel in thirty years if he couldn't.

Would she be broken like Isabel and Andrew?

Connor was inside the cabin sanding down the logs by hand when she walked in. Her heart skipped a beat as she watched him work for a few quiet moments, the *ch-ch-ch* of the gritty paper grinding down the old to uncover the new, fresh life hiding beneath.

She made a beeline toward him, pulled him away from the logs to draw his mouth down to hers, kissed him like it had been weeks instead of hours since she'd seen him. Every moment with him was so precious. She wouldn't take a single second for granted. Not when she'd just seen proof of how quickly it could disappear.

That it could all be gone in an instant.

She should let go of him now, let him get back to work, but she couldn't. Not yet. She ran one hand through his hair, down the side of his forehead.

"Can you take a break for a few minutes?"

He didn't smile then, just slid his hand into hers, let her lead him up the stairs to her bedroom. She'd decorated the room unabashedly girly and colorful, and yet he fit so perfectly in the middle of it all. The missing piece to make everything come together, the intensely male balance she hadn't seen that it needed.

She slipped her hands under his T-shirt, running her hands over the wall of his chest, pulling up the hem to press kisses everywhere her hands roamed.

"Ginger," he said, her name a raw, rough sound on his lips, "do you have any idea what you do to me? How much I needed you right when you walked in?"

Pulling the shirt up over his head, she leaned her cheek against his chest, listened to the beat of his heart. "If it's anything like the way I needed you," she said softly against his skin, "then yeah, I do."

His hands threaded through her hair, tilted her mouth

back up to his as she moved her hands to his jeans, popping the button off, unzipping them and pushing them off his hips so that they dropped to the floor. With her hands, she felt his erection straining the front of his boxer shorts. His tongue slipped into her mouth and she palmed him through the thin fabric, wrapping her hand around his thick length as her tongue met his.

But then he was peeling her fingers off with his own.

"Not like that." He yanked off her pants, her panties, before pulling her down to the rug. "Like this."

And then, he was pushing into her, his hips cradled between her thighs, until he was throbbing against her core.

His eyes were dark and hot as he held himself there above her, perfectly still.

"Sweet Ginger," he whispered before kissing her softly. Tenderly. "I—"

He didn't say anything more, but he didn't need to. She could feel how much he cared in the way he kissed her, in the way he was so careful with her, even when he thought he was being rough.

"I know," she said, and then his mouth was on hers again and they were flying. And afterward as she lay there on the floor beneath him, so perfectly complete, she knew that even if he never actually spoke the word love aloud, at least in that one moment with her on her bedroom floor, he'd felt it.

That night as they ate dinner out on the porch, she had to ask. "How did it go with your father?"

"He wants to help with the cabin."

"Really? Is that the only reason he gave you for coming here?"

Connor was silent for a long moment. "Sam called him. Told him the news. He was worried."

The news. That was all he would say about the phone call that had changed his life.

"What did you tell him?"

He lifted his beer, drank from it before answering. "Same thing I've been telling everyone."

"That you're fine."

"Yup."

Ginger bit her tongue in an effort to keep her mouth shut. But after what had just happened upstairs she felt so close to him, cared way too much to keep listening to the same lie over and over.

"Has anyone believed you yet?"

"Say that again."

His words were cold. Hard. But she couldn't back down. Not this time.

"You keep saying you're fine. But you and I both know it isn't true. You're not. You couldn't be. Not yet. Not when everything you ever wanted was just ripped away from you."

"Jesus," Connor said, slamming his bottle down on the table so hard a crack appeared in the spot it hit. "What the fuck is wrong with all of you? You'd think it was a crime to look on the bright side. Isn't that what I'm supposed to be doing? See how the world is my fucking oyster now? Now that firefighting isn't tying me down, isn't taking up every goddamned second of my life, shouldn't I be seeing the endless possibilities?"

"Yes, Connor. Yes to all of that. But that doesn't mean you can't mourn first, let it all out. Even if it's only for five minutes."

"Don't you get it?" He shoved away from the table. "I could travel the world, see the seven goddamned wonders. Just keep going until I feel like turning around and starting over."

"But that's not what you want," she challenged him again.

"How the fuck do you know what I want?"

She pushed her chair back, went to him, took his hands in hers. "Because I know you. I know who you really are. And I want to help you. Please let me help you, Connor."

"Fine. You want to help me? I'll show you exactly how you can help. The only way you can help."

He spun her around and shoved her into the logs behind them, pinned her hard against the wall with her wrists gripped tightly in his hands above her head. He was breathing hard and she gasped in stunned surprise at his rough handling of her.

"I know you don't mean that," she got out a second before he covered her lips with his in a kiss so rough she tasted blood. She wasn't sure if it was his or hers, and the twisted truth was that as his mouth devoured hers, she didn't really care. Not when all she wanted was to keep tangling her tongue against his. Not when she would gladly take her next breath from his lungs.

But a second later he was wrenching his mouth away from hers and tightening his grip on her wrists, hard enough now that she cried out. She could feel rage rolling off him in waves, almost as if he were even angrier now because she hadn't run from him.

He shoved his thigh between hers, hard enough that a slick of fear ran through her. She tried to pull away from him, yank her wrists from his tight grip, but he only held on tighter.

"Talk to me, Connor," she begged.

"You think you know what I want," he said, his words harsh, utterly at odds with the soft swoosh of waves on the shore. "You're wrong. This is what I want. All I want."

She felt him drop a hand from her wrists, but instead of letting her loose, he ripped off her sundress in one quick movement.

She couldn't see his eyes clearly in the dark, only the shadows beneath his cheekbones, the planes of his face that were so beautiful to her. It was all happening too fast for her to find any words to make him stop—too fast to even know if that's what she wanted—and then he was covering one of her breasts with his palm, squeezing her roughly, branding her with the intense heat that always poured off his body.

Her body reacted instantly to his touch, opening to let him in, moisture quickly coating her thin panties, the top of his thigh.

"Connor," she groaned as she instinctively rubbed herself against him, seeking the pleasure she knew was waiting in his arms, even now. And then his hand was between her legs.

Her hips instinctively bucked up into his fingers, seeking more, but even as he thrust two fingers into her, even as she responded to his touch as she always had, she was struck with the sense that he was stuck in the space between reality and a nightmare. Just like that night up in his room when she'd run in to help him and he'd pulled her hard against him.

And just like then, her fear left as quickly as it had come. Because even out on this rough and ragged edge, she knew he'd never deliberately hurt her.

How could she possibly be afraid of him, when at his core Connor was the most decent, most heroic man she'd ever known?

One word from her and he'd stop.

But she didn't want him to.

"This is who I am now," he said, the words raw as they exited his throat, his mouth moving at her neck, sucking, biting at the same time. He let go of her wrists with his other hand and moved it to her breasts, rolling an erect nipple between his thumb and forefinger, making her gasp again with another shock of pure pleasure. "This is who I've become. And now that you've seen the real me, it's time to make your choice."

"You can try to convince me a hundred times," she managed to get out with the little air she had left in her lungs, "and I'll never believe you."

But instead of calming him, her words seemed to send him even closer to the edge as his fingers dove in, then out of her, his thumb pressing against her clitoris, his palm gripping her breast. And then tremors were taking over her body, her body tightening around his fingers, her eyes closing, her head falling back against a log.

As she came, her orgasm going on for what seemed like hours, he whispered into her ear, "It's your choice, babe. Take me just like this. Or leave me the hell alone."

Through the blur of desire, she could see what he was doing, that he was trying to use sex as a weapon. Trying to break her with it, pushing at her boundaries to see if he could get her to run.

And maybe if she hadn't been running for so many years, if she wasn't so damn tired of going in circles and getting absolutely nowhere, she might have let him scare her off.

Didn't he know she'd already made her choice? That she'd choose him every time? Not just because of the way her body spiraled out of control whenever he touched her. But because loving Connor was what her heart knew to be the most true emotion she'd ever felt.

She'd never thought to announce her feelings to him in this way, up against the wall, trapped in his heat, his overwhelming strength, but now she saw that this was how things with Connor had been from the beginning.

Wild.

Unexpected.

Frightening.

But beautiful and utterly precious all at the same time.

"I love you, Connor."

The relief at finally confessing what she felt, at accepting it fully herself, was so sweet, she had to say it again.

"I love you with everything I am."

"No." His eyes were dark. Wild. "You don't. You can't."

"I do. I can."

She reached up to his face with both hands, made him look at her. "So if this is what you want from me, if this is what you need to break through to the other side, then take it from me. I'm giving myself to you freely."

He closed his eyes, still fighting a war within himself, the same war he'd been fighting for two years.

"Did you hear me, Connor? I've made my choice. To give myself to you. Because I love you."

And then, beneath his eyelashes, she saw a tear emerge, his teeth, his jaw clenched against it even as it fell in a slow trail over his cheekbone, down into the hollow, then onto his mouth.

She moved her lips to his, tasted the salt there.

"Take me, Connor," she whispered against his mouth. "I'm yours."

Darkness was swallowing him up, pulling him down, all the way under as Ginger's words—*I love you, Connor*—swirled around in his brain, wrapping themselves around his chest, the hollow place inside where his heart should be.

She couldn't love him. There was nothing there to love. He was just a shell now. An empty shell. He tried to claw his way back to the top, but he'd never faced a threat so big, not even from the fire that had scorched his skin.

He felt wetness beneath her fingertips as she gently touched his face. He hadn't cried on the mountain, hadn't cried in the hospital, hadn't cried after the phone call. Hadn't cried until he'd shoved Ginger into the wall, made her come apart for him, beneath his fingers, then heard her say—

The wrenching pain in his chest was so intense, he wrapped his hands harder around her hips, digging his fingers into her softness.

"Ginger."

He heard the violence in her name, looked into her eyes, saw the love in them, and knew he needed to stop. Step away. Leave her alone. Before he did something he'd never forgive himself for.

And still, all he could say was, "I can't let you go."

"You don't have to, Connor. I've already told you."

He'd never fought so hard, and yet, second by second, he went down farther, into the black hole at the heart of the undertow.

No fire had ever scared him like this, overwhelmed him so completely. His passion for Ginger, the unending desire that grew every second he spent with her, every time he touched her, was the most intense force he'd ever encountered.

"I should never have touched you. I should have left you alone. You need to run from me. As fast as you can."

He was as hollow as a rotten log, crumbling on the outside, nothing but air at his core.

"I shouldn't do this. What I'm about to do."

It was the only warning he had in him. All he could do was hope that she was strong enough to save them both, smart enough to run like hell.

But instead of running, instead of pushing him away, he felt her fingers ripping at his pants just as he'd ripped her clothes away.

He forced out the words, "No, Ginger," even as he silently pleaded, *Yes. Please don't leave me now.*

And then, as if she could hear his unspoken prayer, she was saying, "I'm not going anywhere," and her legs opened wider, her calves coming around his hips. He felt her hand move down to her panties to pull them aside a split second before she thrust her heels against his ass, driving him inside.

"Let go," she whispered against his forehead. "Just let go."

And then she was wrapping her legs tighter around his waist to ride him just as hard as he rode her, taking him in deeper than she ever had before. But as he roared his release, it was the beating of her heart against his chest that he felt most.

"I'll move out tonight."

Her legs were still wrapped around his waist, her arms around his neck, sweat dripping between their half-naked bodies. And he was an asshole who had just done something he never thought he could be capable of. He'd hurt her, had heard her cry out in pain as he shoved her against the wall. And he still hadn't stopped. Couldn't have stopped.

Abruptly, she untangled herself from him. Pushed him away. And that was when he saw the bruises on her wrists, clear even in the dim lights of the porch.

Bruises. From his hands.

"I hear everything you say," she said. "Even the things you don't say. Especially those. But you haven't heard a goddamned thing I've said, have you?"

She was the only reason he'd been able to hold the pieces together at all, and in return he'd stolen from her sweetness.

In return he'd hurt her.

"I forced you, Ginger. I made you fuck me. Here. Like that."

He felt lost without her pressed against him, a man on a island with nothing left to hold on to. He looked at her ruined dress on the floor, pulled up his jeans with shaking hands.

"I was an animal."

A sound of rage erupted from her throat. "Yes, you wanted to make it *fucking*. You wanted to take what's between us and make it ugly and worthless, but you couldn't do it. Don't you see that, Connor? You couldn't do it."

"I made you come. I put my hands on you and controlled you."

She grabbed his hands, stuck one hard to her breasts, shoved the other between her legs.

"You think you can make me come just by putting your hands on me? Just by rubbing yourself against me? Am I coming now? No!"

She shoved his hands off, whirled away, her skin flushed with anger.

"If you'd been hurting me, if you had really been trying to control me, I wouldn't have come apart like that. I'm in love with you, Connor, but that doesn't mean I'm some puppet you're holding the strings to."

"Your wrists. I did that to your wrists."

She stopped abruptly and looked at her arms. "I've always bruised easily," she said dismissively, before glaring back at him. "Are you hearing a word of what I'm saying? I love you. Just the way you are. All I want is for you to talk to me. To let me in."

He was trying to take her words in, was trying to process the force of her emotion, everything she was offering him, but as soon as he'd heard the word love again, it hit him, a sucker punch in the center of his gut: there was only one thing worse than losing the use of his hands, only one thing worse than losing his entire identity as a firefighter.

Letting himself love Ginger . . . and losing her too.

Because now that everything he'd been absolutely sure of for thirty years had gone up in smoke, all he knew for certain was that everything good eventually slipped from his hands.

It was the only truth he knew. The only thing he could be certain of anymore.

Her frustration echoed out from the porch, out to the beach, the water lapping at the shore.

"I've never thought you were a coward, Connor. Never. But if you leave tonight, I'll know that you are. You might have proved yourself to be a hero a hundred times in a wildfire. Well, this is your chance to prove it to me."

CHAPTER EIGHTEEN

IT WAS a rough night.

Andrew had never needed much sleep—as a litigator, he was often up late into the night poring over briefs, only to wake at dawn to defend his client—but he'd woken up disoriented and confused in the Inn's small cottage bedroom. Making a cup of coffee in the automatic coffeemaker on the kitchen counter, he stood by the window and stared out at the water.

The night before he'd spent hours sitting in the dark on the porch of his cottage on the shores of Blue Mountain Lake. After running his credit card and handing him a large, old-fashioned key, Rebecca, the pretty innkeeper, had said, "I'm afraid our restaurant here is booked up for the night already, but if you're hungry, I can highly recommend the Blue Mountain Diner. Isabel does a fantastic job with the food there."

Although he was starved, he didn't think Isabel would appreciate seeing him show up at her restaurant tonight. Or any other night.

Noting the fruit and cookies on the sideboard in the sitting room, he said, "Thanks, but I'll make do just fine with this spread."

Looking unconvinced, she'd said, "You know what, how about I pop my head into the kitchen and see if the cook can whip up something simple for you and send it down to the cottage in about an hour?"

It was the nicest anyone had been to Andrew all day, apart from Ginger. But he wasn't under any misapprehensions as to why she was being so wonderful. It wasn't because he was a great guy. It wasn't because he deserved her kindness.

Rebecca simply didn't know him.

And being nice was her job.

He'd sat in an Adirondack chair, staring out at the lake, watching the sailboats and speedboats and kayaks go by, but not really seeing any of them.

All night long, the only thing he could see was the hatred on his son's face, on Isabel's face as each of them listed off all the ways he'd hurt them, all the ways he'd failed.

But he couldn't hide out in the cottage forever. And strangely, for all the discord of the previous day, for the first time in years, he felt like he was home.

Thirty years he'd gone without seeing this place. Thirty years he'd stayed away from his mistakes. Or thought he had, anyway. But Blue Mountain Lake was a part of his soul that couldn't simply be thrown away or forgotten.

He'd been a summer baby, born at the small hospital forty-five minutes away. He wondered if his old crib was still in the Poplar Cove attic, or if his parents had gotten rid of it as soon as Connor had outgrown it? Every summer as a kid they'd come to the lake, an extended family that included his grandparents as well. He'd grown up playing on the beach, swimming in the sometimes chilly waters, sailing on whitecaps, roasting marshmallows on sticks. He'd been so certain about the way his life would unfold.

He'd planned to build boats. Handmade sailboats. To sail around the world with a beautiful woman at his side.

He moved away from the cottage window, pouring himself a cup of coffee. It was too late. He'd wasted too much goddamned time being a martyr, spent the best years of his life trying to impress the wrong people.

But even as he thought it, he hoped to hell he was wrong. Otherwise there was no point in sticking around, no point in trying to grow a pair of balls and try again with his son.

But first, he would start his day at Blue Mountain Lake the way he always had as a kid. With a dip in the lake. Quickly putting on his bathing suit, he jogged to the empty beach, down the Inn's dock, and splashed into the water. He was grateful for the rush of adrenaline that shot through him when he submerged beneath the cool waters.

Making his way out of the water, he looked up and saw

Rebecca standing on the Inn's porch watching him. Clearly embarrassed to have been caught, she smiled and waved, then disappeared back inside the building.

The funny thing about discontent, Andrew had discovered over the years, was that he tended to notice it in other people, particularly people who were trying to hide it. Something in the innkeeper's eyes, the set of her mouth, told him that she wasn't happy. Not, of course, that it was any of his business. Still, he knew what it was to search for happiness and come up empty.

After a quick shower and shave, he got dressed and headed into town on foot. The Inn was at the end of Main Street. Isabel's diner was on the opposite end of the two-block center of town. He'd promised he wouldn't bother her, but that didn't mean he couldn't stand across the street, see what she'd done to the place.

His heart was pounding and his palms were sweating as he passed the small tourist shops, the ice-cream store window, the café/bookstore, the knitting shop, the public dock that ran the historic boat tours of the lake, and a handful of business offices.

Arriving at the diner, he was amazed by its transformation. When he and Isabel were kids, the place had been a run-down teenage hangout. From where he was standing it almost looked like she'd rebuilt the whole damn place from the ground up. Why was he surprised? Even as a girl, she'd been remarkable. Smart and funny and talented. Not to mention so beautiful it almost hurt to look at her.

She still was.

And it still did.

A crowd of people was gathering outside and when he caught snippets of conversation about how the diner was never closed at this time, Andrew wondered if something was the matter. A hand-printed sign on the door said, TEMPORARILY CLOSED—WILL OPEN SHORTLY.

And then he heard it, Isabel's voice, frustrated, a few random curses thrown in for good measure.

Before he could think better of it, he was crossing the street and going behind the building. Isabel was kneeling beside an open pipe that was pouring water out all over the parking lot, a wrench in her hands.

"Where are the mains?"

Looking up, her face twisted with surprise—and then annoyance. "Two feet from where you're standing. I couldn't get it to turn. Here."

She threw the heavy wrench at him, and he grabbed it a split second before it hit him between the eyes. Another time, he'd be happy to let her get some much due satisfaction from taking her anger out on him with a hand tool, but right now he needed to get her water shut off before her well emptied out completely.

Someone had painted the valve closed and he had to bear down hard to get it to twist. Thankful that he was religious about going to the gym—otherwise he would have looked like the biggest loser in the world in front of the one woman he most wanted to impress—he cranked down on the valve until not even trickles were leaking out of the tap.

"Thanks."

The word may have been grudging, but he knew he deserved that.

"You're welcome." He tried to hold her gaze, tried to make her see how much he wanted her forgiveness, but she refused to look at him. "I'd be happy to head over to the hardware store for a new pipe, if you'd like."

"This has happened before. I had the plumber leave me some replacements."

"I'll do it for you."

She didn't bother stopping as she walked through the back door. "No thanks. I saw how he did it last time. I can take care of it myself."

But he couldn't let her go so easily. Not when he refused to believe that last night had been it for them.

"There's a line out on the sidewalk in front of the diner. You need to feed those people. I'll get your water up and running quickly. I know how to do this, I promise."

At the word "promise" her eyes narrowed. Damn it, maybe that hadn't been the best word to use.

"Please, Izzy, let me help."

"Isabel." The door slammed.

Why couldn't he, just once, say the right thing?

But then the door opened again and Isabel dumped a plastic bag at his feet. "Don't screw it up."

As the door slammed behind her again, Andrew smiled. Letting him fix her pipe wasn't a big deal, but it was something. A step in the right direction. And a hell of a lot better than being thrown off the property.

He'd take what he could get and he'd work from there.

A car pulled up in the parking lot and Ginger stepped

out. After the way she'd found him yesterday at Isabel's house, pride made him want to walk away before she saw him. But that was what he would have done before.

What he'd done before hadn't worked. It was time to stop repeating the same screwed-up patterns and learn some new ones.

When Ginger was within hearing distance, he said "Good morning."

She jumped. "You startled me."

"Sorry. I'm just helping Isabel with some broken pipes."

She frowned in obvious confusion. "Oh. That's nice of you."

He took in the dark smudges beneath her eyes, her puffy eyelids. It would be easiest just to pretend he hadn't noticed. But then he remembered the way she had reached out to him at Isabel's.

"Everything okay?"

She wasn't a large woman, but up until now she'd struck him as steady. Solid. This morning, however, she seemed shrunken, looked like someone who'd just thrown in the towel.

She swallowed. Shook her head. "No. But I'll be fine." She nodded toward the diner. "I'd better get in there."

Why was she letting him help her, Isabel wondered? She could have fixed the pipes herself. And yet, her feet had carried her back inside, her hands had grabbed the pipes and given them to him.

She hadn't been lying to him yesterday. She wasn't going to forgive him.

Even if he redid the diner's entire plumbing system.

Her fry cook came in from the restaurant where he'd been guzzling his first Coke of the day. "People are about to riot out there. Can I let them in?"

Isabel nodded and moments later, a sea of grateful faces rushed in to take their usual a.m. seats. And although she knew that everyone inside the diner would surely be happier if she had water to make their breakfasts and coffee, nonetheless, a part of her hoped that Andrew wasn't able to fix the pipes. He'd always been handy, even as a teen. With cars, pipes, hammers. Just once, she wanted to see him fail at something.

But a few minutes later, when she momentarily forgot that the water was off and turned on the faucet, it ran beautifully.

Andrew had, once again, succeeded. He'd arrived unannounced like a knight on his shiny white horse to save the damsel in distress.

Damn him.

The orders poured in and soon every burner was covered and she was in the zone where the only thing she should be thinking about was the next order. And yet, every second she was on guard, waiting for him to come through the back door, triumphant. Expecting her thanks. Thinking they could forget everything that had been said.

But breakfast turned into lunch, and still he didn't come. Midway through the rush, the phone rang in her office. Scott picked it up and handed it to her, even though she was in no mood to be friendly to whomever was on the line.

"Blue Mountain Lake Diner. This is Isabel."

"Oh great. I'm so glad I've caught you. My name's Dianna Kelley and I'm hoping you'll be able to help me. The caterer for my wedding just backed out and after asking around, I've heard you're an amazing chef."

"I don't normally do weddings," Isabel said, more curt than normal. "What's the date?"

"July thirty-first."

That was the same date Andrew's oldest son was getting married. Sitting down heavily in her office chair, she asked, "Do you have family at the lake?"

"No, but my fiancé spent summers there as a child. You might know their cabin? Poplar Cove. I know this is short notice, and I completely understand if you can't accommodate us, but Sam and I would really appreciate it if you'll at least consider it."

The woman had just given Isabel a clear out. *Sorry, I'm too busy. I'm afraid it's just not possible.* So then, why wasn't she saying no and hanging up the phone?

The answer hit her clear between the eyes: because she wasn't a coward. So she wasn't going to run. Instead, she was going to face her fears head-on. And she was going to triumph, goddamn it.

A few minutes later they'd worked out the initial details. Isabel was going to cater Andrew's son's wedding.

CHAPTER NINETEEN

ALL HIS life, people had told Connor how brave he was. And he'd believed them. He'd done things no one else could, faced impossible risks and walked out grinning on the other side. He'd skimmed off the surface of life's high moments. Moved from one victory to another.

No question, the fire in Desolation had rocked his world. It was his first-ever brush with his mortality. The first time it had ever occurred to him that he wasn't *Superman*. And still, he'd thought—no, he'd known—that once he got back out there things would be just as they had been before. That he'd be afraid of nothing. That he'd still be invincible, and when push came to shove he'd still know how to make all the right decisions, every single time.

The Forest Service phone call had been the start of his

fall. But it was hearing Ginger say "I love you" that had sent him all the way over the edge.

Because the truth was that he'd never wanted anything, never needed anyone as much as he needed Ginger. He'd never been completely ruled by something that he couldn't control. Even fire had rules. Sure it stunned you every now and again, but for the most part you only paid the price when you'd pushed the boundaries.

But what he felt for Ginger had no boundaries.

Which was why he'd tried to fuck away his feelings for her. It was why he'd tried to make her run. And when she hadn't, he'd done the very thing he'd been afraid of all along, the very thing he'd seen coming.

He'd hurt her.

"Why haven't you come upstairs?" she'd asked him that morning when she'd come down to the living room.

He sat up on the couch in the living room, stunned to see Ginger standing at the foot of the stairs as faint light from the rising sun came in the windows.

God, she was beautiful.

So damn beautiful.

"I can't trust myself with you."

Not after last night. And still, she'd told him she loved him. When he'd deserved it the least.

He stood up, told her, "I can't take the chance that I'd hurt you again. You're the last person on the planet that I'd ever want to hurt."

She came at him as if she didn't hear him, didn't understand that he was trying to protect her from the deep, dark rage that he'd couldn't push down. He hadn't known how bad it was until last night.

The bruises on her wrists had showed him the truth.

She stopped just inches from him, so close that all he could think about was pulling her against him, begging her forgiveness with his mouth, his hands, worshipping her the way he should have last night.

"I've been waiting for you to come to bed, Connor. All night. To come upstairs and talk to me. To talk *with* me. I didn't want to have to do this. To come down here and force you."

Suddenly, she seemed to realize how close they were, and took one step back, then another. Every inch she put between them made the ache inside his chest grow bigger.

And then her hands moved to her chest, almost as if she were shielding herself from him and she said, "I wanted sharing yourself with me to be your choice." He watched her walk out the door, heard her car start, pull out of the gravel driveway.

Everything had been a blur since she'd left. He'd gone out to the workshop, grabbed the heaviest ax he could find, and started slamming it into a thick tree trunk. But all the sweat in the world couldn't push Ginger out of his head, couldn't erase the feeling that everything he wanted was right within his grasp.

Only, in the end, he didn't have a damn clue how to hold on to any of it.

* * *

Stepping out of his rental car behind Poplar Cove, Andrew saw Connor dragging a huge tree stump out of the woods onto the beach. He rushed over to help.

"I'll grab this end."

Connor didn't say anything, but he did wait for Andrew to grab the log. *Sweet Lord*, Andrew thought as he heaved the tree up off the ground, it was heavy. Within seconds he was breathing hard, sweat pouring into his eyes. It was all he could do just to try to keep pace with his son. At the same time, he relished the work.

This was the first time he and Connor had ever worked together as a team.

Finally, they put down the log in front of the cabin. Andrew wanted to throw himself down on the sand and figure out how to breathe again, but Connor was already heading back into the woods.

When he'd offered to help out with the cabin, he'd been thinking about a hammer and nails. Not this he-man stuff.

Time to suck it up, he quickly decided as he watched his son disappear between trees.

But two hours later, Andrew was pretty damn sure he was going to have a heart attack. The pain in his arms and shoulders and legs was relentless. A grunt accompanied every step. But he refused to give up, to cry uncle, to show his son just how weak he was.

And then, Connor dropped the log they were carrying, so suddenly it almost broke Andrew's foot. Cursing as he jumped out of the way, he scowled at his son. "Damn it, you should have said something before you dropped it like that."

But instead of tossing back a retort, Connor was standing in the sand clenching his hands into fists, then flexing his fingers over and over again.

Oh shit. Connor's hands. They'd been wrecked after the fire, were still badly scarred, but Andrew had assumed they were okay now. Because Connor had never said otherwise.

And he'd never asked.

Moving to his son's side, he said, "It's your hands, isn't it?"

"Comes and goes," Connor grunted.

"What does?"

"The numbness. The pain."

Andrew's first instinct was to protect his son. To take care of him in all the ways he hadn't as a boy.

"We should hire someone to do this."

"Like hell we will."

Andrew nearly jumped back at the ferocity in his son's voice. "Not that you can't do it all. I know you can. Just that maybe it'll be easier if—"

"Fuck easy," Connor said.

But Andrew had seen the pain on Connor's face. "Don't be an idiot. You could do more damage to your hands."

"I'm fine."

"No," Andrew said, looking his son straight in the eye. "You're not."

Connor started to walk away, but Andrew grabbed his son's arm and didn't let go.

"Do you have any idea what it was like to see you in that hospital? Lying there wrapped in bandages. Not knowing how bad the damage was. If you'd ever be able to use your hands again or if they were gone. Do you have any idea how hard it is to see your own kid hooked up to machines in that amount of pain?"

Saying the words brought it all back, took Andrew back into those first few horrible hours, where the only thing he did was make deals with God.

"I wanted to be there, in your place. I told God I'd give myself up for you, that he could take me right then if only we could trade places, but he wasn't listening, didn't seem to care that my son was lying there unconscious. I saw everything so clearly. All those years, all those Little League games, Halloween costumes, they were all gone."

He tightened his grip on Connor's arm, gave silent thanks to the man in heaven he'd cursed so thoroughly that Connor was here at all.

"I don't want to lose the next thirty years too."

Connor shook his hand off. "You want to come back here, be a hero, say how sorry you are. But sometimes sorry isn't enough. I should know."

His son's message couldn't have been clearer. Didn't matter what he said, how hard he tried, Connor wasn't going to forgive him. Fine, then there was no reason to pussyfoot around. He hadn't forgotten how upset Ginger had looked in the diner's parking lot that morning.

"What happened with you and your girlfriend?"

Connor had started walking away, but now he stopped cold, turned around. "What the hell are you talking about?"

"I saw Ginger this morning. At the diner. She looked upset. Something happened between you two, didn't it?"

"You want to know what the hell happened? Last night she asked me how things had gone with you."

"With me?"

"She didn't like my answer. Didn't believe a word I said. And when she was right about it all, I lost it. Attacked her."

Andrew recognized the remorse ravaging his son. Thirty years ago, it had been him, hating himself with every breath.

"You were angry at me, so you hurt her?"

"Angry at every fucking thing."

This conversation was like quicksand. But that was good. Because it meant he and Connor were going to have a hell of a time trying to get out of it without each other's help.

"What else happened, Connor? Tell me."

"She said she loves me." Connor stood perfectly still now, almost as if he were bracing himself for impact. "She can't love me. It isn't possible."

"Jesus, Connor. You can't think like that. Can't go into a relationship with a wonderful woman thinking love is impossible. Go to her. Tell her you fucked up. Tell her you're sorry. That you'll spend the rest of your life making it up to her."

They were all the things he'd wanted to tell Isabel. But

it had already been too late by then. Because Connor's mother had come to him with the news that she was pregnant.

"Do you seriously expect me to take advice from you about relationships?"

And this time when his son walked away, Andrew had to let him go. Because Connor was right.

He didn't know the first thing about love.

CHAPTER TWENTY

THE DINER was slammed through breakfast and lunch, but after the last customer left, Isabel said, "Looks like it's time for our regularly scheduled afternoon chat, isn't it?"

Without waiting for Ginger's response, Isabel put her hand on the small of her friend's back and pushed her out the door.

"Let's take it down to the lake this time. Get a little change of scenery."

Families were playing along the shore. Babies splashing. Mothers tickling tummies. Fathers encouraging sons to swim all the way to the buoy. Brothers and sisters goofing around on the floating docks out in the water, hooting with laughter as they shoved each other off.

"That's what I want," Ginger said wistfully.

Isabel lifted a hand to shade her eyes from the sun. "It's

not always this perfect, you know. Later tonight the kids will be bickering in the backseat, while the husband and wife bite each other's heads off over something stupid."

"I'm not asking for perfect," Ginger said. "Just for the chance to have a few moments like these."

"What about Connor? Is there some reason he can't give all that to you?"

Ginger half laughed then. "I come in here looking like this," she gestured to her still puffy eyes, her blotchy skin, "and you actually ask me that. As if there's some way I'll go home today and find Connor waiting for me with roses."

"Roses aren't your style. If he knows you at all, he'll be waiting with a fistful of wildflowers."

"Trust me, there aren't going to be any flowers."

"Tell me something, when you first got involved with Connor, what did you think was going to happen? Because correct me if I'm wrong, but I didn't exactly get the sense that he was riding in on his white steed like Prince Charming. More like he was the villain coming to pillage Poplar Cove."

Ginger flashed back to the first night. To his nightmare.

"You're right," she said slowly. "I knew, right from the beginning, who he was."

Who he couldn't possibly be.

"And you chose to spend time with him anyway. To sleep with him."

Yes. It had been her choice. The same one she'd made again and again, the choice to be with Connor.

He'd never lied to her. Never made her promises he hadn't kept. From that first night, all the way through, he'd been brutally honest.

"We shouldn't do this. I don't have anything to give to you, Ginger. Nothing at all."

She'd told herself that as long as she walked into Connor's arms, eyes wide open, it wouldn't hurt. She'd let herself fall in love with him knowing he couldn't love her back.

But then, last night, when she'd offered herself to him completely, nearly bled with love for him, something had shifted around inside her heart. Because even after she'd told him over and over that she wanted him just the way he was, he'd still stayed away.

Isabel studied her in silence. "Look, I know you've got really strong feelings for him. Maybe you even love him. But honey, you're worth so much more than you know. I thought you realized that by now, that moving to Blue Mountain Lake and starting your life over showed you just how fantastic you are. Any guy you're with damn well should consider himself the luckiest person in the world."

Ginger pulled her knees up to her chin, wrapped her arms around her legs. "After I left Jeremy, I promised myself the next time would be different. That I'd wait patiently until the right guy came. I thought for sure I'd know the real thing when I saw it."

And then Connor had walked in through her door and she'd been lost.

"We all think that," Isabel said with a rueful smile.

"And even though I know better," Ginger found herself

saying aloud, "a part of me keeps hoping Connor will turn into that guy. If I just give him enough time. If I just love him enough."

Isabel's look of concern intensified into worry. "No. No. And no. Listen to me, you cannot change him. He's the only one who can do that."

And that was when Ginger saw the real problem, as clear to her as the blue sky, the sparkling ripples on the water, the happy sounds all around her.

Just as she'd told him again and again, she wasn't hurting from the way she and Connor had come together the previous night. He hadn't been nearly as rough as he'd thought and she really was tougher than she looked. The problem wasn't even that he'd hurt her feelings by choosing to stay downstairs on the couch last night rather than open himself up to her.

No, she was hurting for another reason entirely. And it had just become so painfully obvious that she wondered how she could have gone on this long without seeing it.

The real problem wasn't the way Connor had treated her. It was the way she'd been treating herself.

She'd ached so badly for him, had wanted so badly to help heal his wounds, that she hadn't spared a second thought for herself. She'd put Connor first, just like she'd always put her ex-husband first, her parents, her causes.

Only this time it was worse. Because she'd secretly believed that Connor would see all she was doing for him and reward her with his love. Love she wanted more than anything in the world.

"Have I changed at all, Isabel?" she asked now. "Since you first met me?"

"So much. I've been so proud of you. Especially since I know firsthand how hard it can be to start over after a divorce. You've done a great job of moving on, Ginger."

"If that's true then why am I falling into all the same traps? Why am I working so hard to make everyone else happy?"

Why had she told herself she could feed off scraps? That a little affection was better than none at all?

Isabel's arm came around her. "Oh honey, that's just human nature. You can't beat yourself up for it. All you can do is hope that maybe it'll be easier next time."

"Is it?" Ginger asked her friend. "Easier next time?"

Isabel snorted. "I'm pretty sure you don't want to hear the answer."

"I guess I already know."

The images were still with Ginger: Andrew looking broken as he'd left Isabel's house, Isabel more pale and shaken than Ginger had ever thought to find her strong friend.

"If it makes you feel any better," Isabel said, "I've been giving myself the same advice since yesterday when Andrew blindsided me at my house. I'm working like hell right now not to beat myself up for still having all these stupid feelings for a guy I haven't seen in thirty years. I was so sure it would be different this time. That I could just put up a wall he couldn't cross. That it wouldn't hurt so bad just to be near him."

"I'm sorry that it does," Ginger told her friend, reaching out to hug Isabel back.

"Me too. Especially since I just agreed to cater his son's wedding. The very son he got that girl pregnant with the night he cheated on me."

"Seriously?"

"Seriously."

Isabel was standing in the paint aisle of the hardware store staring at a dozen different greens that all looked the same when Connor came fast around the corner. For a moment she was stunned by his resemblance to his father, got such a clear picture of what Andrew must have looked like twenty years ago it took her breath away.

Connor was clearly preoccupied, barely looking at her as he said, "Sorry, didn't see you there."

He looked tired and beaten down. Pretty much the way Ginger had been all through breakfast and lunch.

She told herself to keep her nose out of their business, but damn it, she cared too much about Ginger to stay quiet. Ginger wasn't just a friend, she was almost like a daughter.

"Connor."

He finally realized who she was. "Isabel."

It wasn't until then that she thought to wonder if he knew about her and Andrew. But judging by how displeased he looked at seeing her, she guessed he did. She got it that no kid wanted to think of his father having feelings for anyone other than his mother, no matter how old they were.

"How's work going on Poplar Cove?"

"All right," he said. "You know how these old camps are."

She nodded, picked up a paint sample, working to find a tactful way of telling him what he needed to hear.

"Ginger is really important to me."

A muscle worked in his jaw. "I know she is."

"Coming here after a bad divorce. Starting over. I know how hard that can be. The lake has been good to her. This town. These people. Everyone loves her."

She paused, let him nod, made sure he got what she was saying.

"Ginger is a wonderful person, Connor. She deserves so much more than she asks for."

He didn't move, barely blinked, but the flash of torment in his eyes almost made her regret saying these things to him. Because in a heartbeat, Isabel had seen just how much he cared for Ginger.

And she knew that if he did end up hurting her friend, it wouldn't be because he didn't have a heart.

It wouldn't be because he didn't care about Ginger.

He did.

But Isabel knew too well that sometimes even loving someone wasn't enough.

The phone was ringing when Connor walked into the cabin and he nearly pulled it off the wall when he answered it.

His brother's voice came across the landline. "Had to check in, see how things are going with Dad."

"You couldn't stop him from coming?"

"There was no stopping him. He was a man on a mission."

It was the first time they'd talked since Sam's message from the Forest Service and Connor knew what was coming next.

"So, how's it going out there?"

"The cabin is coming together."

"Not the cabin. You. How are you doing?"

He couldn't lie to his brother.

"Bad."

Sam's response was just as short and to the point. "Shit."

"I'm fucking everything up."

"No one gives a damn about the cabin. We'll have the wedding somewhere else."

"Not Poplar Cove. Ginger."

"The renter? Are you getting involved with her?"

Connor had to know. "What made Dianna different?"

"Everything."

Connor couldn't have asked anyone but his brother, "How did you know?"

"I couldn't push her away, couldn't get her out of my head. Every single second, she was with me."

Sam and Dianna's relationship had spanned ten years. Not a week, a sledgehammer falling unexpectedly into the center of Connor's heart.

"I'll talk to you later," he told Sam.

He couldn't spend another second in this cabin, not when he couldn't push Ginger away.

Isabel had brought it all home. Her warning couldn't have been more clear.

Leave Ginger alone. Let her be happy. Without you.

Jesus. How was he going to find the strength to do that?

The wind was strong again today. Cold and biting, perfectly suited for his mood. He needed to get out in the Laser, let the whitecaps whip him around. He went down to the boathouse, stripped down and put on one of the suits hanging from a hook on the wall.

The sail was dusty as he carried it waist deep into the water to the buoy. His abs got a workout as he balanced on top of the boat, unrolled and raised the sail and hooked it into place.

As soon as he unhooked the clip from the buoy, the Laser shot through the water. It took him only a few seconds to find his rhythm. The farther he got from the shore, the faster the wind whipped. He felt the hollow pounding of the fiberglass hull hitting the growing waves, hoping it would numb his mind. Rain had started coming down and he welcomed the storm even as the drops turned into pellets.

He gripped the tiller hard as flew over the water, waiting for the moment when all he'd feel was the hail on his skin, the rough pull of the water beneath the hull. But Ginger was still there, in every swirling whitecap he slammed into.

Just like Sam had felt about Dianna, Connor couldn't get Ginger out of his head.

Every single second she was with him.

The wind changed directions and he barely caught the boom in time before it slammed into his head. The sheet bit into his hand, but he barely felt it. He couldn't tell if his hands were growing numb simply from the cold or if it was his usual nerve bullshit. But then he realized it wasn't just his hands going numb, it was his whole arm. All the way up to his shoulder.

In the split second that he lost his concentration, the wind yanked the boat over. He hiked out as far as he could, his body parallel to the water, his abs hard, his quads flexed as they hooked to the underside of the deck. He tried to right the boat, but once the centerboard was no longer in the water all traction was lost. The sail was already dragging into the water, going under, flipping the boat completely upside down. He lost his grip on the side of the deck as he went under and had to swim hard to keep the wind from moving the boat out of his reach.

Jesus, the water was cold out in the middle of the lake and he didn't have enough body fat to withstand it for long. Again and again he crawled onto the turtled hull reaching for the centerboard, but it was too damn slippery, too damn slick for his hands to gain any traction.

CHAPTER TWENTY-ONE

THE CABIN was empty when Ginger arrived home a short while later. Looking out at the beach, she noted that the sailboat was gone from the buoy. Thinking of Connor out there in winds like this had her instantly worried.

No, she told herself. He'd grown up on this lake. He knew when it was safe to go out and when it wasn't.

She needed to stop thinking about him every second. After changing into a paint-spattered sweatshirt and jeans, Ginger brought her easel in from the windy porch and stood in front of her it. This moment was a test. A test she desperately needed to ace.

The acclaimed Blue Mountain Lake Art Show was coming up in two weeks and this was the start of her week off to get ready. The good news was that she'd just sold another one of her paintings off the wall of the diner this morning during breakfast, but it did mean that she had one less painting to put on display.

All week she'd need to paint like a whirling dervish to get everything done on time. Especially since she'd given up so many hours this past week for the pleasure of being in Connor's arms. At the same time, though, she was thankful for the way her time with him had fueled her. A few sweet days in his arms, loving him, had provided her work with a much deeper emotional sensibility.

It was only if her creativity had become intrinsically tied to him that she was completely screwed.

Taking a deep breath, as she lifted a brush she decided she couldn't let Connor take this from her too. He already had her heart.

She deserved to keep something for herself.

It wasn't an easy start, but thank God, she finally started disappearing inside her paints. She didn't know how long she'd been working—time simply fell away when she hit her groove—when she looked up from her easel and saw that the wind had turned into a full-on hail and rain storm.

And that's when she realized Connor was still out there.

In the kind of storm that could destroy a small sailboat.

She ran out of the cabin, down the beach to the dock. The cover was still on the power boat and she ripped at it, tearing a couple of fingernails in her panic. The storm had sent a thick fog in addition to the rain and wind. With the boat uncovered just enough for her to be able to sit behind the wheel and steer, she quickly untied the ropes holding it to the dock and turned the key in the ignition. She wanted to go fast, shoot out onto the lake to find Connor, but she could barely see five feet in front of her and had to creep along.

Where was he?

She prayed then, harder than she ever had before, and then she saw it—a quick flash of something that looked like the white of the upside-down hull—and drove toward it.

She had to get within twenty feet before she could clearly see the boat. She didn't see Connor at first. She lost her grip on the steering wheel as the shock of losing him almost took her down, but then, a second later she saw his head, his shoulders, bobbing up and down in the water as he tried to climb onto the upside-down hull.

Connor was trained for saving people. Not Ginger. But now that their positions were reversed, she knew she needed to not only draw from her own strength, but his too.

Steadily, she drew the boat up alongside him, needing to get as close as she could without hitting him. With the wind and huge swells knocking them both around in the lake, it was difficult, but she refused to back down, to give in to the fear trying to break her.

He saw her then, coming for him. She cut the engine and leaned as far as she could out of the boat without falling into the water. He was just out of reach, just beyond her fingers, but she knew she couldn't jump into the water, couldn't let the power boat get away from them.

She reached again for him and this time, her fingers were able to catch his.

Pulling from a strength she hadn't known was in her, she wrapped her cold hands around his near-frozen flesh and pulled him away from the sailboat. He could barely close his fingers, and she knew that the combination of the cold and wet with his nerve damage must be making even the slightest movements nearly impossible.

But then, he was the one pulling her toward him and as the two boats slammed together, he leaped into the power boat.

She should have known better than to doubt his strength, even in conditions like this. She forced herself to hold focus until she had the boat safely tied up to the dock. They'd worry about recovering the sailboat later.

Only then did she let herself look at him, put her arms around him. Oh God, his skin had lost its color. He was so cold, he was shaking. Somehow she needed to get him inside, get him warm, make sure he was okay.

But he had more strength than anyone else would have; when she got out of the boat and reached in to help him out, he was quickly on the dock, moving with her through the hail into the cabin.

The minute they were inside she stripped him down, then pulled a thick blanket off a nearby chair and wrapped it around him. Somehow, she got all caught up in the blanket, her body pressed hard against his, but when she tried to pull away to go make some tea to warm him, she realized his arms were holding her fast.

"You scared me," she whispered into his chest. She was

trembling, more from the fear of almost having lost him than from the cold.

"You saved me."

His skin was still so cold, his hard muscles like blocks of ice against her, his hands and arms stiff as she tried to massage life into them with her fingers.

"You need to get warm."

Fortunately, the mud room in the back of the house had a shower, so they didn't need to go all the way upstairs. Seconds later, they were standing together under the spray, holding each other, Connor naked, Ginger fully clothed.

Quickly warming, she'd never been more glad to feel his lips on her than she did as he bent his head down to kiss her.

Her nipples beaded against his chest and when he started pulling off her clothes, the only thing she could think was that it must mean he had feeling in his hands.

And then she was naked too and he was sinking down onto the tiled shower floor and she was going with him.

One last time, was all she could think as she felt the thick head of his cock press into her, as he slowly filled her with his heat. She worked to memorize every last thing about him, the passion in his blue eyes, the emotion etched into his face.

One day she'd find another man to marry. She'd have children. And she'd work like hell to be happy.

But there would never be anyone like Connor.

After what had just happened, she deserved these last few final stolen moments in his arms.

And then she'd be strong.

She gasped with pleasure as he wrapped his hands around her hips and pulled her down hard, all the way onto him. She never wanted to let go, never wanted to give him up as he told her how much he wanted her, needed her, had to have her. Her muscles started to contract around him and his roar of pleasure vibrated all the way through to the center of her.

One last time.

Thank God she was back in his arms. It was right where she belonged, the only way he could feel any peace at all.

Connor couldn't believe how stupid he'd been to go out in the sailboat in the middle of a storm like that, without a life vest.

The worst part of it was that he hadn't just put his own life at risk, he'd risked Ginger's too. She shouldn't have come out in that storm to save him, but she had.

He felt her shift in his arms and, selfishly, he almost didn't let her move. But her arms were strong as she pushed away from him and stood up.

He watched her step out of the shower and wrap a towel around herself, then he turned off the water and did did the same, his heart thumping hard.

"Connor. We need to talk."

Oh fuck. He could feel what was coming—what had to come after the way he'd behaved last night and this morning.

Wanting desperately to stop her from leaving him, he

said, "You were right. When you said I've been lying to everyone. Knowing I can't go back to my job, to my crew—" He stopped, tried to put the loss into words. "It's worse than the way I felt when I woke up in the hospital. I knew my skin would grow back. But I'll never get to be out on the mountain again, never get to feel that rush of facing down the flames."

He ran a hand through his wet hair, forced himself to say, "I was embarrassed by how much it hurt. That's why I didn't want to talk about it."

There was no going back now. Time to lay it all out on the line.

"If it's not too late, if you think you can ever forgive me for being a complete asshole, I don't want to lose you."

She stared at him. Every other time he'd been able to read what she was feeling on her face. Not this time.

"For how long?"

He shook his head, didn't get her question, especially after his difficult confession.

"How long?"

"How long do you want to keep me?"

Oh shit. This time he got it, but that didn't mean he had an answer for her. "This is more than just a summer fling. You know that."

"Okay then, throw fall in too. Then what?"

Ginger was well aware of the fact that he didn't exactly have the future mapped out right now, that he was moving day to day without any sort of plan.

"I don't know."

She turned and left the bathroom. He wanted to pull

her back into him, rewind five minutes, start this conversation over. Better yet, forget the conversation altogether and just lose himself in her again.

"When we started this," she said when they were both out in the living room, "I thought I could do it. That a summer fling could work for me, that if I was really lucky it might bleed into fall. Winter even. I know we had an agreement. I'm the one who told you not to be such a hero. I'm the one who practically begged you to make love to me. I realize I'm suddenly changing all the rules. But I can't keep going on like this. I can't pretend that two or three seasons are good enough."

Not reaching for her as she spoke was the hardest thing he'd ever had to do.

"I want it all. Passion. Devotion. Kids. Love." Her gaze didn't waver. "I want a husband and a partner. I want a man who wants to figure out our plans and future together." She pulled the towel tighter around herself. "I want to be with a man who loves me as much as I love him."

Connor would have given anything to make the words come. To be able to tell her everything she needed to hear. Because she was right, she deserved all of those things and more. Isabel's words rang in his ears: *"Ginger is a wonderful person, Connor. She deserves so much more than she asks for."*

Damn it, he didn't want to think of her in some other man's arms, looking back on her summer with him with a distant smile of remembrance.

It should be so easy. Three little words. That was all he needed to say and she'd be his.

But he couldn't get them out.

Fuck. What was wrong with him? An incredible woman was giving him the chance to be with her, to spend the next seventy years loving and being loved by her.

He looked at her then, her curls damp and dripping on her bare shoulders, her skin rosy from the heat of the shower and their lovemaking, and even though her green eyes were glassy with unshed tears, the determination to hold out for the kind of love she deserved shined through.

Suddenly, he realized the truth. He'd been in love with Ginger from their first kiss, from the first night at Poplar Cove when she'd held his hand after his nightmare and refused to let go.

Everything he'd been trying to hide from slammed like a fist into his gut, took the air out of his lungs with it. Because now that he knew he loved her, it was impossible to deny the rest of it.

He loved her too much to pretend there wasn't a better man out there for her.

She needed to be with a man who already had the future figured out. She deserved a man who wasn't working like hell just to make it from one minute to the next. She belonged with a man who wouldn't keep taking and taking from her until she ran out of anything to give.

"You're right," he forced himself to say, his throat as raw and inflamed as if he'd swallowed fire. "You deserve all those things, Ginger. And I need to step aside so you can get them."

She flinched as if his words had been a physical blow. He'd never felt worse, never felt so low. Especially after the way she'd risked her life to save him.

"You're an incredible woman, Ginger. I've never met anyone as strong as you. As beautiful."

The selfish part of him fought like hell to get him to say how much he loved her. To beg her to keep giving herself to him, even if he didn't have a damn thing to give her back.

"If I could love anyone," he finally let himself say, "it would be you."

She sucked in a shaky breath. "If I could stop loving anyone," she said softly, "it would be you."

CHAPTER TWENTY-TWO

THE TENSION—the misery—that pervaded every inch of Poplar Cove was so heavy Andrew was almost choking on it. It didn't take a genius to see that things between Connor and Ginger had gone from bad to worse. No more accidental brushes against each other. No more knowing glances. No more kisses good-bye.

Four days turned into five as they each worked in their corners. Connor cutting out the old rotted logs from the wall, Andrew sanding down the new logs, Ginger painting fast and furious.

Connor barely said two words. Ginger brought out sandwiches, but didn't join them as they ate. Andrew wished like hell he could wave a magic wand and get these kids back where it was so obvious that they needed to be, but he knew it wasn't that easy. He kept hoping they'd work it out, that the next morning he'd return and everything would be fine.

Just when he didn't think he could take it anymore, was actually considering locking them into the coat closet together and not letting them out until they'd worked it out, they both left the cabin, each going in opposite directions on the beach. It was such a relief to have the place to himself, he almost felt guilty. But as much as Andrew cared about his son, Connor wasn't the only one with problems.

Here he was, finally near Isabel again, and he couldn't think of a single plausible reason to go see her. Not when she'd made it perfectly clear that he needed to stay the hell away. He felt the clock ticking down, and even though a handful of days added to thirty years shouldn't matter, they did.

Seeing her again, holding her in his arms, had brought him right back around to the nineteen-year-old boy who had been so in love with her.

He was rechinking a couple of fresh logs when the phone rang in the kitchen and without thinking anything of it—it had been his house once, after all—he answered it.

"Josh never showed."

It was Isabel and she sounded harried. Irritated. Panicked. He recognized the name Josh immediately.

"Your son? Is anything wrong?"

"Andrew. Why the hell are you picking up Ginger's phone? And how the hell do you know my son's name?"

He'd been unable to stop himself from keeping tabs on

her all those years while he was in California. But this wasn't the best time to tell her that.

"Never mind," she continued before he could reply, "I don't have time for this right now. I need to talk to Ginger. ASAP."

"She's gone. So's Connor. What do you need?"

"I can't believe this is happening," came first, then "Josh was supposed to be my dishwasher. We're about to be buried under dirty dishes. If I don't get someone on it soon we're done for the day."

"I'll be right there."

He hung up before she could argue with him, broke the speed limit the entire way into town.

"You couldn't drive any faster?" she shot at him before jerking her thumb toward the back sink when he walked in the back door. "I'll show you how to work the Hobart."

After her demonstration of the big silver machine that spray washed and dried the plates, glasses and silverware, she asked, "Any questions?"

"None," he said, quickly getting to work on the enormous stacks of dirty plates and glasses, so many that they'd overflowed the stainless steel counter to the floor. Side by side they worked in silence, their rhythm as good as if they hadn't spent thirty years apart, until the situation was partially in hand.

And even though he'd never thought the day would come when he'd enjoy doing something like washing dishes, the truth was he hadn't felt this good in years. Simply because he got to be close to Isabel.

Hours later when the last of the customers had gone

and he was running the floor mats through the machine, he was surprised to hear her say, "Thanks for your help. I hate to say it, but you completely saved the day. And you don't totally suck at washing dishes either."

"You know what, I actually enjoyed myself." He shrugged and said, "I've forgotten how much pleasure there can be in a job well done. Any job, as it turns out."

Clearing her throat, she said, "I'll just go grab some money out of the till to pay you."

His laughter rang through the kitchen. "I don't want any of your money, Isabel. I just wanted to lend you a hand."

Her back stiffened. "I know you've probably got a fancy job—"

"Not anymore."

She seemed stunned by that.

"They fired me. Called it early retirement, but those are just fancy words."

"So that's why you're here."

"Not having a job made it easier to come," he agreed, "but I already told you why I'm here. My son needed me."

"Must be nice coming in and playing hero."

Her words hit too close to home for Andrew's comfort and he opened his mouth to argue, but instead found himself saying, "I haven't done any manual labor in thirty years. My body is killing me. Working out five days a week at the gym does nothing to prepare you to hammer nails for eight hours straight."

"You used to love hammering nails."

It struck him, powerfully, that only Isabel knew that

about him. "You're right. I did. And I'm learning to again." He nodded toward the Hobart. "I don't know if dish washing has quite the same magic, but just using my hands again is good. Regardless of what I'm using them for."

She turned away quickly, but not before he saw the way her skin had started to flush, the way she'd quickly sucked in a breath. God, he wanted so badly to pull her into him. To run his hands through her hair, over her skin.

But it was too soon. He could see the truth of it even through the force of his desire. He needed to leave before he did something stupid, but at the same time he had to make sure he could see her again.

"Do you have anyone lined up for dinner?"

He could tell she didn't want to answer, saw how much she hated saying, "No, I don't."

"What time should I be here?"

She picked up a knife, ran it under water, then wiped it off with a clean cloth. "Five thirty."

He took the light glinting off the stainless steel blade as his cue to leave.

"Don't be late. And don't think that just because I'm letting you wash my dishes means I've forgiven you."

"I won't," he said to the first, even as he hoped he could change the second.

Three hours later, after running a whole host of errands in town on foot, even though it was another cool and windy day, by the time Isabel got back to the restaurant she couldn't wait to get out of her sweater and coat. If her hot flashes got any worse she'd need to spend the entire afternoon in the walk-in refrigerator.

No, she thought, as she laid out a half-dozen orange and yellow bell peppers, there really was no point in lying to herself.

Andrew had done this to her. He had made her hot all over. That afternoon she'd actually wished for one stupid second that he'd just stop talking, stop letting her tell him to stay the hell away, and take her right there on the stainless steel counter.

It shouldn't have softened her to see him standing at the dishwasher, wearing the thick plastic apron, the big yellow gloves, but it had. And knowing he'd be back any minute now to do it all again—to save her ass—only set her nerves more on edge.

And filled her with sick anticipation.

The only way she could protect herself was to keep being suspicious of his motives, to look for the real meaning behind his smooth words.

Planning to grill the peppers, she turned on the gas on her stove and picked up her lighter, flicking it over the gas. The flames jumped higher than she expected and she was about to take a step back when strong hands wrapped around her waist, hoisting her out of the way.

She'd know Andrew's touch anywhere. She'd never had such an intense reaction to anyone else, been covered in goose bumps at the same time her insides were burning up.

She whirled out of his arms, even though everything in her wanted to lean in closer.

"What the hell are you doing?"

A muscle jumped in his jaw. "You need to be more careful."

Well, he wasn't the only one who was angry. "This is my fucking restaurant. You don't think I know how to operate my own stove?"

"Jesus, Isabel. Those flames were only an inch from your face. You could have gotten burned."

She opened her mouth to tell him where he could stick it, when his words finally penetrated her brain.

Burned. He'd been afraid she was going to get burned. Like his son.

"Seeing your son get burned. I can't imagine what that must have felt like," she said before she could pull the words back.

He blinked at her as if he'd only just realized how extreme his reaction had been to her lighting the gas ring.

"I'm sorry. You're right. I overreacted."

She started to reach out to him, and it was only at the last second that she stopped.

One touch, a split second of skin on skin, wouldn't be enough.

"It's just that ever since Connor's accident—"

He swallowed hard and she saw all the love—all the fear he'd felt for his son—imprinted in the lines on his face.

"I can't stand fires. Any kind of fire. Fireplaces. Fire

pits. Even seeing people's campfires glowing across the lake gets to me."

"That makes perfect sense."

"I wasted so much time, Isabel. I should have come here with Connor and Sam when they were kids. Should have been out there teaching them to sail instead of leaving it to my parents to show them how great the lake was."

She didn't know what to say, not when she'd been selfishly glad he hadn't come. How could she have possibly faced seeing Andrew every summer with a wife and kids?

"You're here now."

"I'm afraid it might already be too late, though."

"Then try again. And keep trying. Because that's what parents do. Even when our kids act like they don't want or need our love, that's when they need it the most. So stop worrying about yourself, stop worrying about how you feel for once. And just do what you need to do for him."

"Thank you for reminding me," he said softly and Isabel instantly saw that she'd just jumped in so much deeper than she should have.

"I need to get ready to open."

He nodded, moved back to the dish-washing station without another word. But she already knew it was only a temporary reprieve.

Fortunately, the diner had been incredibly busy and Isabel had no choice but to keep on task. The only problem was that she couldn't possibly tell Andrew to go home early. But even though she wasn't alone in the kitchen with him—Caitlyn and Scott plus two of her waitstaff were all there—he remained far too close for her comfort.

After plating her final order, she pushed out the back door, desperate for some air. The wind had picked up and she was wearing only a T-shirt, but she welcomed the chill.

Walking through the parking lot toward the water, she saw a young couple kissing and stopped cold. That was her son. And the blond girl he'd gone off to the movies with just a few days ago.

She didn't notice Andrew was beside her until he said, "Can you believe that's how young we were when we met?"

"That's my son. I didn't realize he had a girlfriend."

"We didn't want our parents to know about us either. We thought we were so grown-up," he said softly. "But looking at the two of them now . . ." He shook his head. "We were just kids, weren't we?"

Looking back at her son tentatively embracing his girlfriend, she suddenly saw just how right Andrew was. Her son wasn't even close to being an adult. He would, inevitably, make many mistakes over the next few years as he grew and changed.

For the first time in thirty years, her past with Andrew was painted with a different sheen, the black haze that it had been buried under for so long suddenly peeling up at the corners.

She turned to look at him, taking in the lines on his face, the gray streaks of hair, and realizing that, even so, he was more beautiful than he'd been as a perfect nineteen-year-old.

"We didn't have a clue what we were doing, did we?" she said softly.

"No, we didn't," he agreed. "Especially me."

The way the rough timbre of his voice reached down into her chest scared her. "I need to get back inside."

She half expected him to reach out and stop her. Instead he simply said, "Fine. Go. But one day you won't be able to find a reason to run away from me."

That got her back up, just as he must have known it would. Still, she couldn't swallow the words, "I'm not running."

"You sure about that?"

A swift rush of anger had her moving closer to him. "I have no reason to run from you."

"How about I give you one, then?"

And then his lips were on hers and a rocket ship was launching inside her belly.

Oh God, how could she have ever forgotten how incredible his mouth was, how sweet his kisses?

His hands came around her next, one on her waist, the other in her hair, pulling her closer, and soon it wasn't just their lips that were touching, but their tongues, swirling together in a dance that was so natural, so perfect, she found herself moaning with pleasure as she leaned closer.

He leaned her against the hood of a car, pressing himself hard against her, and she gladly went with him, wanting more of his heat, more of the sweet rush that only Andrew could bring her.

Sex with her husband had been good, but now that she was back in Andrew's arms she had to wonder how she could have possibly settled for anything less than this all-consuming passion. How could she have accepted anything less than the need to take her lover's next breath as her own?

Her hands were on him now, just as hungry, just as full of need. His arousal pressed into her and she couldn't help but rub herself against him. She ached to give herself over completely to this moment, to let Andrew take her as far she could go.

He reached up under her shirt, his fingers skimming her rib cage before he pressed both of his palms over her breasts, her heart beating against his hands.

And then, through the thick haze of desire, she heard, "Mom?"

She was too far under to process the voice as her son's until he said, "Fuck. That's my mom. Making out on the car with some guy."

Oh God. Josh.

Andrew moved first, pulled his hands out from under her shirt before her son could see. She moved as quickly as she could with limbs that felt like melted butter, tried to stand up to go after her son, but before she could he said, "You make me sick," and was gone.

Andrew tried to put a hand on her back to comfort her and she flinched at his touch.

How could she have done that? How could she have kissed Andrew? And if her son hadn't found them there, how much further would she have gone?

But she already knew the answer to that. Andrew had always been the one person who could make her lose control. And yet, even though he was the one who'd kissed her first, none of that was his fault. She'd wanted it just as much as he had. Had been more than willing to pull him down hard over her in the middle of a parking lot.

"He'll get over it, you know. Seeing you kiss me."

"I just don't know what I'm doing anymore. He used to say I was the best mom in the whole wide world. We were friends. We had a good a time together."

She wanted to cry. Scream. Sleep for a week.

Kiss Andrew again.

"But now it seems that I can't say or do anything right. I feel like I'm losing him. And it's killing me."

"He's trying to figure out how to be a man. I know from firsthand experience how hard that is."

Andrew was the last person on earth she should be spilling her guts to, and yet it felt so natural. As if, despite everything that had come between them, he was still the person who understood her best.

"Did your sons go through this?"

Pain flashed across his face in the moonlight. "I don't know," he said, and she was stunned by the heavy emotion in his words. "I was always working, always on a business trip. One day I left and they were boys, came home and they were men. Men who wanted nothing to do with their father."

"I'm sorry."

"I am too. But you were right this morning. I can't go back and change the past, but if I'm lucky, if I don't wimp out, I might be able to work on the future. Here. Now. With Connor. I want them to know how much I care about them." His eyes met hers, held them. "But I'll also understand if they don't see it. If they can't see it. Because sometimes if you screw up bad enough, there isn't any way to fix what you've done."

It all came back around to them. Every single time.

"So that firsthand experience about boys trying so hard to become men that I was talking about is mine alone." Her breath caught in her throat as he continued with, "I know you don't want to hear me say this again, Isabel, but I was a stupid kid who didn't know which way was up."

She didn't know what to say to him anymore. They were past yelling. Past her frantic attempts to hold him back with anger, with sarcasm. Past her up and walking away when she didn't know what else to do.

But not past forgiveness.

Clearing his throat, he said, "I should go, shouldn't I?"

She didn't look at him, couldn't look at him. "Yes, you should."

"What's wrong with you?"

Josh realized Hannah was practically running to keep up with him on the beach. He couldn't believe what he'd just seen, couldn't stop playing it over in his head, that guy practically humping his mom on the hood of a car.

He felt sick to his stomach.

"My mom shouldn't be doing that. Out in public." Or anywhere. Ever.

"I thought it was kind of romantic, actually. Your mom's been single a long time, right? Don't you think it'd be nice if she could find someone?"

"It wasn't romantic. It was disgusting."

Hannah stopped walking. "Why?"

Something was in her voice, a warning to watch how he answered her question, but he was too pissed off to care.

"She's my mom. She shouldn't need to do . . . that."

"But you told me your dad dates all the time."

"It's okay for him."

"How? Because he's a guy? Whereas she's just supposed to be happy and fulfilled being your mother for the rest of your life? You're the one who keeps saying how you wish she'd get a life and leave you alone. And then when she does you act like a complete jerk."

She turned and started walking away.

"Hannah, why are you mad at me?"

She barely stopped, only turned her face halfway to say, "Because you just treated your mom like garbage. And I don't want to be with a spoiled brat."

Isabel was waiting up for Josh when he got home.

"What you saw tonight. It's not what you think."

"Of course it is." He scowled. "You were practically doing it on a car with some random guy."

Bile rose in her throat at what her son had seen. At the

same time, it didn't feel right to apologize to him for being a normal human being with normal sexual needs.

Still, she wanted him to know she hadn't picked some random guy to go to town with.

"I knew him. A long time ago. Andrew grew up next door. At Poplar Cove. We dated." The words, "I was your age and I loved him," fell out of her mouth before she could think better of who she was saying them to.

She watched in horror as Josh's expression changed from angry and disgusted to just plain crushed.

"Dad was the only guy you've ever loved."

Oh no. She hadn't thought of how hard it would be for him to hear that she'd had a life before him, before his father.

"I did love your father. And even though we're not together anymore I'll always love him for giving me you."

But Josh wasn't listening. "I saw you tonight. I saw what you were letting that guy do to you. The only person you should be in love with is my dad, not some asshole who used to live next door. And now Hannah hates me because of you."

She reeled from what her son had said, that she wouldn't have been doing those things with Andrew if she didn't still love him.

"I don't love him," she said almost to herself, even as the last part of his sentence finally registered. "Hannah? Your girlfriend, you mean? How come she hates you?"

But he was done with her. "Why don't you just go back to lover boy and forget all about me. Since it's obvious that he's the only one you really give a shit about."

The last thing she heard was his bedroom door slamming and the music kicking in.

It occurred to her, then, that everything she'd said to Andrew about Connor pushing him away right when he needed his father most was also true for her and Josh. The more he pulled away, the more he told her he hated her, the more he needed her to be there for him.

Yes, she understood his growing pains, remembered only too well how hard it was to be fifteen and feel like your whole world was turning inside out. But even though she knew she needed to pull back a bit to let him find his way, that didn't mean she couldn't be there for him if he fell along the way.

Which he would. Because they all did.

Every single one of them.

CHAPTER TWENTY-THREE

DURING EXTREME wildfires, Connor sometimes went up to seventy-two hours with little to no sleep. He'd keep running on nothing more than adrenaline and fistfuls of high-calorie food, with the knowledge that when it was all over he could crash, satisfied over a job well done.

This past week he'd had just as little sleep, but there was no satisfaction coming on the back end.

All day, every day, as he worked on refinishing the logs, Ginger wasn't just a room away, she was there in his head with him every second, her words *"I want a husband and a partner. I want a man . . . who loves me as much as I love him,"* on constant repeat.

He never thought he'd be so glad to have his father around. The days were easier, with Andrew a silent buffer between them. But after his father left, as soon as the sun gave way to darkness, Connor's resolve would slip into dangerous territory.

He hadn't even tried to sleep in the cabin. Not when all it would take was one weak moment and he'd be upstairs, kicking open Ginger's door to steal another few minutes with her, doing anything he could to convince her to be with him one more time, and then one more after that.

Each night he'd gone out to the workshop as soon as the sun had set. That first night he'd done push-ups, sit-ups, pull-ups until he was dripping sweat all over the cold concrete floor. But it hadn't done a damn thing to clear his head. So he'd gone for a run. The first mile, his body felt sluggish. Heavy. As if he'd tied lead weights onto his limbs. Which only made him more determined to push through the pain, to run faster. Mile after mile passed as he ran away from Poplar Cove, his pace picking up with each new stretch of ground that he covered.

But Ginger stayed with him every step of the way.

Her beautiful face. The way she looked in the morning, her curls fanned out on the cover around her, her mouth soft and lush and so kissable. The way she'd looked when she'd told him she loved him on the porch, the truth in her eyes telling him they weren't just words said in the heat of passion.

He'd turned back around to the workshop, none of his usual tricks worth a damn. And that was when he'd found himself standing in front of his father's sailboat. It was a beautiful piece of work, even unfinished.

The storm he'd gone out in had wrecked his grandparents' old sailboat. The morning after Ginger had asked for everything he couldn't give her, he'd taken the speedboat out to retrieve the small craft. It was lying limp against the far shore, nearly smashed in two from slamming again and again into the rocks.

He couldn't put his grandparents' boat back together, but he could finish building this one. After a thorough search, he found the plans for the boat, neatly folded up in the bottom of a drawer.

It became his goal, his focus during the difficult days in the cabin with Ginger. Working on the sailboat didn't drive Ginger from his mind, but at least it was a way to pass the hours until the sun came up again and he could secretly watch her paint out on the porch, breathe her in as she walked by.

Every day, the agitation he'd carried around since his accident in Desolation—only when he was with Ginger had it eased—was multiplying exponentially. The couple of hours he slept on some thick canvas in the workshop were plagued with nightmares. His hands went from oversensitive to numb more and more and he had to be constantly on guard against dropping his hammer and caulk gun and sander.

He was bent down over the sailboat, putting in the finishing touches. The sun was almost rising and he was planning to drag it out on the water. He almost prayed for another storm, for the universe to force him and Ginger together again.

But since he knew that wouldn't happen, he was

tempted to take a hammer to it instead and start over. Because when he was done with the boat, what the hell was he going to have to focus on to keep himself away from her?

The day before, a neighbor down the lake who also had an old log cabin had been sent by a couple of guys at the hardware store to see Connor's work. Clearly impressed, the man had mentioned that it was pretty much impossible to find anyone to work on a place like this, that modern day contractors all just wanted to tear the cabins down and start over with a Lincoln Log kit. He asked what Connor's plans were going forward, if he might consider helping out some of the other log cabin owners on the lake with their homes.

Although Connor enjoyed the work, even though there was something immensely satisfying about running a paintbrush over a log in smooth strokes, coating it with a fine layer of varnish to both protect the log and bring out its natural golden sheen, despite the fact that seeing his great-grandparents' cabin come back to life was a rush, he couldn't stay here and work on fixing up old cabins full-time. Not because he didn't like the thought of becoming a carpenter, not even because he didn't think his hands could take the work, but because he couldn't stay at Blue Mountain Lake if Ginger was here too.

Watching her marry another man, have his children, would be hell on earth.

He'd rather jump into a pit of flames than stick around to watch that.

* * *

Andrew lay on the bed in his room at the Inn for hours, staring up at the ceiling, Isabel there with him in his head, his body the entire time. He remembered her softness pressing into him, the salty-sweet taste of her tongue sliding against his, the way she'd pulled him down onto her, pulling him closer.

Come five a.m., his eyes having been open straight through, he hoped like hell a jump in the lake would snap him out of it. But although the water was cold, and he was physically tired, his insides still buzzed and snapped as if it had been thirty seconds since he saw Isabel instead of hours.

The sun was just starting to rise when he got back into his car and headed toward Poplar Cove. But when he pulled up to the cabin, he realized it was way too early to bother either Ginger or Connor. He couldn't just sit out here in his car, so he got out and started walking the path he knew by heart to the one place he'd managed to avoid since coming back to Blue Mountain Lake.

His grandfather's sanctuary, his most prized place in all of Poplar Cove: the workshop.

Standing outside the old red barn, which his grandfather had preserved on the original property when they bought it in 1910 and started building the cabin on the waterfront, Andrew could almost see his lost dreams worming their way up out of the dirt, the dry leaves on the ground shifting beneath him so fast he lost his balance.

His heart pounding, he put his hand on the wide door-knob and pushed it open. There it was, his wooden sloop at the far end of the barn, right where he'd left it a little more than thirty years ago. He couldn't believe no one had taken it apart to use the wood for other projects, or at the very least, moved it out of the way. Why on earth was it still there?

And then he realized he wasn't alone, that his son was squatting down beside the boat.

"Connor?" he said, coming closer. And that was when he realized that the boat was no longer half built. "Did you do this? Finish building my boat?"

"It was a waste of perfectly good wood the way it was."

Despite Connor's unemotional words, Andrew was incredibly moved as he kneeled beside the boat, running his fingers over the smooth, golden wood he'd so painstakingly planed and sanded as a teenage boy.

He hadn't been much older than Isabel's son when he'd started building the boat, but it had been his dream to make his living with sailing as far back as he could remember. His father had put him on a sailboat as soon as he could walk and they'd spent hours together out on the lake in the *Sun Fish* and then the Laser.

Andrew had always assumed he'd end up in a boat of his making on the lake with his own sons.

"You're right," he finally said. "I shouldn't have left it unfinished all these years."

"It's just a boat," Connor said and Andrew knew his son was trying to steer them back out of the gray area. But there was no point in trying to steer clear of stormy weather. Not when it would find you no matter how hard you tried to hide from it.

"No, it wasn't just a boat. I loved to sail. It was what I was going to do, build boats and sail them. I was going to sail around the world."

"Why the hell didn't you come back then?"

"God, I wish I had come back, wish I could change everything, but I was just too much of a coward to face up to my mistakes."

"I get it you had a thing with Isabel, but who cares. You could have come anyway with Mom. You could have spent time with me and Sam. You could have taught us to sail instead of Grandpa."

"It wasn't that simple."

"I don't see how it could have been any simpler. You had a wife and kids who needed you."

"I was going to marry Isabel," Andrew confessed before he could grab the words back. "As soon as she graduated from high school, while we were both in college, we were going to be together. Instead I got your mother pregnant. One stupid, drunken night. And just like that I screwed up everyone's lives."

Realization dawned in his son's eyes, and then a rage Andrew'd yet to see, even those first days in the hospital bed when Connor's frustration had been a palpable thing.

"Mom was pregnant with Sam? That's why you married her?"

"I wouldn't have married her if I didn't have feelings for her."

"But you never loved her like you loved Isabel, did you?"

Andrew knew he'd have to work like crazy to make his son understand. "I never wanted your mother to feel like she was second best. And when she got pregnant, neither of us could just go our separate ways and make the best of it. It wasn't the way either of us had been raised. It wasn't the right thing to do. We made the decision together to put a ring on each other's fingers and we tried like hell to make it work. We didn't want Sam—or you—to grow up in a broken home."

"You made the wrong choice."

"I know that now," he tried to say, but Connor cut him off.

"You never gave a damn about any of us, did you?"

Something in Andrew snapped. He was done just sitting here and taking crap from his son.

"How dare you lecture me about love. Not when you're too damn scared to let that beautiful girl of yours love you."

There was murder in Connor's eyes, but Andrew didn't care. He wasn't going to shut up until he was good and done.

"I did everything I could to be a good father when you and Sam were little, but the house was such a war zone, so much your mother's territory, she practically forced me into hiding out at work. Any time I showed up to a baseball game, she'd give me grief about the other five times I didn't go. There was no way to win."

He held up a hand to stop Connor from interrupting again.

"A stronger man would have been a good father in spite of it. And I wasn't. But I wouldn't have traded you boys for anything in the world. And I'm hell-bent on being that better man now. Which is why I'm not going to let you get past me until you tell me what in God's name has gone wrong between you and Ginger."

Connor's hands were hard fists and Andrew wondered if they were going to come to blows. He almost hoped they would, that he could let Connor work out his frustration, taking away some of Andrew's guilt with him.

But instead of coming at him, Connor said, "She deserves more than I can give her."

They were simple words, words that shouldn't have meant much at all. But the pain behind them knocked the air out of Andrew's lungs. Thirty years ago there'd been no way out for Andrew or Isabel or Elise.

But his son still had time to get it right.

"I've never known you to back down from a challenge. Have you even tried to give her what she wants?"

"Didn't you hear me?" Connor shouted. "I can't fucking do it! I can't live my life thinking about her every single second, wanting her so bad I can't see straight, worrying that something will happen to her."

"You love her."

"Of course I love her," Connor said, his voice raw, rough with emotion. "But I've hurt her again and again. I'll just keep hurting her."

Andrew wanted to reach out for his son, but he didn't

know how. "We all screw up at one time or another. We hurt each other. But the big mistake isn't screwing up. The big mistake is wasting time being bitter. Being angry. Letting guilt eat you up inside. Letting one stupid moment change you into someone you never wanted to be."

"Don't you get it?" Connor growled. "I've got nothing to give her. She deserves a whole man who can give her everything she deserves right now. Not in five, ten years. She shouldn't have to wait for me to figure out my future. To see if I even have one."

"Those are all just excuses, Connor. You know that as well as I do. Of course you're good enough for the woman you love. She wouldn't love you if you weren't."

Connor didn't respond and as a thick silence hung between them Andrew told himself he'd tried. That he'd done all he could do. He was about to walk away, give his son some space, when Isabel's words came at him.

"Try again. And keep trying. Because that's what parents do. Stop worrying about how you feel for once. And just do what you need to do for him."

He'd come back to the lake to prove to everyone—especially himself—that he had it in him to be a better man. He'd been so sure that all he needed to do was decide to do the right thing and it would be so simple. He'd expected all of the relationships it had taken him thirty years to screw up to be tied up with little bows by now.

That first day back in Isabel's bedroom, he'd told her that he was a changed man. But he hadn't been. He'd still been looking out for himself first.

It was long past time to change that.

"You don't need to be a hotshot, Connor. You don't even need your hands. Life is what you make it. And you've still got the world at your feet. Along with a beautiful young woman to love. And the only thing I know for sure is that if you let her go, you'll never forgive yourself."

And then, as his strong son stood beside the sailboat looking utterly lost, Andrew knew what he needed to do.

It was one of the most frightening moves he'd ever made, taking those first steps toward his son, and only got worse the closer he got. But he wasn't in it to see what he could get right now. Andrew's happiness was already lost.

He'd do anything he could to help Connor save his.

Andrew put his arms around his son and refused to feel the slightest bit embarrassed by the tears running down his cheeks as he spoke.

"I know I haven't told you this nearly enough times, but I love you. I know I was a shitty father, that I screwed up a hundred different ways, and even though I didn't know how to show it, I always loved you. And I always will."

CHAPTER TWENTY-FOUR

GINGER GROANED as the phone woke her up out of a rare patch of sleep.

The past week had been utterly exhausting. Worrying about accidentally touching Connor every time she walked past him, knowing that was all it would take to throw herself in his arms, to forget everything she was trying so hard to remember. Trying so hard to be mature, to not be spiteful in the little things by making only herself a sandwich at lunch.

Every night she'd waited for him to come up the stairs, her heart pounding like a lovesick fool. No matter how hard she tried to turn over and go to sleep, she'd lie there wide awake hoping and praying that tonight would be the night he'd turn the knob, walk in, and get down on his knees to beg her forgiveness, to tell her he was wrong, that he loved her after all.

But he never had.

Why did it have to hurt so much to try for happiness?

And why did moving forward after loving Connor have to be so damn hard?

Grabbing the phone off the table, she'd barely grunted out a hello when Isabel said, "Ginger, I didn't wake you up, did I?"

"Don't worry about it," Ginger said. She went to sit up in bed, but when she moved her stomach began roiling with nausea.

"I swore I wasn't going to call you—I know how much you need this week to focus on your painting—but can you come over? I asked Scott to cover for me at the diner. I'll make you breakfast."

The thought of eating anything made bile rise in Ginger's throat, but she said, "Of course. I'll be right there," anyway.

So many times since arriving at Blue Mountain Lake, Isabel had been there for her. First with a job and then with friendship. So even a sudden attack of the stomach flu wasn't going to keep her from helping Isabel.

But as soon as she walked into her friend's house and smelled eggs frying in the kitchen, she had to run to the bathroom.

Isabel found her there, throwing up.

"Oh my God," her friend said as she pulled her hair away from her face, wound it into a knot. "The only time I had that kind of reaction to breakfast was when I—" She paused, finished in a gentle voice. "Ginger, could you be pregnant?"

Ginger hadn't even had a chance to wipe her mouth off yet when round two hit her. A couple of minutes later as she sat back against the cool bathroom wall, wiping her face with the wet hand towel Isabel had handed her, she found she couldn't say anything.

Not even to tell her friend it couldn't possibly be true.

How many times had she and Connor been too rushed to use a condom? Nearly all of them, she realized now. She'd been so hungry for his touch, so desperate to be with him, that apart from their one stilted conversation about using protection, she hadn't given it another thought.

"I'm going to buy you a test," Isabel said. "Next town over so no one thinks anything."

Something pinged in the back of Ginger's brain. Slowly, as if the thought was being dragged through the mud by its hair, she said, "You needed something. Tell me what it is, Isabel. I came here for you."

But her friend had already grabbed her keys and purse. "My deal can wait. Finding out about yours can't. Don't go anywhere until I come back," she pointed a stern finger at Ginger, "especially not Poplar Cove. I'll throw the eggs away outside on my way to the car. Go take a shower in my bathroom and then try to relax. I'll drive fast. I promise."

Ginger was glad to have Isabel's directions to follow. Staying in the shower until it went cold, she wrapped herself in a towel, put her clothes back on, then went back downstairs to sit on Isabel's living room couch to wait. There were plenty of magazines and books she could have thumbed through, a hundred channels on cable to watch, but her spinning thoughts were already providing more than enough stimulation.

She'd wanted a baby for so long that she couldn't help but pray Isabel was right, that she was pregnant.

But at the same time, she wasn't living in a fantasy world. Not anymore, anyway.

She'd been so adamant about not using her parents' money, about not wanting to use her husband's money, about making it on her own. But there was a big difference between feeding herself on tips from the diner and bringing a kid up right. She wanted to be able to pay for ballet lessons and go see pirates at amusement parks. She wanted to make sure she could always send her child to the best doctors, the best schools, give him or her the best of everything.

Even Isabel, one of the strongest people Ginger had ever met, had said how hard it was to raise a kid alone, that she'd often wished she had a partner to share the burdens and the joys of being a parent.

Examining her thoughts one by one, Ginger knew all along that she was leaving the most important one out.

Connor.

Isabel walked in carrying a white plastic bag. "I bought two. Just to make sure."

Ginger took the tests into the bathroom. Two minutes later, a blue plus sign stared back at her.

Joy—pure joy unlike anything she'd ever experienced outside of Connor's arms—roared through her. Ripping open the other box, she mustered up more urine and waited again. Tick-tock went her heart, pounding so hard she almost thought her ribs might splinter from the inside. But long before the two minutes were up, the open oval on the little white stick read PREGNANT in bright blue letters.

Catching sight of herself in the small, rusted mirror, she saw tears of joy streaming down her face.

She'd wanted a baby for so long, and now, entirely by accident, she'd managed to get pregnant.

No more watching new mothers try to jam their strollers into the diner's narrow front door and wishing it was her. No more looking into the future and wondering when, if ever, having kids was going to happen for her.

But then, it hit her, had it really been an accident? If she'd slept with anyone but Connor, wouldn't she have been more careful? Had she fallen in love so fast, so hard, that she'd secretly wanted to get pregnant with Connor's baby every single time they came together?

Isabel knocked on the door. "You okay in there?"

Ginger walked out of the bathroom only able to say one word.

"Pregnant."

Isabel screamed, threw her arms around her, hugged her hard.

"I'm so happy for you," came first, before, "It's going to be okay, whatever happens."

"I need to go tell him. Right now."

Isabel nodded. "Do you want me to come with you?"

"No."

This was between her and Connor, no one else.

Joy and fear knocked into each other again and again as she made her way across Isabel's beach to Poplar Cove. And then she saw him standing on the beach and her legs almost failed her.

It's going to be okay, she repeated several times in her head, before taking a deep breath and heading toward him.

It was time to tell Connor he was going to be a daddy.

CHAPTER TWENTY-FIVE

CONNOR'S HEART jumped when he saw Ginger walking across the beach to him.

He'd thought the stronger path was to walk away from her, to deal with his demons on his own. In his world, a hotshot never gave up, never admitted weakness. But was that because they were all so tough? Or was it because they knew there were nineteen other guys backing them up on the mountain? A skilled crew of friends and family who would pull their ass up out of the flames if they ever needed it?

A sudden thought hit him hard in the solar plexus: Ginger was his crew.

How had he not seen it before? She'd supported him, understood him, had risked her life for him. She'd given herself up to him completely. And instead of doing the same for her, he'd run.

A thousand times he'd faced physical threats, but this was the first time his heart had ever been on the line. This was the first time he'd fallen in love, harder and deeper than he'd known was possible.

His father was right. All of his reasons to give up Ginger were just excuses. Just as she'd always been there for him, he wanted to be there for her. To hold her hand when she was hurting. To celebrate her successes.

To love her no matter what the future held. And to let her love him back without doubt.

He wasn't going to run scared anymore. And he'd do whatever it took to get her back.

As he moved toward her it was almost as if everything was moving in slow motion. He could feel the grains of sand beneath his bare feet, the sun hot on his shoulders, hear the loons calling to each other across the lake. Finally she was standing right in front of him.

He drank in the sight of her. She looked tired. Like she'd been crying. But radiant all the same.

"I've missed you, Ginger."

He watched her start in surprise at his words, then look down at the sand, close her eyes and take a deep breath.

"I need to tell you something, Connor."

"Ginger, please. Just let me say something first."

"No," she insisted. "I need to say this." She squared her shoulders, lifted her chin. "I'm pregnant."

The sun emerged from behind a tree and he was momentarily blinded.

"Say that again."

"I'm going to have a baby." Her voice was shaking now. "Our baby."

"You're pregnant." He needed a second to process the shocking news.

"It must have happened the fir—" She stumbled over the word. "The first night. Or that next morning. The timing works out right."

He braced himself, wondered if the walls were going to start closing in. A baby meant his life as he knew it was forever over now.

Instead, he was blindsided by relief.

And pure joy.

He took her hands in his, threaded his fingers through hers. "I love you."

She looked down at their hands, then up at him, her eyebrows furrowed in a deep frown. And then, she abruptly pulled her fingers from his. Took a step back.

"Don't say that now, just because—"

He reached for her again, but this time he pulled her against him. "Damn it, Ginger. I just told you I love you. You're the first woman I've ever said that to."

"I'd also bet I'm the first woman you've gotten pregnant."

What the hell was happening here? He'd just confessed his true feelings to her and she was throwing them back in his face?

"I don't get it. I thought this was everything you wanted. A baby. A man who loves you."

"I don't see any wildflowers."

"What the hell do wildflowers have to do with anything?"

"I already asked you for everything," she yelled. "And you already said no. So don't you dare tell me you love me now and expect me to believe you."

Her chest was falling and rising and her face was flushed. Visibly working to calm down, she said, "This doesn't have to change anything. You'll be going back to California soon. We can figure something out that makes sense. I know this is your child, too, and I'll make sure you get plenty of time with him or her."

"Like hell this doesn't change anything. Everything is different now. You're going to have a child. My child. And no kid of mine is growing up without a father."

"If you say the M word I'll deck you."

"You're right, marriage doesn't necessarily make sense. But what if my wanting to marry you has nothing to do with having a child? What if I want to marry you because I can't imagine a life without you?"

Her mouth opened in a small "o" of surprise a split-second before irritation took over.

"I don't have amnesia. Four days ago you were *stepping aside,*" she put the words in air quotes, "*giving me the chance* to find Mr. Right. Now you're trying to step inside his shoes."

His hands tightened on her shoulders. "They're my shoes, damn it!"

How had it come to this? The two of them standing here on the beach yelling at each other? He worked like hell to calm down.

"How many times am I going to have to tell you I love you before you believe it?"

"I don't know, Connor. I just don't know." She put a hand over her stomach. "This is all too much for me today. All of it. I need some time to think things through."

"How much time?"

And how the hell was he going to keep it together until she decided?

"I don't know. All I know is that I can't talk to you right now."

Their positions had just reversed. This time he was the one asking for everything . . . and she was the one leaving him without it.

Josh waited until he heard his mom leave the house to call his father. "Hey Josh," his father said, "didn't expect to hear from you. Especially not this early."

He looked at the clock, realized it was only 7:30 am. But he'd waited as long as he could.

"I want to come live with you."

There was silence on the line. "You mean you want to come out for a visit again?"

"No. I want to live with you full-time."

"Have you talked to your mother about this?"

"No, but she'll probably be happy to have me out of the way so that she and that guy can finish what they were doing on the hood of that car."

"There's a guy? On the hood of a car?"

"She was making out with some dickhead she said she used to be in love with."

"Andrew."

"Yeah," Josh said, getting more and more frustrated with this conversation. Why wasn't his father telling him to pack his bags already? "So it's cool for me to move in, right?"

"Hey kid, you know I'd love to have you but I'm going to be in Asia most of next month."

"I can hang on my own," Josh said, but just then he heard a girl's voice and then his father answering, "It's just my son, honey. I'll be right back."

Just his son.

The message couldn't have come in clearer. Both of his parents were too busy fucking around to give a rat's ass about him.

"Forget it," Josh said right before slamming down the phone.

Isabel had just walked into the diner when Scott handed her the phone. "It's Brian."

It just got better and better. First Andrew. Then Josh. Now Brian. All the men in her life ganging up on her.

"What's up?"

"I knew he'd come back for you."

"Who? What are you talking about?"

"I just got off the phone with our son. He told me Andrew's back."

How was it that after ten years, whenever the subject

of Andrew came up, her ex still managed to sound wounded by it?

And she still managed to feel guilty.

But Andrew was none of Brian's business. "Why did Josh call?"

"He wants to move in with me. Full-time."

"No."

"Don't worry," he said quickly, "I already told him it wouldn't work."

"Jesus, Brian. Is that how you said it? Did you give one second's thought to how that would make him feel?"

"How about you? When you were on the hood of the car with long-lost Andrew, were you thinking about your son then?"

Fuck you warred with *touché* on the tip of her tongue.

"Thanks for the warning," was what she finally managed. "I'll have a talk with Josh this afternoon."

She hung up the phone, her heart heavy for Josh, for how hard fifteen was treating him.

At the same time, though, her heart was heavy for herself.

It didn't matter if she ever got beyond forgiveness with Andrew, if she ever learned to trust him again. Because there was no way her son would ever accept him.

Maybe if Josh hadn't seen them in the parking lot, maybe if she hadn't admitted to him that Andrew was one of the big reasons her marriage hadn't worked, then things could be different.

But they weren't different.

And never would be.

* * *

Josh fingered the half-empty pack of cigarettes in his pocket. He'd swiped them from the new dishwasher's stash a few days ago, told himself the guy wouldn't miss the last few in the box. It had been a long time since he'd stolen anything, when he was five years old and had pocketed the water pistol his mother wouldn't buy him at the grocery store. He hadn't gotten caught, but just as he had then, he felt guilty.

Pushing out the back door of his house, he headed through the trees, to the wood pile between his property and Poplar Cove.

The house that fuckhead who'd been boning his mom grew up in.

Josh hated feeling guilty for stealing the cigarettes. Just as much as he hated feeling like nothing he did was right anymore, that no matter where he was, he didn't fit in.

He'd tried to call Hannah but she kept letting it go through to voice mail. And the worst part of it was, he knew it was his fault, that she had been disgusted by the way he blew up at his mom.

'Cause that was the thing, there were times when he could see it all so clear, when he could see that his mom was doing her best and that he was the one fucking up. But then, other times, he couldn't get a hold on his anger, his frustration.

The cigarettes and pack of matches bounced around in his pocket and he took them out, held them in his sweating palm. He wasn't really feeling it now, but only a loser would walk away without at least smoking one, right?

Popping one out of the pack the way he'd seen people do in movies, he lit a match and held it to the cigarette. Hopefully he'd lit the correct end of it, he thought as he put the other side between his lips.

Standing in the woods, a lit cigarette in his mouth, for a second he felt completely badass. Like he was finally in control of his own destiny.

And then he took a puff.

The cigarette went flying out of his mouth into the dry leaves as he coughed and choked. Shit, that was the most disgusting thing he'd ever tasted. How could people actually smoke those on purpose?

Smoke whipped up around his feet, the dry leaves quickly burning up near the rubber soles of his tennis shoes, and when his eyes stopped watering he realized the leaves were catching on fire, all of his stupid childhood fantasies going up in smoke too.

Doing a panicked rain dance on top of the leaves and dirt, feeling like a bigger idiot that he ever had, all he wanted was to go to his mom's diner, sit at the counter with a comic book, and have her make him a triple thick chocolate milkshake. Just like she had when he was a kid.

Finally, when he'd stamped the small fire entirely out, he went home and he buried the pack of cigarettes and matches in the bottom of the kitchen garbage before heading into the bathroom to shower off the smell of smoke.

CHAPTER TWENTY-SIX

THANK GOD, Ginger thought as she worked quickly on the final touches of her painting. She might be as emotionally confused as she'd ever been, but at least she hadn't lost her mojo. All she wanted was to focus on her art instead of all the crazy things Connor had said to her out on the beach.

I love you.

What if I want to marry you because I can't imagine a life without you?

Didn't he know she'd already written him off? That he couldn't just up and do an about-face about everything and expect her not to question him?

She put down her paintbrush. She was lying to herself. She wasn't in the zone at all. How could she be when her entire future was hanging in the balance? When Connor was waiting for her answer?

Her first big art show was in less than a week, a show she'd been eagerly anticipating for months. By God, she needed to make the most of it. With or without the man she loved by her side.

She was reaching for her paintbrush again when she noticed the smell of smoke wafting by. Strange. Why would someone have lit a campfire in the middle of a sunny day?

And then, in a flash, it hit her. She wasn't smelling a campfire: something was on fire.

Her hand immediately went to her stomach. Working to remain calm, she slipped her feet into tennis shoes before running out on the beach to try to figure out what was burning.

Her hand went to her mouth when she stood at the water's edge and looked up. The trees behind Poplar Cove were smoking and every few seconds a new orange burst of flames popped up over the roofline.

Her first thought, her only thought, was about Connor. About how upset he'd be if the cabin burned. He'd poured his heart into renovating it, but more than that, his summer home had been such a happy place for him as a child, and held the best of his memories inside its log walls.

She couldn't let it burn.

She ran toward the house, searching for a hose and a ladder, even though she knew what Connor would tell her if he were here. *"Get away from the building. Get as far away from the fire as you can and stay safe."*

And she would. But first she needed to do what she could to save his family's cabin.

She'd just propped the ladder up against the side wall, just turned on the hose full blast, when Josh came running across the beach, obviously drawn by the smoke.

"Go back home and call 911," she yelled. "Call your mother. And call Connor and his father."

The boy's eyes were wide with fear as he yelled, "Okay," and ran back to his house to make the calls.

It was the strangest thing, but even though the fire was close enough that she could feel its heat, she wasn't afraid of getting on the roof while lugging a heavy hose. Not when she had such a clear purpose.

I need to save Poplar Cove. For Connor.

She didn't know how long she'd been up there, but it was quickly getting hotter and smokier as the fire made its way down the mountain to the cabin, jumping trees one after the other like tinder.

The Adirondacks were known for their flash rainstorms, for the huge amount of water that could, abruptly, fall from the sky with no warning for fifteen minutes and then disappear just as quickly. But since the storm that had tipped over Connor's sailboat it had been hot and dry, with temperatures almost in the triple digits.

Oh, how she wished one of those storms would decide to roll in right now to give them all a good dousing. But when she looked up at the sky, behind the layer of smoke and ash all she could see were blue skies, not a cloud in sight.

She didn't have to be a firefighter to know that it was the perfect day for a wildfire.

Moving as quickly as she could, she wet down the entire roof. She hadn't yet heard sirens, and didn't have any idea how far away the volunteer firefighters were. She'd stay as long as she could, but make sure to get down before she was in any real danger.

When she heard yelling, she looked down to see Andrew climbing the ladder up to the roof. She was on the back edge of the building, so close to the trees she could practically grab one and jump on.

"Ginger!" Andrew's face was a picture of panic. "You need to get off the roof. Now!"

She opened her mouth to answer him, to tell him that she was still okay, when she felt a sharp, unexpected whoosh of wind at her back.

But the breeze had never been this hot, this thick. The fire had moved faster, come closer than she'd calculated.

"Drop the hose and run," Andrew yelled over the crackle of flames and she was just about to drop the hose when she saw a thick spark of flames jump over her head. It looked like one of those small firecrackers the kids were playing with on the beach July Fourth.

Despite her efforts to keep the roof wet, the sparks caught and lit on the wooden tiles, a wall of flames separating her from Andrew or any way to get down.

As the flames danced before her, she could only think one thing: She was going to die without ever finishing her conversation with Connor.

She'd thought she'd had plenty of time to think things over, to chew on everything he'd said, to weigh both sides.

She'd thought she deserved at least a handful of hours to be mad, to make him suffer the way he'd made her suffer.

But the fire had come on so fast.

And now she thought, as she started coughing and couldn't seem to stop, it looked like she might be all out of time.

Unless Connor found a way to her before the flames did.

Yes, Connor understood that Ginger had needed time, but that didn't mean he'd agreed to sit back and wait.

All his life, he'd gone for what he wanted. Made it happen.

He didn't plan on losing Ginger. Not now that he'd finally pulled his head out of his ass and realized his life wouldn't be worth a damn without her.

Isabel was one of her closest friends. He needed her on his side.

Not long after Ginger left him on the beach, he was walking into the diner for the first time since learning of his father's relationship with Isabel. She was making coffee behind the counter when she looked up and saw him.

"Connor."

"Ginger's pregnant," he said, not bothering with small talk. "I love her. She doesn't believe me. Help me find a way to convince her."

Isabel didn't look nearly as stunned as she should have. "She took the test at my house."

Ah, that's why she was walking back down the beach that morning.

"I know she loves me."

"Yes," Isabel said. "She does."

"She's being stubborn."

"You hurt her."

"I know. And I want to spend the rest of my life making it up to her."

"You're really going to have to grovel."

"Trust me, it's going to be groveling like no one has ever seen before."

Isabel finally smiled. And for the first moment since Ginger had walked away from him, he felt like maybe everything might work out after all.

And then the phone rang just as someone said, "There's a fire. Across the lake."

Connor ran outside, looked up at the sky and had to blink a couple of times to clear his vision. Smoke was still billowing up out of the trees on the other side of the lake.

Right at the spot where his great-grandparents' cabin sat.

He was half in his car when he realized Isabel was opening the passenger-side door. "I'm coming with you."

He pulled out of the parking lot in a flurry of dust under his tires. The speed limit was forty-five on the road around the lake, but his speedometer continued to climb. Sixty. Sixty-five. Seventy. Seventy-five. And still, Connor tried to drive faster, because the closer they got to Poplar Cove, the worse the situation looked.

Please, he silently prayed, *I need to know Ginger's safe. Please let her be safe.*

In all his years of fighting fire, he'd never prayed harder, never wished for the safety of someone more.

Ginger meant everything to him. Everything. And if, by some horrible chance, she got caught in the fire . . .

No, he couldn't let himself think it.

If he did, he'd be lost. Completely lost.

"They're out there, fighting it," was the only thing Isabel said during their drive, the terror of her words filling up the car, making it impossible for Connor to reply, to soothe her fears.

Finally pulling up beside the cabin, he jumped out of the car. Ginger.

Where the hell was Ginger?

His eyes scanned the property quickly, just as he would in any other fire, only this time it was taking everything in him to keep the panic at bay. To try to keep from losing it.

He couldn't see her.

Where the fuck was she?

Someone grabbed his arm, but it wasn't Ginger so he didn't break his stride, didn't turn his focus from his search for her.

"Connor, she's up there. On the roof. She's trapped by the flames. And she's already inhaled so much smoke."

Finally, it registered that his father was speaking. "I tried to get her off," his father was saying, but Connor was already halfway up a ladder propped up against the side of the cabin.

He didn't have any turnouts and was wearing tennis shoes that would melt almost instantly if he came face-to-face with fire, but none of that mattered. The only thing that mattered was getting Ginger off the roof as quickly as possible.

Seconds later he was on the roof, looking straight into flames. And then, as the afternoon breeze came in, good and strong, moving the smoke and flames away for a split second, he saw her.

Ginger was standing in the back corner of the roof, holding a hose, still wielding it to try to fight the flames despite the fact that she was in mortal danger.

Too high off the ground to jump and with fire coming at her from both sides, Connor knew that anyone else would have been screaming. Crying. Begging for help.

But even through the flickering flames, he could see her focus, her determination to save his family's cabin.

Amazing. She was amazing.

In his turnouts, maybe he could have run through the flames to her. But if he tried that in his shorts and tennis shoes, they'd both die up here. He had to find a way to her, and fast, since the flames were growing hotter, the smoke thicker with every second that passed.

He knew he should be running, looking, finding, but suddenly his feet wouldn't move.

Jesus, he was frozen.

A chilling wave of panic moved through his cells one by one, further paralyzing him, making it hard for him to breathe, to think. His chest clenched as the possibility that all was lost became more and more real.

And then, he heard a voice calling out his name. Ginger's voice. Followed by the horrible sound of her coughing out the smoke she was inhaling.

Smoke and flames clouded his vision, but just hearing her voice, hearing her yell for him to go, to get off the roof, to save himself—it broke the deadly spell that had tried to wrap itself around him.

An unexpected smile moved across his lips. Never in his life had he thought to love someone as much as he loved her.

He would save her. And himself.

Because they deserved a life together.

All fear leaving him, he went to a place of pure instinct and muscle memory, a place where everything he'd learned from his decade of experience fighting deadly fires came into play. Quickly scanning their surroundings again, he decided his best option was to make a running jump for the large poplar tree directly beside the house. It was the same tree that had dropped the widow maker on them. But now, he gave thanks for it.

Gauging the distance between the gutter and the tree, he pushed aside any voices or thoughts that wouldn't get him where he needed to go and jumped.

As he landed, the bark bit into his palms, the skin on his bare knees, hard enough that he could feel the warm trickle of blood down his shin. Holding focus, he climbed up one limb and then over to the next, again and again, until he was as close to Ginger as he could get.

"Time to get off the roof now, sweetheart."

Leaping from the limb he was on, he landed on the roof again, only this time, he could feel the heat of the tiles beneath the soles of his shoes.

She ran to him, threw her arms around him. "I knew you'd come."

That her faith in him could be so unwavering when he'd failed so many times before moved him more than anything ever had. She started coughing again and it took every last bit of control to keep his voice easy.

"And I knew you'd be up here with a hose," he said, pushing the teasing words past the lump in his throat in the hopes of keeping her calm. "I'm going to need you to hold on to me and not let go."

"Okay," she scratched out, coughing even as she climbed onto his back, her arms and legs tight around his neck and waist.

Her soft warmth against his back made him feel invincible, as if there wasn't anything he couldn't do.

How, he wondered even as he ran across the roof, had he not seen it before? Firefighting. Not firefighting. Who cared? It was all just details.

Because as long as Ginger was beside him, he could do anything.

Reaching for the tree, he jumped. But once they were in midair, he realized he'd misjudged their combined weight and that they were falling faster than he'd planned. Fortunately, Ginger was one step ahead of him and he felt her let go an instant before he could stop her. Together, they grabbed the only branch left to save them from the final fifteen feet to the ground.

Just as his hands went around the tree, he heard the air knock from Ginger's body as she slammed into the limb. Tightening his right grip on the tree, he reached out with his left to grab her.

He wanted to tell her a thousand times over how much he loved her but hanging from a tree while a fire raged all around them wasn't exactly great timing. Especially since two dozen people were rushing under the tree, all talking at once, throwing a ladder against the trunk, reaching for them. He'd have to be happy with once.

"I love you," he said as he helped her climb down the ladder.

Her lips opened, but all that came out was more ragged coughs, and then the paramedics were taking her from him.

Everything in him wanted to hold on to her, but he couldn't deny years of disaster experience. The medics needed to check her out ASAP, needed to do something to calm her coughing, to make sure the baby stayed with her through the shock.

One of the local volunteer firefighters was telling everyone to clear the area. Bystanders went back to their boats that were pulled up on shore, but his father remained at his side as the volunteer firefighters crew ran onto the beach in their turnouts and began the work of keeping the fire from spreading.

Connor didn't let Ginger out of his sight, not for one

second, even as the fire chief approached Connor and Andrew on the sand.

"This is your house?"

Even as Andrew said yes, Connor knew what the chief was going to say.

"We've got to put our focus on putting the current fire out, so that it doesn't spread to the other houses down the lake. My gut is that your cabin is already too far gone, but if we've got the manpower to work on it later . . ."

Connor knew that if he stayed to help, with just one more set of hands and legs, he might be able to tip the balance in favor of keeping the house. But he had to take care of the woman he loved.

The paramedics had made her lie down on a stretcher and as they lifted her into the ambulance, her eyes were locked on his.

"I have to go," he told his father. "I need to stay with Ginger."

He expected to hear anguish from his father as their family camp burned before them. Instead, Andrew told him, "Ginger needs you far more than a bunch of smoking old logs do."

Connor pushed through the back of the ambulance just as they were shutting the doors.

"Hey, you can't—" one of the paramedics started to say, but Ginger's soft voice cut through his protests.

"I need him," she managed before she lost her breath again and one of the paramedics covered her mouth and nose with an oxygen mask.

"I'm here, sweetheart," he said as he slid into the seat beside her.

He held her hand, stroked her hair. They were putting an IV in and her eyes were already closing as the oxygen, the hydration, made their way into her depleted system.

"She's pregnant," he warned the paramedics. "Be very careful with her."

She was asleep by the time they got to the local care center. The paramedics quickly took her away to be examined by a doctor and even though he knew he couldn't be there, it killed him to have to be separated from her at all. He wanted to be beside her when she opened her eyes. Wanted to keep her safe in his arms and never let her go.

Connor was pacing the small waiting room when Isabel, Josh, and Andrew rushed inside. Isabel threw her arms around him. "You saved her."

She wasn't crying as she said it, but it was clear that she'd only just stopped. "Are you all right?"

"No, I'm not. Not until I know Ginger's okay."

"And the baby."

All he could do was nod.

"Ginger is a tough cookie," Isabel said as she squeezed his hand. "She'll be all right. They both will."

Just then, Josh tugged on his mother's sleeve. His face was white, his eyes wide, his fists clenched.

"Mom. I need to tell you something."

CHAPTER TWENTY-SEVEN

"I STARTED the fire," Josh said.

It was just about the only thing that could have snapped Connor out of his anxiety about how Ginger was doing.

"What happened?"

The kid scrunched up his eyes, a couple of tears squeezing out. "I went out back, to the woodpile behind our houses. To smoke."

Isabel's mouth was pinched, her face pale with horror. With fear. Andrew moved behind her, put a hand on her back, and Connor had a feeling his father's support was the only reason she was able to stay upright.

"But it made me sick, so I ground it out under my shoe. The leaves started smoking and burning so I stomped them out." Josh took a shaky breath. "But I guess I didn't get it all out."

Connor had done this a hundred times, heard the confession of an accidental arsonist, worked to calm the person down. But it was different this time. Not because it was his cabin burning.

"Ginger could have died up there."

The kid really started crying then, had to wipe his nose on his sweatshirt. "I'm so sorry. It was an accident, I swear. I didn't mean to hurt anyone. Especially not Ginger. She's great. I would never want anything to happen to her."

That made two of them, Connor thought angrily as Andrew moved between them.

"I'll go with him to talk to the fire chief. Make sure he doesn't say anything they can twist later to try to pin this on him as anything other than an accident." He put his arm around Josh's shoulders, which were shaking with fear and remorse. "Isabel, you should be there too."

She nodded, turning to say "I'm so sorry," to Connor before she followed her son and Andrew back to the car.

The receptionist cleared her throat from behind her desk. "Excuse me, are you Connor MacKenzie? Ms. Sinclair has asked you to come back to see her."

All his life, Connor thought as he moved through the waiting room and down the hall to the triage area, he'd been the steady one. The guy who everyone could count on to keep it together. Even after his stint in the burn ward, he'd been a rock.

It was almost as if the events of this past two weeks had been put into motion to test him, to see what he was made of.

The Forest Service call.

Losing control every time he touched Ginger.

Learning he was going to be a father.

Ginger throwing back his words of love.

Poplar Cove burning down, one hundred years of history, gone up in smoke.

And now, Ginger lying in a hospital bed.

The curtains were drawn and when he pulled one back to step inside, his heart stopped at the sight of her hooked up to an IV, propped up by pillows, lying beneath a thin white blanket.

"Hi," she said with a small smile.

It was only then that his heart started beating again. She sounded fine and her color was good. But there was no way that he could look at her as just another fire victim, no way he could scan her stats and be satisfied that she was all right.

He told himself to be gentle with her, but once she was in his arms, he couldn't stop kissing her, couldn't help but pull her closer.

His throat was dry, cracked, as he asked, "How is the baby?" His hands automatically moved to her still flat stomach. "Is it—"

She put her hands over his. "Perfectly fine."

The breath he'd been holding came out in a loud whoosh of air.

"Thank God," he said, and then, "Seeing you up there on the roof, I've never been so scared. And when I realized there was no way to get to you—"

It had been the worst moment of his life.

"Nothing else mattered but getting you off that roof."

"I had to try to save the cabin," she said. "Even though I knew you'd be furious with me for not leaving at the first sign of fire."

"Promise me you'll never do something that brave—or stupid—again."

She winced at the "stupid," but held her ground. "I can't make you that promise, Connor, not when something I love might be at stake. Are they going to be able to save the cabin?"

"Probably not."

A tear fell down her cheek. "It's not fair that the first chance you've had to fight fire in two years is because your own home was burning. I'm so sorry, Connor."

"I don't care about any of that. Not the cabin. Not even firefighting. The cabin was there when we needed it, to bring us together, to make it impossible for us to ignore our feelings for each other."

He wasn't going to hold the words back another second.

"I love you, Ginger. Please, marry me. Not because you're pregnant, but because we belong together."

She didn't pull her hands out of his, but he felt her fingers grow tense.

"I don't want us to repeat a bad pattern, Connor, to do the same thing as your parents and just get married because I'm pregnant."

"My father was in love with someone else when he got

my mother pregnant. I'm in love with you, Ginger. He was nineteen. I'm thirty. He wasn't ready to get married, not to my mother, anyway. But I'm ready for this, Ginger. I'm ready for you. For a life with you. With our child."

He watched her try to take in everything he was saying, but even so he knew he had to give her more. After the way he'd hurt her, she deserved every last piece of him, no matter how hard he'd fought to hold himself back from everyone for so long.

"That night you told me you loved me, I've never felt so overwhelmed by sensation before. Not even when my hands were melting. It scared me, Ginger. More than anything else I've ever faced. It seemed easier to go numb."

He lifted her hands to his heart, held them there.

"But now I know I'd rather feel too much than nothing at all."

She'd made herself say that stuff about repeating a bad pattern, even though her heart wasn't really in it. Just to make sure they'd covered all the bases. So she'd know that nothing had been left unsaid between them.

Because when she looked deep into her own heart, she believed that he loved her. Connor wasn't the kind of man who would lie about being in love simply to get what he wanted, to get her to agree to marry him. Connor would never try to keep her in an emotional prison like so many others had.

Connor was her first love.

Her true love.

"I've never felt this way before, either," she admitted. "My feelings for you scare me too. You're a part of me now. In so deep that I'll never just be me again. And all I could think as I was up on the roof and the fire was closing in was that I was never going to get the chance to tell you yes."

Nothing had ever moved her as much as the pure joy on Connor's face.

"Yes? As in yes, you'll marry me?"

"There was never any other answer, Connor. No other choice I could have possibly made. I've loved you almost from that first moment you walked onto the porch. Every time you lost control, I was right there with you, already lost. But this morning on the beach, my feelings were hurt. I wanted to make you work for it."

"Believe me, no one is ever going to work as hard as I will at making you happy."

"No, Connor, you don't have do anything other than just be who you are. Be the man I already love. Because no matter what happens between us from here on out, I'll never doubt your love for me again. Not when I'll always know that we're both giving each other everything."

He kissed her, then, slow and sweet.

"Firefighters call it our good-bye list."

"Good-bye list?"

"If you knew there was no way out, if the fire was closing in and you were about to go, who would you make your last phone call to?"

"You would want to call the people you love most, tell them one more time."

"Two years ago, Sam and my mother were at the top of that list."

"And now?"

"It's you, Ginger. It will always be you."

CHAPTER TWENTY-EIGHT

ISABEL HAD never felt so wrung out, so utterly depleted. It had seemed as if the day would never end as the fire chief questioned Josh, and then the fire investigator, Andrew standing beside him each time. Protecting her son.

Josh had burned down Poplar Cove. Ginger and Connor had nearly died. Thank God Andrew had been there reminding everyone over and over that it had been an accident. He'd assured her at least a dozen times that nothing was going to happen to Josh, that nothing was going to go on his permanent record, and no charges could possibly be filed by the investigator.

By the time the sun set, Josh was already fast asleep in his room. Andrew was sitting in her kitchen, holding a cup of coffee and she was amazed to find that he looked just right.

Somehow, he fit right into the lakeside world she'd created for herself and her son.

"It's been a hell of a day, hasn't it?"

It was the understatement of the century. All Isabel wanted was to get away from it all for a little while.

"How about we row out to the island?"

She looked back at Josh's room, wondering for a moment if she should stay in the house just in case he woke up, but in truth she knew he was just an excuse not to be alone with Andrew again.

Because she was frightened to death of the depth of her feelings for him. Especially after today.

Andrew grabbed a couple of oversized towels off the porch as they walked out to her dock and climbed into the rowboat. The wooden paddles swooshed through the black water, beneath an equally black sky.

They didn't speak as he rowed, and she could barely see him in the inky darkness, but it calmed her—pleased her—to know that he was right there with her, sitting only a couple of feet away.

Thirty years ago, he'd been the one man she'd wanted in her lifeboat in an emergency.

For the first time in three decades, she wondered if it were possible that he could be that man again?

After pulling the boat up on shore, he held out his hand and she let him lead her to their "private" beach, the special place they would sneak off to as teenagers when they wanted to be alone. And as he walked beside her, his hand warm over hers, she expected memories to come, one after the other, all the memories she hadn't wanted to replay.

But instead of retracing their old steps, she realized that they were taking new ones. She would never forget the past, but she could finally see that he hadn't come back to the lake to revisit the past.

They were here together to build a future.

They spread out the towels over the sand and it was the most natural thing in the world for her to lay her head on Andrew's shoulder.

"I'm so sorry you lost your cabin," she said and as he pulled her in tighter against him, finally safe in his arms, she let herself crumble.

"I almost lost you today. Up on the roof—" She couldn't manage to say anything else, not when the sheer thought of Andrew getting caught in the fire made her sick to her stomach.

He shifted them so that her head was cradled beneath his strong forearm and he was looking down at her. His thumb brushed softly across her cheek as he gently wiped away her tears.

"Don't cry, Izzy. I'm still here. And I'm not going anywhere. I promise."

"I'll never be able to apologize enough for what my son did. Before he went to sleep he told me he was wrong about you. That you're not a bad guy after all. I hope you can find a way to forgive him one day."

"Don't get me wrong, it still hasn't exactly set in that Poplar Cove is gone, but I can't help but wonder if maybe it's all for the best."

"How can it possibly be for the best?"

"Well, for one, it's a new start for me and Connor. Lord knows we both needed it."

"Ginger too," Isabel murmured.

And her too, she silently admitted. She hadn't realized until Andrew's return just how stuck she'd been in the past.

"Now Connor and I might get a chance to rebuild the cabin together. Spend a few months working as a team on something that matters to both of us. Maybe Josh could help us, work through some of his guilt with a hammer and saw. Might also be a good way to burn off some of that teenage energy, keep him out of trouble for a while."

"You're planning to stay?"

And he would actually consider asking her son to work with him after what he'd done?

"I want to, Izzy. More than anything. But I don't want to hurt you again, so if you don't want—"

She put a finger to his lips to stop him. "When my son found us . . ." Her face grew hot. "Well, when he found us kissing, I behaved badly to you. Just because he couldn't deal with his mother behaving like a normal adult doesn't mean I should have tried to act like it didn't happen." Her eyes moved to his face, held his gaze. "Because the truth is that I wanted it to happen. I wanted you to kiss me."

"You did?"

"Yes. I did. More than I've ever wanted anything. But I was torn, because I still wasn't sure I could ever trust you again. Until today, when I saw you with my son, the way you protected Josh, even though he was the one responsible for your loss."

"He's just a kid who made a mistake. A bad one, but a mistake nonetheless."

"Watching you with him made me see that I can trust you. I do trust you. Your mistake and his mistake weren't so different, really. Two kids who didn't know what to do with all of their energy. Their passion. I keep thinking about those things I said to you that first day you came by the diner, when I said a real man would have made the best of his situation."

"You were right. Completely right."

"Maybe I was," she said, "but if I can dish it out, I should be able to take it, shouldn't I? Because there I was saying you should have figured out a way to make your marriage work, but did I make mine work? No. Not at all. Because all the time I should have been loving my husband, the father of my child, I was still in love with you."

"You love me?"

"I've always loved you, Andrew. I never stopped loving you, not even for a second, not even when I was so angry with you I wanted to come at you with a kitchen knife."

She heard him chuckle at her honesty, and then he was whispering, "My sweet Izzy, how I love you," a moment before his mouth came down over hers.

Their kiss was sweet, gentle, and then, without warning, they were both taking, tasting, testing each other with tongues and lips and teeth, a whole summer's desperation taking away any hesitancy or patience.

And then he was repositioning her, laying her on her

back on the towel and as he stripped off her clothes, she looked up at the moon through the trees, the scent of the blueberry bushes filling the air with sweet perfume. Every patch of skin his fingers touched as he slid off her shirt, and then her bra, and then moved to the waistband of her pants, made her gasp with pleasure. He cupped her breasts and she leaned into his wonderfully large hands wanting more, as much as he could give her. His mouth found her next, his tongue moving in long strokes between her legs and she forgot where she was again, could only focus on the man giving her the kind of pleasure she'd never felt anywhere else.

Higher and higher she climbed as he loved her with his mouth, but she wanted him to share it with her, so she reached for his shoulders and dragged him up her body. Her hands shaking, she fumbled with his pants, but then he was kissing her again and she couldn't figure out how to make her fingers obey her instructions. Andrew took over where she left off and soon his clothes were off and he was propping himself up over her again, naked this time.

Another time she'd stop, breathe, stare, relearn every inch of his body. But for now, all that mattered was taking him inside, opening herself up to him and feeling the long slide of his shaft take her breath away.

He stilled, asked "How am I ever going to get enough of you?" and then he was thrusting, and they were grabbing at each other's bodies, trying to get closer, moving together in a rhythm that was sweetly familiar, and yet brand new. He was kissing her like he'd been waiting his whole life to find her and she gave herself completely to him in the very moment that they took each other over the edge. His roar of pleasure was swallowed by the trees and then her mouth as she kissed him.

And as they came back to earth, lying sweating and panting on the twisted towel, she put her hands on his face and kissed him again with all the love in her heart.

No more regrets.

No more anger.

After thirty years, love was what remained.

CHAPTER TWENTY-NINE

Two weeks later . . .

Art in the Adirondacks had been a spectacular day for Ginger. Fortunately, she'd stored most of her finished canvases in the Blue Mountain Lake recreation center basement—along with the handful on display on the diner's walls—so although she'd lost several of her most recent paintings in the fire, she had enough to show.

Connor had helped her hang the sign above her tiny open white tent, "Paintings by Ginger Sinclair," and each time she looked at it she'd started grinning like an idiot. Every time a stranger stood in front of one of her canvases and told her how much he or she liked it . . . frankly, it didn't even matter whether or not they bought one. Being a part of a community of artists was pleasure enough. Better still was the fact that she'd not only almost sold out, she'd also been asked to do several commissions for various homeowners on Blue Mountain Lake as well.

She was thrilled that her dreams of becoming a full-time painter were coming true, but the best part of it was sharing her joy with Connor. Every day he'd gone out and picked wildflowers for her. Vases of wild blooms filled every room of their rental house, petals were strewn across the sheets.

And now, she'd just witnessed the most beautiful wedding out on the island in the middle of the lake. She felt utterly privileged to sit on a towel on the sand and listen to Sam and Dianna's touching vows.

As soon as Sam and Dianna had been told about the fire, they'd both changed their schedules to fly out to the lake early. With Poplar Cove nothing but a pile of hot coals, the wedding venue had to be changed. Andrew was the one who had suggested the island, and everyone had immediately agreed it was the perfect location.

It hadn't been easy to get so many people and decorations and food out to the island, and all of them had been praying for the rain to hold out until after the wedding, but in a way scrambling to get everything together had been part of the fun. And Ginger was thrilled to know that she was going to be related to Sam and Dianna in the near future.

Most likely very near, she thought as she put one hand on her stomach. She and Connor couldn't see any reason to wait, not with a baby on the way.

She felt a familiar heat rush through her and she looked up to find Connor, who was standing beside his brother as best man, smiling at her.

He mouthed, "I love you," and her stomach did a little flip-flop of joy as he followed the bride and groom down the informal aisle.

She blew him a kiss, then stood up to help Isabel serve lunch.

Flanked by his sons on each side as the photographer took pictures for the wedding album, Isabel had never seen Andrew look happier.

Forgetting she was holding a tray of grilled shrimp hors d'oeuvres as she watched them, she was surprised when a smooth voice asked, "Could I help you with anything?"

Andrew's ex-wife, Elise, took the tray from Isabel's suddenly limp hands. "Thank you for doing so much to make this wedding happen. And the food is wonderful."

"You're welcome," Isabel replied, powerfully glad that the ice had finally been broken.

Letting herself finally take a long look at the woman Andrew had been married to for thirty years—Elise was still a beautiful woman, slim with a dark brown bob and keen fashion sense—Isabel smiled and said, "You've raised two fine sons. You should be very proud."

"I am." They stood together in silence for a few moments, watching the three men. "I've wanted to talk to you for a long time," Elise admitted in a soft voice. "I've wanted to tell you that I'm sorry for what happened more than thirty years ago."

Isabel met the woman's gaze. "I'm sorry too."

"But I wouldn't change it. I wouldn't have given up my sons for anything."

The final piece of the puzzle slid into place inside Isabel. Everything happened for a reason.

"I couldn't agree more," she said with a smile. "And if you wouldn't mind, I would love a hand with the food."

Elise smiled back and although they'd never be friends, Isabel was glad to know they'd never again be enemies.

Watching his ex-wife approach Isabel was as close as Andrew had ever come to having a heart attack. Through it all, he continued to smile for the photographer, but his heart didn't start beating again until the two women smiled at each other.

What the hell did they just say to each other? was his first thought, quickly followed by, *Just be glad that water seems to be running under the bridge.*

He was a lucky bastard, had thought so ever since the moment Isabel kissed him. And these past couple of weeks, with both Connor and Sam together, he'd finally gotten the chance to sail across the lake with his sons in the boat that Connor had helped build. It had been even better than he'd dreamed all those years ago. He hoped to sail Blue Mountain Lake with them—and their children—many more times in the coming years.

After Connor was pulled away by the photographer for

a photo with Ginger, Sam said, "You went above and beyond pulling this wedding together, Dad."

Andrew knew that scrambling to make this wedding happen on the island barely made up for the mistakes he made. But they weren't talking about the past anymore. They were moving forward, into a much better, much brighter future.

"There was nothing I would have rather been doing." Dianna, his new daughter-in-law, waved at them from where she was speaking with the officiator and he told his son, "I'm so happy for both you and Connor."

"So," Sam said slowly, "apart from staying here to help rebuild the cabin, what are your plans exactly?"

Andrew was done hiding things from his kids. "I'm going to marry Isabel."

Sam surprised him by laughing out loud. "Hell, we should have just made this a triple wedding."

That mist that had been coating Andrew's eyes all day came washing back. "I don't think I've told you yet today, but I love you, son."

And for the first time since he was a little boy, Sam said, "I love you," right back.

Connor wrapped his arms around Ginger from behind. "I don't think I've ever seen my brother and father laugh together."

Leaning her head back into his chest she said, "I know he wasn't much of a father, but I'm betting he'll be a great grandfather to our child."

He pulled her closer, rested his hands on her stomach. "Our children."

Catching his grandmother's eye across the stretch of beach, he knew she'd seen her son and grandson connect as well from the joy on her face. Surprised as always by how quickly his grandparents moved, he grinned as his grandmother swept Ginger into a hug.

"We're so thrilled that we're going to have another granddaughter-in-law soon."

When he'd told them about the engagement his grandmother had simply said, *"I knew this was going to happen. Weren't we smart to rent out Poplar Cove?"*

He and Ginger had decided to keep her pregnancy to themselves until the second trimester, and he could see how much his fiancée wanted to spill the secret. Somehow, though, he sensed his grandmother already knew about the baby. She'd always had eyes on every part of her head. Clearly, nothing had changed from when he was a kid.

His grandfather cleared his throat and reached into his coat pocket. "We've given your brother the deed to the empty lot beside Poplar Cove. And this one," he held out a piece of paper, "is for you. Your father told us your renovation made the log cabin look like new. Your grandmother and I believe you've already made it yours. This simply makes it official."

The day after the fire, Connor had joined the volunteer crew to clean up the structure. Each of the guys on the crew had come up to Connor at one point or another to tell him they wished they'd been able to save his camp and how sorry they were that it had burned.

He was profoundly glad he'd been there during the cabin's last hours. And he was greatly looking forward to rebuilding it over the coming months, along with doing some work for several other log cabin owners on the lake. Already, he'd booked as many hours as he was willing to work. He and Ginger had rented a house down at the end of the bay and would stay there until Poplar Cove was standing again.

The photographer pulled his grandparents away a moment later and Ginger said, "I'm so happy for you, Connor. I know how much you loved Poplar Cove. Now it's yours."

He turned her in his arms to face him. "Not mine. Ours. First thing Monday morning, we're going to the courthouse to put your name on this. Together, we're going to build a new life here."

Just this morning as he'd run some last-minute errands for the wedding, he'd seen a ring in the shape of a flower, each petal a different, brilliant color in a window on Main Street. He reached into his pocket and held it out.

"A wildflower," she breathed in wonder.

"When I saw this ring I knew you were meant to wear it, that it had been made for you." He slipped it on her ring finger then threaded his scarred fingers through her soft ones. "All my life I thought I needed fire to feel alive. But now I know all I need is you, sweetheart. This ring is a promise from me to you that I will love you—and cherish you—forever."

And before she kissed him to seal the deal, it was the most natural thing in the world for her desperate words from weeks ago on the porch to blossom into something truly beautiful.

"Take me, Connor. I'm yours."

Available this month from *Rouge Romance*:

Tessa Dare's 'Stud Club' Trilogy:

ONE DANCE WITH A DUKE
Spencer Dumarque, the fourth Duke of Morland, has a reputation as the dashing "Duke of Midnight." Each evening he selects one lady for a scandalous midnight waltz. But none of the ladies of the ton catch his interest for long, until Lady Amelia d'Orsay tries her luck.

TWICE TEMPTED BY A ROUGE
Brooding war hero, Rhys St. Maur, returns to his ancestral home on the Devonshire moors following the murder of his friend in the elite gentlemen's society known as the Stud Club. There, he is offered a chance at redemption in the arms of beautiful innkeeper, Meredith Maddox, who dares him to face the demons of his past.

THREE NIGHTS WITH A SCOUNDREL
The bastard son of a nobleman, Julian Bellamy plotted to have the last laugh on a society that once spurned him. But meeting Leo Chatwick, founder of the exclusive Stud Club, and Lily, his enchanting sister, made Julian reconsider his wild ways. When Leo is murdered Julian vows to see the woman he secretly loves married to a man of her own class. Lily, however, has a very different husband in mind.

THE HUSBAND TRAP by Tracy Anne Warren
Violet Brantford has always longed for Adrian Winter, the wealthy Duke of Raeburn, who is set to marry Violet's vivacious twin sister, Jeannette. But when Jeannette refuses to go through with the ceremony, Violet finds herself walking down the aisle in her sister's place in order to avoid a scandal. But keeping up the pretence with a man as divine as the Duke will take all of Violet's skills…

THE WARRIOR by Nicole Jordan
Ariane of Claredon is betrothed to King Henry's most trusted vassal, the feared Norman knight Ranulf de Vernay. But cruel circumstance has branded Ariane's father a traitor to the crown and Ranulf is returning to Claredon, not as bridegroom...but as conqueror. But though he has come to claim her lands and body as his prize, it is the mighty warrior who must surrender to Ariane's passion and her remarkable healing love.